HER Devoted *Protector*

ALESSA KELLY

"Duty is what I do for others. Devotion is all of me that I faithfully give to you." ~ Mark Connor

1

IVY WREN CAVANAGH

Helena, Montana

THE CAR DOORS open one by one. The wind rushes in, and soon I hear boots hitting the ground. It must've been the men jumping out.

I'm blindfolded and gagged, and my hands are tied behind my back. Those men have abducted me from my home, and we've traveled less than an hour, so I'm likely still within the city limits. But you don't need to go far to find a secluded space in Montana. Hearing widespread grass and leaves blowing in the wind, I sense that I've been taken to a place where the only eyes witnessing proceedings are those of owls or coyotes.

Someone pushes me off my seat, and I tumble out of the vehicle. Then I feel two men passing their hands under my arms, dragging me. Their moves are so rough and swift that my feet almost lift off the ground. It must be ten yards or so before we finally stop.

Something creaks in front of me. I think someone is

opening a door. It sounds woody, but the ground I'm treading feels like concrete. The smell of moss is strong, and it's so damn cold in here. I'm sure I'm in an enclosed space now—perhaps it's part of the Mosaic headquarters.

The men shove me forward, so I walk on my own for a few steps. Soon I'm forced to kneel. One of my captors pulls out my gag but leaves the blindfold and keeps my wrists bound.

The silence is eerie. It's not absolute silence. Rather, it's frigid air filled with harsh breaths released by men who, I guess, will do anything to hurt me.

One taps their boot from one end, followed by another behind me. They're certainly trying to toy with my psyche. I think they removed my gag to figure out how frightened I am behind my lack of response.

Then I hear steady footsteps ending right in front of me.

"Attorney General Cavanagh." His voice is sandy and deep, just like the voice I heard on the phone before I was taken—only here, it has a touch of grandiose thanks to the echo. He calls himself Deuce. No one knows who he is, but many believe he's the man behind the feared and powerful drug syndicate Mosaic.

"Deuce," I greet him.

"You're shivering."

"I didn't know Mosaic was this broke. Can't even pay for heating. Fentanyl business hitting a rough patch? And I haven't even started!"

"Ah, that's exactly what I admire about politicians. They always see things through rose-tinted glasses, even when they can't see at all." The sound of his footsteps circles me. "You might've rattled the industry with your war declaration. But don't flatter yourself. Mosaic is stronger and more prosperous than ever."

Deuce moves away. There's a splash as his feet land somewhere, maybe on a puddle. And when I listen carefully, there's water dripping.

"What, AG Cavanagh?" Obviously, he knows I'm trying to figure out the environment around me.

"Was that you pissing yourself?"

He slaps me.

But I stay upright, challenging him. "I didn't know you're the slapping type. The coward type. Let me see you!"

Silence falls again. Then a man steps behind me, and my blindfold is removed.

I immediately look up.

"There you are!" Deuce hisses.

I should've known it wouldn't be this easy. The prick is wearing a mask, but not a ski mask like his soldiers. It's white and sturdy, like the Phantom of The Opera. Only it covers his whole face. It's hard to judge his height from where I am, but he's six-foot-two or thereabout. His hair is hidden under a black beanie, and he's wearing a tan overcoat that falls almost to his ankles. It's impossible to make out the exact shape of his body, but from what I can see, he's a well-built man—just like his soldiers.

"You didn't think I would show my face, did you? You haven't earned it."

"And you're not as brave as I thought you were." I look around—four others are surrounding me.

"Oh, I have more men guarding this place. So don't you think about escaping. I even have spares who are busy getting rid of those two corpses from your house."

I'm hoping he's referring to the Mosaic casualties. Although I don't know the fate of my two bodyguards, who were shot in the attack.

"What do you want?"

"Ah, getting impatient, are we? In time, I will tell you. But first, why don't we get to know each other?"

"I know you've got blood on your hands, Deuce. Young lives you never give a chance to flourish."

"Another thing about politicians. They give you lectures without looking at themselves." He then gets his man to show me something on an iPad.

My God. Those boys on the video—some could be as young as fourteen or fifteen—are packing bottles, counting tablets, and smoking like they've been addicts all their lives.

"Those are the very people you swear to protect, aren't they, AG Cavanagh? You declared war against fentanyl. But look at them! They're gladly contributing to the industry. I can even say they're thriving."

"You brainwash them."

"You and your lawmakers can try until you all die of exhaustion and despair—with your policies, bills, and what-not. But you'll barely make a dent."

"Watch me!"

"Those youths are just products of failed marriages and fucked-up families. You're not that different," he mocks. "I can imagine someday Noah will be sitting among those boys, working hard on my factory floor." He bends down to say to my face, "Too bad the boy's not here!"

I'm sure he intended to take my son tonight, but I know he's safe.

"Fuck you!"

"He's a loose cannon, that boy. What do they say? The first seven years of a child's life are the most important. How old is he now? Eight? Whatever he's gone through, the effect is likely to be irreversible. I've got a feeling sooner rather than later, he'll unleash his potential and step into the dark side."

I'm not a perfect mother, but I will never let Noah be a slave like those boys.

"What did your mother do to you, Deuce?"

He hisses and steps closer to me. "She did okay. Look at me now. The most powerful woman in Montana is kneeling in front of me."

"What do you want?" I repeat.

"You put someone in jail—I'm sure you remember him. I want his release."

"Too many to count. You've got to be more specific."

"Oh, I'll give you his name. Don't you worry."

"If you want him to be pardoned, ask the governor."

"You were a fearless prosecutor then. Now, you're at the top of the justice food chain, and the Montana State Prison is your oyster. You'll be able to do anything."

"Who is he, Deuce?"

"Later. Right now, I just want to have fun with you. Perhaps we can prove that lawmakers and criminals can get along after all."

"Oh, we *will* get along. Only at the end of it all, there'll only be one of us—and it won't be you."

"Mosaic is bigger than you can ever imagine. It's bigger than the State of Montana itself. Even if the whole Helena PD or State Troopers rally around you, you'll never be safe."

Deuce circles around me again and continue with his warnings, "Not to mention your little family secret. Hm? One that will destroy everything you've fought for."

"I will keep hunting you, Deuce. Whether I'm still in the Justice Building or in hell."

"I know you'd say something like that. You're a strong woman. I applaud you. Thirty-six years old. Fighting for her second term as the attorney general of Montana. The youngest in US history when first elected. But you're not alone in this—and that will make you weak."

I know where he's going, and I don't like it.

"If you satisfy my demand, I'll guarantee that you, Noah, and your other family will be off-limits. Hands off. Protected. And I don't mean protection like those hillbillies. What do they call themselves? Red Mark?"

No one should underestimate the men of Red Mark.

When Noah managed to escape the attack tonight, I know the first thing he would've done was to call one of them—his 'watchbear,' Mark Connor.

And no one should *ever* underestimate Mark Connor. Or they'll be as good as dead.

Deuce forces my chin up. "When I say his name, say you'll release him."

"Fuck you twice, Deuce!"

He rises swiftly, looming over me like dooms day. But I look up at him, telling him I meant it. I've barely met his masked gaze before his knee crashes into the side of my head.

I fall to the ground.

In the haze, I see a shadow move. It's another of Deuce's soldiers. Although covered in black from head to toe, I recognize his skinny frame. The elusive teenager had told me he's the best among the Mosaic troops, and I don't doubt it.

But the deepest part of my heart cries out for him.

I know Mark is on his way. If he could only save one person in this room, I'd tell him, 'Save that boy.'

2

MARK CONNOR

A week ago

WHEN IT COMES to saving a life, we have little margin for error. And when the life you're trying to preserve is that of a child, your mission becomes more than just strategies and probabilities. Your physical and mental being belongs to that child. You live for that child—and nothing else—until you get them to safety.

At the Red Mark Rescue & Protect command center, we're monitoring two of our guys who are storming a suburban house in Billings. After days of searching, we believe that's where a ten-year-old girl and her younger brother are being held hostage.

A two-hundred-thousand-dollar ransom has been demanded for each of them, but we know nothing will buy the kids' freedom. The tone of threats and prior records show that the man spearheading the kidnapping is ready to ship the siblings to the highest bidder. Worse, to kill them if things go wrong.

Having cleared the ground floor, the team is now proceeding to the basement.

"Watch out for traps," I order as they're about to kick open a door. They know the targets are almost in their sight, but they're moving a little too fast.

"It's clean, sir," Tyler Hunt replies. The former SEAL marksman joined our organization six months ago and has so far proven that the Red Mark blood runs in his vein. Even without his sniper rifle, he's an asset. He's a hound when it comes to tracking instincts, and the man is able to calm any distressed kids with his words and, more often, just by being there.

"We're going in!" he announces and then kicks the door open.

"Do you see them?" Sam Kelleher, my business partner and best friend, asks in anticipation. He keeps rubbing his dark scruff as if it would trawl a 'yes' out of Tyler.

"Negative."

Sam leans forward, his hands now planted firmly on the dashboard. Red Mark is no longer a two-men band, but I must admit, being in the command center is not the same as getting our boots dirty. But I trust Ty and his partner as much as I trust my own partner. Otherwise, I wouldn't have declared them ready.

"What's happening with their cameras?" Sam stares at the black screen.

"I think they're passing a thick wall, sir." Cora-Lee Rancic, Red Mark's head of tech, punches the keyboard while switching her views between four monitors. "Boys, change your transmission mode, and I'll take it from there," she informs the team. Then she turns to Sam and me. "Picture quality may degrade, but we'll have visuals back. Give me a minute." Despite speaking in zeroes and ones when she's in the zone, the programmer is an effective communicator when it's crunch time, and she mans the command center like a boss.

"It's okay. We'll rely on audio for now," I advise. "Ty, the BPD still with you?"

"Yes, sir."

Most of Red Mark's missions are carried out in collaboration with the local police, and this time it's the Billings Police Department. We handle the rescue, and they deal with apprehending the criminals.

Suddenly, shots are fired.

"Ty! What the hell is going on?" Sam calls out. "Tyler, do you copy?"

No reply.

"Goddamn it!" His hands are now gripping the edge of the dashboard like he's riding a roller coaster.

After a few mutters, we hear Tyler. "We're okay. We had company, but the police took him out. The suspect's dead, sir."

"Any signs of the children?"

For a few seconds, we're getting rustles and static as a response.

"They're here!" Ty's voice blares above the noise. "I have eyes on them!"

"Video's back," Cora-Lee reports.

And we see Ty's P.O.V.—a girl hugging an unconscious boy in a corner of a dark room. Only the team's flashlights illuminate the area.

"Hey, I'm Tyler," he says to the girl. "Don't be scared."

The girl cowers, screaming into her hands.

Holding our breaths, we anticipate Tyler's next move. Ty and his partner have been through intensive training with Sam and me. I really hope they come through on their first independent mission. Sam is about to say something, but I hold his shoulder, hinting to let the team handle the situation themselves.

"We're here to get you home," Ty comforts her. His point of view lowers. No doubt he's kneeling close to the girl now. "Your parents sent us. Look, they gave me this photo." I'm sure it's a family photo that the kids' mother had passed on to Ty.

The girl raises her eyes to him. The pictures we're receiving are fuzzy and in black and white, but there's no doubt she's warming up to him.

"Please help my brother," the girl sobs. "They forced him to take a drug. He hasn't woken up in hours."

Ty takes the boy's pulse. "He'll be okay. Come on, let's get you two out of here."

"He'll beat us," the girl pleads.

"No. No one will harm you anymore," Ty softens his voice. "The police are upstairs and outside, guarding us. That bad man is gone. You don't have to be scared anymore."

The girl reaches out for Ty, letting his partner take her brother. Her face zooms into view as Ty takes her in his arms. They finally step out of the house, where paramedics await.

"Good work, boys," I thank them, then nod at Sam. "You've trained them well."

"*We've* trained them well, buddy!" Sam pats my shoulder.

We started our training together, but as I focused on newer recruits, my partner has been out there with Ty on recent missions, and the two former SEALs were unstoppable.

"All right, boys. Time to leave the Midland Empire," Sam quips.

"Gladly, sir."

"Good work, Cee," I praise Cora-Lee. "Couldn't have done it without you."

The young head of tech smiles as she removes her headset. Sam and I leave the command center, making our way downstairs. The Red Mark headquarters is three levels. The top floor houses our offices and secure storage spaces—files, server rooms. The second is mainly occupied by our command center, IT, and meeting rooms. The ground floor is the largest, holding the reception area, lounges, gear storage, and our ever-expanding training facility.

Surprisingly, someone is waiting for us. Precisely, two people who are legit part of the Red Mark family, even though they're not our personnel.

"Dad!" Grace runs to Sam as soon as we join the mother and daughter in the media lounge.

Dad.

I still remember the days when Grace was calling him 'Sam.' Barely a year ago. As soon as Sam and Grace's mother got married, Sam adopted Grace, and the girl has called him 'Dad' ever since. After multiple break-ups and trying to copy my life as a bachelor forever, I couldn't be happier that he's now a proud father of one and soon two.

"Hey, Pup." Sam hugs six-hear-old Grace. "Have you been waiting long?"

"No, not really," she replies.

Cassidy Winter-Kelleher, Sam's wife—and the reason he can flash a smile full of pride and love like that—maneuvers her bulging belly to lean into him.

"Hey, sweetheart." He kisses her, caressing her bump. She's due anytime now. It's incredible how calm she looks.

"Hi, Mark!" Grace comes to me. Being an uncle to this feisty girl is as close as I can get to being a family man. Nevertheless, it's an honor.

"Did you find those kids in Billings?" Cass asks.

"Yeah, the guys did. Training and tough love—works every time," Sam replies.

"Oh, thank God!" Cass gives him an 'I'm proud of you'

gaze. "I won't keep you. I just dropped by to see how you were. And to drop off these. New menu from the bar."

I smell well-seasoned poultry inside the 'Thirsty Fox' branded brown bag. The downtown bar is only a couple of blocks away from here. It's Red Mark's official watering hole and Cass is the manager.

"Five-spice chicken burgers with Cajun fries," Cass describes. "Plenty to go around. Let me know what you think."

"You're the best, wifey." Sam doesn't wait to dip into the bag.

"All right, we've gotta go," Cass tells Grace.

"Bye, Dad." Grace puts her arms around Sam's hips.

"I'll see you at home, Pup." Sam chews his fries fast and then kisses Grace's crown.

Grace then waves at me. "Bye, Mark!"

"Bye, sweetheart." I watch Cass and her mini-me leaving hand in hand.

"I saw you," Sam hails when we're alone in the room.

"Saw me what?" I challenge him.

"I saw you twitch every time you hear Grace call me 'Dad.'" Noticing my mouth move, he quickly adds, giving me no chance to reason, "Don't say I'm seeing things."

I roll my eyes, which earns a scoff from him.

He chatters on, "Yes, buddy, this will be one of those lectures of mine. There's a woman who's head over heels in love with you. And I know the feeling is mutual. You want a life with her? You want to be called 'Dad'? You tell her!"

I pass him a bottle of ale.

"I carve my own path. And it doesn't include a woman in it."

"Come on. She's not just any woman!"

It's true. Ivy Cavanagh is not just any woman. I admire her. I may even love her, albeit secretly. But love had once burned my life to ashes. So the only thing I could do was to dedicate what's left of me to my work.

Sam takes a bite of his burger. "God, this is good." He then carries on, "Mark, brother. There's no one I'd rather have by my side in any situation. But that love brain of yours—whatever happened to it!"

"My amygdala is just fine," I deadpan and continue devouring my lunch. Goodness—this is what you call a chicken burger.

Sam starts the television, letting the news roll without paying attention to it. While he's snacking on the last pieces of fries, I get up. "I'm gonna make some tea."

"You and your hibiscus tea," he comments, his head following me. "But don't walk away from our conversation."

We're crossing live now to The Capitol, where the attorney general is giving a press conference.

"Hah!" Sam yells victoriously. "Even NBC Montana agrees with me. Look who's on the news! It's a sign."

I ignore him, looking into the tea canister as if the hibiscus leaves would give me an answer to a question I don't even want to ask. I take my mug of tea and a jar of honey, keeping cool as I sit beside Sam.

"I see that!" he elbows me. "You twitched again."

Hell, yeah. This time I know I did. Something stirs in me every time I see that man with an earpiece by her side. The retired Army ranger turned bodyguard is in his late forties and not looking for love. But where he's standing—that used to be my place. I remember how good it felt to be her protection. How right it felt.

Ivy Wren—I like to call her by her first and middle name in my head.

She sits tall, looking straight into the camera. While facing the public, her diamond-shaped face doesn't usually give much. But when she speaks, it's her eyes as much as her voice.

The trajectory of illicit fentanyl use is alarming—especially among our youth. In Montana alone, there's been a one-thousand percent increase in fatal overdoses linked to fentanyl in the past five years.

Those ridiculous hazel eyes—mostly brown in the middle, with a tinge of green around the edge of her irises. Even through a television screen, they have the same effect on me. Whirs disturb my chest as if she was in this room, stripping me defenseless.

Strength defines Ivy Cavanagh. Yet, I've seen firsthand how that strength can yield to gentleness. Among egos and tensions, she won't hesitate to put politics aside and cool down the temperature. And she has never lost her human heart. One particular case stayed with me, where a girl with a learning disability was taken from her home. Because of Ivy's encouragement, the girl's grief-stricken father was able to talk and help with the investigation. It wasn't her role as the attorney general, and she could've left it to the police. But she stayed, and I believe her action came from a place of genuine compassion.

Today, I declare the State of Montana at war with illegal fentanyl. Now I'll be taking questions.

Her head slants as she listens to a reporter from ABC Fox. The wavy end of her hair bounces over her chest. Then she swipes her fringe aside as she gives her answer, revealing her whole face—determined, full of intent.

"The Mosaic is going to go after her," Sam comments.

Her words are indeed targeted at the alleged biggest fentanyl trafficker in the state.

"She knows what she's doing." I sip my tea, switching my

attention to her bodyguard. I sure hope that man is up to the task.

"She's lost weight, don't you think?" This is the first time we've seen her in weeks, and Sam is right. "Perhaps it's time you called her. I know small talk isn't your forte, but I'm sure she'll appreciate it."

The whirs in my chest are forming words which I maybe, possibly, could say to her if I made that call. But truly, small or big —talking to Ivy is not my forte. "What has it got to do with me?"

"You're unbelievable!" Sam cringes as I cringe to myself at what I just said. "Rena might've broken your heart." God, I haven't heard that name in years! "But I know for a fact she didn't brainwash you."

If brainwashing had been on the table, I would've chosen it in a heartbeat. What that woman did to me was a hundred times worse.

Nevertheless, everything about Ivy has got everything to do with me—because deep down I care about her. But there's a reason why I never show it.

My best friend looks me in the eye. "Remember what I told you happened when you lay unconscious in St Peter's Hospital? After you took a bullet for Grace?"

All lives are precious, but saving that girl was the best thing I've done in my life.

Sam continues, "Ivy was the first one to get to you. She was by your side when I got there. Waiting, whispering to you to hold on. And dammit, Mark, you squeezed her hand. You fucking squeezed her hand. If it takes unconsciousness for you to be aware of what's in your heart, I'm going to drag you to her and kick you in the head."

"You can't wait to see a tale of redemption?"

"You've got nothing to redeem, Mark. None of it was your

fault. Rena betrayed you. She hurt you heartlessly. You and Ivy —it's not a tale of redemption. It's about why you're here in Montana. It's why you left New York. It's about you coming out of your monolithic cave."

"She's harboring a secret."

"Who isn't?"

"Well, that's precisely why. I have secrets too."

"Do you?"

I look at him seriously.

His lips flatten. "Mark, we've known each other for how long?"

"You don't even know the half of me."

"That's an insult!"

"Didn't you say everybody harbors a secret?"

"Gah! You're annoying," Sam sulks. "Still, you're like my brother, so I'm telling you this again. She loves you."

I never deny it. Besides having confessed to Sam, she had been giving out signals. Cautious, restrained—but I knew. As a Green Beret, I was trained to read people—friends or foes. As a civilian, inadvertently, I've become an expert in reading my clients, including Ivy.

There's no mistaking a woman in love. I saw that in her every time we met—her eyes sparkled, and elation rose in her face.

Back when it was just Sam and me running Red Mark, she never failed to check on us after every assignment. She'd hug Sam with a warm smile and a firm, friendly hold. But when she came to me, her face angled down, her arms softened... She'd let her glorious brunette hair drop and caress my arm, and her neck would open up to me.

I'd never found out if it was worse to try to repel her or risk it all for her. Opening up to Ivy would've been like undoing the stitches that hold my heart together. I wasn't ready to gamble on whether Ivy Cavanagh could stem the bleeding.

In the end, I let the pain of the past win. I kept my distance and built a fortress. That's the path I've carved for myself. Because I knew the moment my heart bled again, I would stop being human, and I didn't even want to think what I'd be capable of.

Ivy's love for me is neither accepted nor rejected, and I feel responsible if she ever feels hurt. So far, she's taken it all in with finesse and regard. She keeps it professional between us, respecting our boundaries. I'm no longer her security, but since Red Mark switched focus from guarding to rescuing missing children, we continue to work together.

Sometimes I ask myself why she keeps hanging on. She doesn't need me. For god's sake, she has brought down many dangerous, powerful men with her wit and intelligence. And with her power and looks, she could have any man. But somehow, I understand her. A human heart is a beast that can't be tamed. She's the type who stands tall and has the strength to bear love alone.

Sam clears up the table, throwing away the trash-filled Thirsty Fox bag. Then something catches my eye. My protective instincts kick in seeing what's unfolding in the press conference. "What the hell is that?"

Ivy's assistant interrupts and whispers something in her ear. She immediately gets up and leaves the podium. Just as she's about to disappear off camera, I notice her taking her cell phone out.

Like a show coming straight into one's living room, my phone rings.

"Mark."

It's her.

"Ivy, are you okay?"

"Someone has taken Noah."

I put the phone on speaker so Sam can listen in.

"He was at school and... I don't know, Mark. Apparently, he followed someone and never came back. Meet me at Noah's school."

"We're on our way!" I gather my gear.

Sam does the same. "It's got to be the Mosaic!"

"We don't know that. Noah followed someone. Perhaps he knows the man."

"When you get there, take her hand, and tell her everything will be okay. Got it? Don't just stand there like an insurance salesman."

I glare at him.

"Or hug her. That'll be even better," my best friend insists.

"She's the Attorney General of Montana, and right now, she's our client."

I take the wheel, driving straight to Noah's school. By now, Sam seems to have lost his will to reason with me.

After a few moments, he starts fidgeting, rubbing his chin. I know he still has something to say.

"Mark," he drawls. His round, gray eyes settle on me as if looking for an explanation. "What did you mean when you said I don't even know the half of you?"

"Not a good time, Sam."

He quits looking at me, puffing. "I really don't want this to happen, brother. But the longer you go on like this, the stronger my vision is of you dying alone."

"I won't die alone, buddy. I'll take my killer with me."

3

IVY

Noah's classroom has been converted into a makeshift investigation quarter. I sit straight as I watch the CCTV footage, my hands resting on my thighs, out of view under the teacher's desk. My knuckles stiffen, save a finger that's been scratching a spot on my skirt.

Behind me are Captain Zander from the Helena PD and Noah's school principal. Standing by the door is Jones, my bodyguard. I wish he had been with Noah. Our intel suggested an imminent attack on me leading up to the press conference this afternoon, so the Helena PD has been focusing their efforts on *my* security. There has been police presence around the school—as a 'just in case'—but no one caught anything.

I'm not the type who looks back, but this time I can't help thinking this wouldn't have happened if Mark had been with Noah.

He used to be our security, but—

"Do you recognize that man?" Captain Zander asks.

"No." I squint at the figure next to Noah, covered up from

head to toe with a hooded jacket, sunglasses, and baggy jeans. They're walking along the outside of the school fence.

It's not so much *how* for me at the moment. It's *why*. Why did my son walk off like that with a stranger? Willingly, eagerly, as if the two had made a pact.

Whatever the reason, I can't help thinking about what happened last weekend. Noah is a rebel by nature, but we'd never fought like that before. Perhaps now he's trying to get even with me.

My head hurts like a spear had been lodged through my temple. Is an eight-year-old really capable of getting even with a parent?

"It's clear they know each other," Zander adds, pointing at the way the stranger holds my son's hand and the way Noah glances smilingly at him.

"It appears so, yeah," I admit. "I didn't see them exit the school, though."

"That's what we need to find out. Are you sure Noah never mentioned anything about a new friend or something?"

"No. And I'm telling you, I don't recognize that man, Zander." I study the captain's expression to gauge where he's at. His eyes become sharp as if reminding me this isn't the first major incident involving Noah. Two years ago, a psycho *took* him—so it was different. The creep demanded that I admit to the public I was a Russian spy after he had found out my grandmother was from Russia.

"And even if I could see his face, I don't think I'd know him," I add.

"Hm." His head bobs down, then tilts up toward the school principal. "Have you noticed a change in Noah?"

"No. This is a complete shock," she replies. Then her phone beeps. "Sam Kelleher and Mark Connor are here. I'll fetch them."

We're left alone in the room, and Zander restarts, "For the second time, have you received a threat? A demand?"

"No." I rewind the footage to observe the stranger some more. He's skinny, not overly tall. Noah stands just below his chest, so he must've been about five-foot-eight. He wraps his shoulders forward when he walks. "He could even be a boy, an older boy."

"Perhaps. Maybe someone who has been groomed to do this." Zander leans in as if trying to get my undivided attention. "We go back a long way, Ivy. I have to warn you again. It's re-election time, and the Mosaic is getting wary of you."

"I will never put my son's life in danger. You know that!" I eyeball him. "This has got nothing to do with my job. Even if I was a stay-at-home mother, I wouldn't have known this would happen. Noah didn't want me to know. That's the problem."

The doors fling open. Mark and Sam enter the room, bringing with them a sense of urgency and reassurance. If anyone can find Noah, it will be them. As usual, they're both dressed in their smart suits. They mean business, but it's not just their attire. It's in their eyes and their stances.

"Gents," Captain Zander welcomes the Red Mark leading men.

Sam comes to me first, giving me a light hug. "Ivy, How are you holding up?"

"Thanks for coming so quickly."

"AG Cavanagh." Mark reaches out his hand to shake mine.

Whatever has stiffened my knucklebones since I watched the CCTV footage, it's gone. I feel my blood starts to flow again. It may be the side effect of seeing my secret love after so long. But I know in my heart I feel what I'm feeling, because I believe Noah will be back in my arms. Today.

In true Mark style, he opts for formality in the presence of Zander and the school principal. Still, the hand I'm holding is warmer than anything I've felt since my assistant whispered in my ear, 'Someone has taken Noah.' And those cobalt eyes looking at me—they appear aloof, but I know he's with me all the way.

"What have we got?" His attention lands on the laptop as soon as he lets my hand go.

Despite his youthful appearance, Mark Connor commands authority. He's two years younger than me, but his mere presence can ground me like he was an old soul who had been with me all my life, and his words can comfort me as if he knew what the future holds. He stays cool in the middle of a fire, and he endures when others give up. Sam isn't wrong to call him stoic.

The principal drags a couple of extra chairs. Mark takes the one closest to the laptop. Then Sam gives the other to me, so I sit right next to Mark.

How I miss this. Being next to him, breathing next to him. I watch his thick hands taking over the laptop. The keys look so small under his fingers. He's not as big as Sam, but the former Green Beret's six-foot-two body is a house of muscles. The man could carry me with just one arm—and I'm speaking from experience.

"At recess this morning, Noah walked away with a young man. Or it could be an older boy," Zander recaps.

"None of your older students or staff—employees or contractors—could resemble him?" Sam questions the principal.

"I can't say for certain without looking at his face, but I don't recognize him at all."

"Is this all the footage?" Mark asks.

"From today, yes."

"All entrances and exits have been covered?"

"Yes."

"Show me the main gate again," Sam requests.

"There!" Mark points at a man walking out with a group of students and their teachers. He's not wearing a hooded jacket or sunglasses—but he is with Noah!

"I'll be damned!" Zander curses.

"He knew where the cameras were. So even when he looked 'normal' just like the other adults in that group, we still can't see his face," Mark says. "And here..." He switches to another footage. "He put his disguise back on as he fronts another camera."

"Who were those students and teachers? Coming out at once through the same gate?" Sam queries.

"We had a visit from another school, five-graders from Wyoming."

"And no one noticed that Noah had snuck into the group?" I glare at the principal.

"I'm sorry, Ms. Cavanagh." She raises her eyes at me remorsefully.

It's not good enough, but I'm not going to waste time grilling her.

"This man knows this school very well," Zander remarks.

"But I've got a feeling he's not from around here," Sam conveys. "He really looks like a stranger—a stranger who blends in, ironically."

Mark ponders. "We've got to talk to Dylan Roberts."

I feel a tug in my chest. He still remembers my son's best friend.

"Every student has gone home now," the principal informs.

"Then let's go to his house," I suggest. "I'll come with you, Mark."

"All right," Mark agrees.

"I'll stay and interview the staff." Sam pats his partner's shoulder as he gets up. "I'll let you know if I find anything."

"Stay with Sam," I instruct my bodyguard when he starts following me out.

Jones glances at Mark, the same look he always has when my former bodyguard is around. "Ms. Cavanagh…"

"Stay with Sam."

"Yes, ma'am."

"Send the footage to my phone," Mark tells Zander as we walk out.

"Consider it done."

Keeping up with my impatient pace, Mark escorts me to his car.

"Seriously?" I react when he opens the back door.

"It'll be safer."

I ignore him and climb into the passenger seat.

"As you wish," he mutters, and we get going.

Not surprisingly, he still remembers the way to Dylan's house.

"You okay?" Mark checks in on me. It's only then I realize that I've been scratching my skirt again.

"Yeah."

"Here." He passes me a bottle of water.

"Thanks."

"And perhaps it'll be wise for you to take your medication now."

I grant him an admiring smile. "You notice." The rearview mirror reveals my ghostly-white face. Everyone has to see that —but only Mark knows.

I pop a couple of fludrocortisone tablets and gulp half of the water. Then I tell him, "I grounded Noah over the weekend. No games, no tv, no phones, no computers."

"You think he's doing this because he's mad at you?"

"More than that. We had a fight at a toy store. He wanted a realistic-looking gun with pellets and all. You know my stance on guns and kids—toys or not. Noah made a real scene out of it."

"You're his mother. It's your job to discipline him, Ivy."

"I'm not sure if I went too far with the grounding. I was outraged, but mainly for his father. I knew he allowed Noah to play with those kinds of toys when he was at his house. Over the weekend, the father wasn't there to face me, so perhaps I unintentionally put it on Noah."

Mark makes a gentle turn toward the street where Dylan lives. "What did you do to him?" he asks.

"Besides the grounding? I did yell at him, desperately trying to get into his head, that he's got to listen to me, not his father—on the toy gun matter anyway."

"What happened today is not your fault," Mark assures me. "You saw how well Noah and the man interacted. This had been planned way before last weekend."

My shoulders slowly ease. Temptation almost draws me to show my gratitude by leaning into him, but I restrain myself. His words and his presence would have to do for now.

Dylan's mother greets us at the door. "Ivy, I heard what happened. Any news?"

I shake my head. "Rose, this is Mark."

"I remember. Good to see you again, Mark."

"Mrs. Roberts, can we talk to Dylan?"

"Sure. Come on in."

Dylan's room is open. The boy is playing with Lego, apparently building a space station.

"Dylan, honey, Noah's mom is here."

He tilts his head up. "Hello, Ms. C."

"Hey, Dylan. Can we talk to you for a moment?"

"Yeah." He shifts himself toward the other side of the rug he's sitting on as if giving me and Mark space to join him.

Mark unbuttons his jacket and then sits next to Dylan.

"I'm Mark. Remember me?" The big man smiles. He doesn't do that often. But when he does, his smile reveals a set of lovely dimples. Like that, he could get away with being a fresh graduate. But his deep gaze shows that he's a seasoned warrior. He's a man you want in crisis, and nothing fazes him.

"You're Noah's bodyguard," Dylan replies.

I join them, kneeling on the other side of the rug, facing the two.

Mark passes a scoop of Lego bricks that he anticipates Dylan might need. He wasn't always like this with kids. The little ones used to be afraid of him, including Noah, in the beginning. To this day, I still don't understand why—because it definitely wasn't how he looked. Maybe he took his stoicism too far. But he'd learned from Sam, and now he's a natural.

"When was the last time you spoke to Noah?"

"This morning, before recess," Dylan answers.

Mark hands over some astronaut mini figures to Dylan, asking, "Did Noah tell you anything about someone? A secret friend, maybe?"

"No."

Then Mark takes out his phone and plays the CCTV footage in front of Dylan. "Do you recognize this man?"

Dylan puts the phone close to his face. "Hm... no." Then he extends his arm, observing the man from a distance. "Wait... isn't he the painter?"

Mark glances at me, then angles his face so he can see Dylan's expression. "The painter?"

"Yeah. The guy with white paint, making the lines on the basketball courts and football field. I don't know if it's him, but he sure looks like him."

"When did you see this painter?"

"I don't know. Two weeks ago, maybe."

"Thanks, Dylan."

We rush back to the car as Mark calls his partner. "Sam, get CCTV from a couple of weeks ago. That man may be someone the school hired to repaint their sports facilities. We'll be there in fifteen."

I tap the dashboard. "You were right. This has nothing to do with that fucking toy gun."

Mark takes off his jacket. He's wearing a white shirt under it, revealing the shape of his broad shoulders. I could look away, but my eyes are shamefully unable to pass the tantalizing view—the contour of his pecs behind the fabric and those poking nipples. He doesn't seem to mind as he calmly unclips his holster, transferring it to what he calls a tactical belt which already carries his other gear. He then secures the belt around his waist—that tapered, impossibly tight waist.

He notices my lingering scrutiny, but he simply puts his jacket back on, saying, "Get Zander's best men to guard Noah twenty-four-seven. Or hire an additional guard."

"You know bodyguards drove Noah crazy. Well, he was okay with you—eventually. But after you left and we changed our security personnel, he really went berserk. The more he was guarded, the more he was convinced someone was out to get him."

Red Mark was our security for a couple of years or so. Not full-time. It was mainly when I traveled on official duty. Noah was taken by that psycho from our home when I had a late meeting with the vice president. My ex and I still lived together at the time, even though we were divorcing, and we hardly ever had guards at our house. Following Noah's rescue, that changed. Mark stayed with us twenty-four-seven for a few months—and became Noah's official 'watchbear.'

Then things settled, and Red Mark ceased providing personal security services to focus on rescuing missing children. Besides, as I embarked on life as a single mother, my love for Mark scared the hell out of me at the time. So I let him go.

If only I hadn't.

Mark inhales, showing his understanding. "I don't blame him for being frightened. The boy had gone through a lot. But the therapy worked, yeah?"

"Yes, it did. There hadn't been anything—until today."

I stare at my own lap, murmuring, "Mark..."

"Yes, Ivy?"

An invitation, not a provocation. Non-judgmental, only encouraging. He always listens before he speaks. In fact, that's the Red Mark way.

"Tell me," he says.

"There's another thing." I pause. "But you've got to keep this to yourself. A man called Deuce sent me a message. Something... about my past."

"Do you know him?"

"Heard of him, but I don't know him, no. It hasn't been proven, but so far, things point to the possibility that he's the top boss of Mosaic. You know, the organization behind the in-fashion EM2. It's basically a cheap-but-potent cocktail of meth, Tylenol, and fentanyl. No one knows what he looks like, though."

When my gaze returns to him, I'm confronted by his thinking eyes. There are a lot of questions flying in his head, I'm sure.

"What is it about your past?" he probes.

I take time to gather words that might make sense. "I don't even know if what he's claiming he knows about me is true."

"What did he say?"

I pause again, releasing nervous breaths.

"Ivy, what did he say?"

I take out my phone and show him the message.

I know you better than you know yourself, AG Cavanagh. Whatever they told you then, it was all a lie.

-Deuce

"No demand?"

"No. That was all he sent."

"When was this?"

"A couple of weeks ago."

His eyes haven't settled when he says, "You've got to know something. Otherwise, you would've told me this as soon as you were here with me."

I stay silent.

"Ivy, Noah is missing. You've got to tell me everything you know!" he raises his voice.

"I have thirty-six years of the past, and I've been lied to by so many people."

"Look, everyone has the right to keep their secrets. I respect that, but it's Noah we're talking about here. You've got fifteen minutes. If what Sam finds back at the school doesn't yield anything, you tell me everything. I don't care if it'd take you all night to tell me the thirty-six years' worth of lies you've been subjected to. Got that?"

He knows how to keep me in check, but I can't figure out what the hell the message meant and how it's connected to Noah's disappearance.

And Mark has got to know that, so I spell it out, "Whatever

lie Deuce was referring to if it wasn't another lie, that means I don't even know my own secret. You know I'll do anything to keep Noah safe. I'm his mother. And I'm not hiding anything because of re-election, if that's what you're thinking. Even if I have to show myself to the public covered in shit, I'll do it. You know that!"

Deuce's message could simply be a trick, sent just to confuse me. But if it was true, his choice of words led me to believe whatever he knew about me had nothing to do with law or politics. It was personal and intimate.

When I received that message, my immediate thought went to my parents. I never got along with them, so I figured they might not have been my parents. But I'd analyzed my birth records with a fine-toothed comb, had a DNA test done, and unfortunately, they were. Then I thought perhaps my Russian grandmother had some kind of secret connections that might jeopardize our country's security. But I couldn't find anything on her either. I even scoured through my ex-husband's history, but similarly, I came up with nothing.

Mark is still pondering hard, but his grip on the steering wheel loosens. Slowly he shifts his hand and places it on top of mine. My scratching finger may have finally gotten to his nerves. Or perhaps he simply wants to touch me.

The contact urges me to fall onto him and convince him that I'm in the dark as much as he is. But there is a boundary between us that I don't intend to cross because I can't afford to lose him.

Almost four years of unrequited love. It's long and lonely, but it has taught me a lesson nonetheless. A lesson that real love will never disappear.

It's Mark or never.

And I'm saying that with my head high, not as a fool in love. I know who I am and where I am in life. I accept that 'never' will be more than an acceptable option if Mark declares himself off-limits forever. When a man comes into your life, and he catches you when you falter—again and again—you hold on to him, even only in your heart.

Nothing fazes Mark Connor—except me. And I won't let him go just because he's too afraid to be with me.

4

MARK

I might've left my hand on hers for too long. But regardless of what kind of lies I may be dealing with, I have to let her know that I'm on her side.

Ivy receives threats on a daily basis. But that message from Deuce—even though it wasn't a threat, per se—unsettles me in a deep way.

Could that be her secret that I've been dreading?

While I'm hoping that Sam will get something on the school painter from the CCTV, I can't help going back to the first day Ivy and I met.

Townsend, four years ago. Newly elected Attorney General Ivy Forbes drove thirty-five miles from Helena to visit the Red Mark office. It wasn't much of an office then, as it was only our second day occupying the premises, and we were cash-strapped.

With no appointment and no warning, she emerged among boxes of files and gear, glowing like a saint with her shiny long hair. Her smile was intense but polite, with a degree of embarrassment because her presence had caught me, and herself, off-guard. Precisely, she caught me almost naked. But being the professional adults that we were, we got over it. As soon as she removed her sunglasses, her eyes greeted me with gladness and affection—not that different from how I saw her in Noah's classroom earlier.

She was there seeking security arrangements for her trip to a mine near the Canadian border. There was a dispute that had every chance of getting violent. The conversation that followed should have been as simple as a 'know your customer' chat. But when I asked her how many children she had, it took her a moment to answer, 'One. Just one.'

Such a simple question. Why the delay? She then tried all the tricks in the book to stop me from studying her further. In the end, she decided it was time for her to leave. Only, she fainted. That was the first time I found out about her chronic low-blood pressure condition. But with how sudden it came, I was sure extreme stress contributed to her episode that afternoon.

My assessment of people is rarely wrong. Now the question is, has that got to do with Deuce's message? And the 'lie' that Ivy claimed she didn't know?

I might know the answer soon, and I might not. For now, Noah is my priority. Unless Ivy is an unbelievably good liar, I think she's telling the truth—that she has no idea what Deuce was referring to. So I'm relying on Sam to deliver a breakthrough on who took Noah. From there, we can figure out where the boy might've been taken. Because I swear, the last thing I want is to have to tear Ivy apart. I want to protect her, not hurt her.

This whole thing—her secret, the Mosaic, Deuce, the painter—is scattered information without any connective tissue. But above the murky water, Ivy is a mother fighting to find her son, and that should be my clarity right now.

As soon as we're back at Noah's school, we join Sam,

Zander, and the school principal, who are still working in the same classroom.

"We found him." Sam shows me the CCTV footage from two weeks ago.

"That's him," I exclaim. "The Painter." From now on, it'll be his nickname.

The video keeps rolling. He's moving and finally facing the camera.

I shake my head in disappointment. Wearing sunglasses and a respirator mask, we still can't see his face. But I know it's the same person.

Ivy gasps as the pictures keep rolling. Noah has approached him on more than one occasion across multiple days.

"Oh, Noah..." She slumps back. "I never thought he would—"

"Hey, don't blame yourself," Sam says.

"Sam," I call out as something flashes in my head. "Play that footage we started with today—when he and Noah walked hand in hand."

Sam finds the segment.

"There! He threw away something!" I point.

"A piece of paper?"

"Looks like."

"That's just ten yards from the main gate. I'll take you there," the school principal says.

"I hope the wind hasn't blown it too far," Zander grits.

We inspect the ground around the footpath, scanning surfaces and scouring between shrubs.

"Got it!" Sam yells.

You're lucky this time. Take this note as my present to you. Noah is safe. He's where life reflects, and the meadow of Helena sprouts to life.

"Where the hell is that?" Sam frowns.

"I don't know. Reflects, maybe a lake?" I suggest.

"Meadow... there are hundreds of meadows around here that he could reach within—" Sam looks at his watch. "Five hours, give or take."

I think hard. "Sprouts to life. Spring?"

"Spring Meadow Lake!" Ivy exclaims. "It's only five minutes from here."

Sam and I dash to our car as Zander orders four of his men to follow us. By now, Jones the bodyguard has joined his boss, stopping her from following me. That man reminds me of Colin Farrell with a John Selleck mustache. Not that I'm trying to criticize her taste.

"Listen to him," I tell Ivy when she starts arguing with Jones. "You stay here. When we find Noah, you'll be the first to know."

She relents as Zander and Jones usher her back inside the school building.

As we hurry to Spring Meadow Lake, Sam blurts, "You haven't changed."

"Why should I change?"

"You looked like a salesman in there."

"I look like a man who's going to rescue a child. Now, focus!"

The sky has darkened when we arrive at the lake. Torrential rain is forecast. I sure hope Noah is really here and that we find him soon.

"Mark!" Sam gestures at a bench where a mound of blankets spreads across its length.

"Noah?" I approach to uncover the face of the person lying there.

"Yer motherfucker!" an old homeless man yells at me.

"Sorry!" I retreat.

We press on, canvassing the park.

"Sam!" I nudge my partner, pointing at a figure leaning against a tree. "I think it's him!"

"Noah," Sam calls. The boy is unconscious, wrapped in two layers of blankets. "He might've been sedated."

"Noah, hey, it's Mark and Sam," I whisper as I lift him into my embrace. "Call Ivy. I'll call the paramedics."

"Yeah. I'll get her to meet us at the hospital."

"You really think she'd do that?" I look at my partner. Ivy won't wait. I know that one hundred percent. "Let her come here."

I take a three-sixty-degree view of my surroundings, trying to catch any movement in case The Painter is still here. It's common for a perpetrator to linger around a scene to watch the aftermath of their crime. He could be one of the Mosaic, or he could be trying to impersonate Deuce. But I don't think he is the real Deuce. He's too young to lead such a massive and powerful organization.

Four of Zander's men crowd around us, and Sam says, "Keep looking. The kidnapper may still be around."

"Yes, sir." The squad leader directs his men to disperse around the park.

Noah writhes in my arms, then drawls, "Mark?"

"Noah. Are you okay?"

"I'm fine. Don't tell Mom, please! She'll hate me."

"Your mom doesn't hate you, Noah. She knows, and she's worried about you. She loves you more than you know."

Paramedics arrive and immediately assess Noah.

"Noah, did you see who took you?" I slowly ask.

He shakes his head.

"Okay. That's okay," I calm him down, caressing his hair. "If you remember anything, you'll tell me, won't you?"

"Yeah."

"Good boy. Rest up now. Your mom will be here soon. In fact… she's here."

"Mom!"

"Noah!" Ivy runs so fast Jones is struggling to keep up with her. The mother and son hug. "Are you okay?"

"I'm sorry, Mom," Noah begs. I've never seen the boy so distraught.

Ivy hugs him. "Apology accepted. You're here. It's all that matters. But don't you run away like that again. Please, promise me, honey."

"Yes, Mom. I promise."

"Did he hurt you?" She inspects him all over.

Noah shakes his head, then yawns.

"We'll go home soon. And you'll have a good sleep tonight. I can feel it." Ivy grins.

By now, I should be leaving them discreetly. My job is done. But my feet are weighed down by a pain coming from my chest. Stitches in my heart are starting to unravel.

No. I'm not ready to leave just yet.

And as if she knew, Ivy catches my hand. With Noah still in her other arm, she pulls me into her.

"Ivy…" I murmur.

Her pull is so strong the only thing I can do is to embrace her back. I'm a salesman no more. For the first time in my life, I touch something so beautiful I can't even describe it. A mother and son are in my embrace. They're not my own family, but it's the closest thing I've ever got to one.

"Thank you, thank you," Ivy whispers.

"You don't have to thank me," I whisper back, so close to her ear I almost kiss her.

But I loosen my hold, and the lead paramedic uses the opportunity to get things moving. "We should take Noah to the hospital now," he tells us. "He was probably sedated with something mild, like cough syrup. He'll be fine. But, just as a precaution."

"Of course." Ivy draws herself from my feeble grasp. "I'll come with him." She throws a glance at me.

"I'll follow you," I suggest, which she welcomes with a grin.

But a disquieting conversation is unfolding behind me. When I spin around, Sam is gritting, sweat coating his face as he speaks into his phone. "Cass, stay with me... Tell me where you are. Call an ambulance... Stay calm, sweetheart, okay? I'm coming!"

"What the hell was that, Sam?"

"Cass is in labor, and she's trapped in some parking garage. The gate wouldn't open."

"Oh, Sam..." Ivy sighs, hugging him. "Mark, you go with him."

"No, you stay with Ivy," Sam insists.

I wish I could be in two places at once, but Ivy makes the decision for me. "Go! Jones is here," she assures. "And Zander will have his men stationed around the clock at my house for the next few days. We'll be fine."

I swivel to face her bodyguard. "Don't let them out of your sight."

"That's my job, Connor," he boasts.

"Anything. Anything at all, you call me, got it?" I lock eyes with Ivy until she says yes.

After stopping Sam from taking the driver's seat, I unlock the car. Between us, Sam is usually the daredevil. But this time, he's a father in distress.

"I'm gonna get you there, buddy," I assert. I won't let anything happen to his wife, and I won't let him miss the birth of his child.

5

———

IVY

I'm still lying beside Noah in his bed when I receive the news that Sam and Cass have just welcomed a baby boy. Phillip Redley Kelleher.

"Oh, bless them..." I peruse the family picture, which also includes Grace, Cass' daughter from her previous marriage who looks as loving as a big sister can be.

I kiss Noah's nape, recalling the day he was born. A little chubby at the time. But in a flash, he shed his baby fat, and he's now only growing taller. His hair used to be blond like his father's, but now it's gotten darker. His other facial features are almost a carbon copy of mine. No one disputes that he is a mommy's boy.

The other day, we fought over a pellet gun. It was the first time I saw his intimidating deviance, standing upright like a big boy who could handle getting hurt. But now, asleep next to his teddy, I'm reminded how much he still needs my protection.

Noah is not an easily contented boy. He doesn't say 'yes, mommy' without trying to push his luck first. But at the same time, he'll be the one who brings me water when I'm tired.

He'll pick up flowers from the garden when he senses I'm struggling with something. And then he'll say, 'you'll be okay'…in a way. Like Mark does, sans the flowers.

Last night before bed, I tried to fish out information about who took him. But he either shook his head or shrugged at me, and I let him be, not wanting to push him.

I lie with my boy until my phone buzzes again. A call this time.

"Ivy, how are you?"

Just the voice I want to hear.

"Mark. I'm okay. I just received the news about baby Philip."

"Ah, yeah. He's adorable. Thank God the drama with Cass last night turned out to be nothing. She got to the hospital in time."

"Must've been a relief for Sam, especially."

"You bet."

I continue the conversation as I head to the kitchen, passing Nanny Linda. The fifty-year-old has been Noah's nanny since he was two years old. She's an angel—a far cry from her predecessor, who seemed to think that opening her legs to my husband was part of her job description.

Mark says. "Hey, how's Noah?"

"He's all right. Considering. Any updates?"

"The police are still processing Noah's clothes from yesterday," he explains, then takes a deep breath. "They found a few pellets in his jacket pocket."

"What do you mean?"

"I'm sorry to say this, but perhaps the toy gun may have had something to do with Noah willingly joining The Painter. I think the two were out playing the very game you banned Noah from playing. That was the lure."

"Shit, Mark."

"Still, you weren't wrong to discipline him, Ivy."

"Anything else?"

"Not so far," he replies. "Are you really okay?"

"Yeah," I sigh.

Nanny Linda gestures to me, offering tea, but I decline.

Suddenly I hear Jones opening the front door, saying, "Wait here." But the guest surely makes himself feel at home.

"Mark, I've gotta go!" I hang up.

"What the hell, Ivy?"

It's Darren Forbes, my ex-husband.

"Keep your voice down! Noah is still asleep." I gesture to him to come into my office. "Close the door."

"I'm taking Noah with me, and he'll stay in San Francisco until you've got your shit under control. And *I* will decide if that shit has really gone away."

"Not today!"

Darren stands close to me. He's not a violent man, and although I don't always agree with his choices, he is a loving father to Noah. But his presence can feel like a threat some-times. "I can't believe this happened again!"

"Noah stays with me, whatever happens. If you're not here to help, you can leave."

"Noah is not safe with you."

"What happened yesterday is my responsibility. I'm not running away from it. But taking him away from normality is the last thing he needs."

"What kind of normality are you talking about? Being in danger all the time?"

"He needs school. He needs his friends, and he needs his mother."

"His mother who's too worried about her second term being the most powerful woman in Montana? Huh?"

"Darren, enough."

"And you're talking about his friends? Like that hooded man he followed at will?"

My teeth grit. Then I blurt, "Noah followed that man because he wanted to play guns with him! And I wonder who gave our son the idea that shooting pellets was fun?"

"Don't you put this on me."

"Like I said, I am taking responsibility for what happened yesterday. But you've got to stop feeding our son things that I don't allow here."

"Fine. No more shooting." He raises both hands, then adds, "Look, I get it that you're ambitious. You want to be the woman who can have it all."

"Darren!"

"Just remember, your career has cost us our marriage. Don't let it cost us our son. Yesterday wasn't the first. May I remind you about that psycho?"

He was taking care of Noah the night when that psycho took our boy. But I'm not going to go into that.

"I'm proud to dedicate my service to Montana. It's an honor, and it's bigger than just me and you. But I won't stop being a mother to Noah. And fuck, Darren. You know our marriage breakdown wasn't just because of what you called 'my ambition.' It ended when you decided to dip your dick into that young nanny's pussy. Now, don't blame me for that!"

Darren purses his lips.

"Noah will have Jones as his full-time bodyguard," I resolve. "And the Helena PD will provide security for him and for me until we get to the bottom of the kidnapping."

Darren looks at me. "No Connor?"

"What do you think?"

"Two strikes, Ivy. The third one, I swear I'll get custody of Noah."

"You know that's not going to happen."

Darren about-faces but halts at the door. He slants his face to me. "By the way, your mother's hospice called."

I frown at his statement. "Why would they call you?"

"Because you kept ignoring them!" Darren swings one foot out of my office. "Your mother is dying."

He marches away.

Mother. Oh, Mother!

I sit in my chair, hands behind my head.

She has been out of my life since I could get out of hers. She hasn't been on my mind, and she shouldn't be now, especially when she's dying—or even dead if it's that quick.

Let her rot—in her bed or underground. I don't give a damn.

"Fuck!"

I don't give a damn, but she still manages to unleash the anger within me. I don't have long to deal with it, though. Another message from Deuce arrives on my phone.

They told you he remained nameless. But trust me, AG Cavanagh, he has a name.

My spine stiffens as if a cold hand had just pinched the back of my neck. This second message—there's still no demand or threat—it's like a beacon leading me to a place in my past I thought had never been a part of me.

Him.

I thought he'd died with the half of me that I have long forgotten—or forced myself to forget.

I rest my face on my palm, digesting the surrealness of Deuce's message. How the hell an underbelly lord knew about *him*? And what does he want out of finding *him*?

My vision blurs. It's not time for my medication yet, but I feel the need for it like a junkie craves meth. Everything is stacked against me. If there's anyone I'd want to be by my side right now, it'd be Mark.

But how far can I stretch Mark's understanding nature?

Not even his stoicism will save me. In fact, it will doom me.

No. This is too personal to share with Mark. All I have to do is get air-tight security on Noah, so Deuce can't touch him. I will deal with this secret alone even though it's bigger than anything I've faced before. This is shame, guilt, and hurt all in one. The 'he' Deuce is alluding to destroyed me. Yet, *he* defined who I was. And I loved *him* with all my heart.

Before asking someone else to understand, I have to understand it myself. When I told Mark that I might not know my own secret, I meant it. Because Deuce has brought up the impossible. That precious life—*he*'s supposed to be dead.

I call my assistant. "Cancel all my appointments today."

If Deuce is right, and that person is who I think *he* is, I won't let my mother take that secret to her grave.

6

MARK

I return to the hospital with a few goodies for the happy parents—most of them are items that the hospital doesn't supply, or they can't get from the on-site pharmacy.

I head straight to the maternity ward with both hands and elbows full.

"Hey, pal," Sam meets me at the lobby. Despite the dark smudges under his eyes, my friend has transformed from a stress ball yesterday into a proud dad this morning. Philip Redley Kelleher was born ten minutes after midnight.

"How are Cass and Phil?" I ask.

"They're doing fine, pal. Just fine."

"And you?"

He pats my shoulder a couple of times. "Never happier!"

From the constant smile gracing his face, I know my partner has taken fatherhood in his stride, as if he's been a dad for a long time. I guess with the number of kids he has saved, that instinct has always been in him.

"Let me take that," Sam offers, reaching to take a couple of bags off me. "Everything on the shopping list, I presume?"

"Yep," I answer.

He observes the bag that remains on my elbow. It actually looks more like an oversized padded bag. "Mark, I told you not to buy diapers. The hospital has plenty!"

"I know! I know! But look at the prints. They're so cute. And you can take them home if you don't need them here."

"Peter Pan?" Sam observes the pattern shown on the packaging.

"Boys ought to love those rather than the plain ones from the hospital."

"Actually, they have Winnie The Pooh."

We both laugh as I wonder what a day-old human would know about the difference between a green-clothed boy versus a yellow bear. At the end of the day, those diapers are destined for the trash once they've done their job.

"You certainly bought a lot of them." Sam scans the bulky bag one last time.

"It was an impulse buy."

"Since when do you do impulse? You think about every-thing at least twenty-four hours prior."

I smirk. Sam is like a brother to me, so I'm now acting like a proper uncle, and yes—a few things have changed in me. "Coffee?" I extend the tray to him.

"What would I do without you!" He pores over the tray and picks a plain cup, leaving the one labeled 'decaf.' He knows it's for Cass. He motions for me to follow him, in the process eyeing the flowers I'm cradling. "Cass will love those."

"I hope so. I'm still conservative, you know. Blue for boys kind of thing."

"There's nothing wrong with that," he convinces me.

"Grace still here?"

"Her uncle took her home. But man, you should've seen

her. She's just over the moon—over the moon. She's so sweet and gentle with Phil. I guess she learns from her mom," Sam gleefully explains.

"I wish I was here to see it."

"Well, Grace isn't here, but *someone* is." He winks at me and slows his pace as we approach Cass's room. "Cass is feeding Phil at the moment. Wait here."

Something whirls inside my gut.

First, at the mention of 'someone,' and second, at the prospect of being so close to a newborn baby. I saw Philip this morning through a glass window. But thinking that I might actually be asked to hold him is turning me into a nervous wreck. Rescuing missing children hasn't prepared me for this —it'll never do. Most of all, seeing a mother and baby bonding in their first days is going to create a chain reaction within me. I can feel it, although I don't know what it's going to look like yet.

But today is not about my disastrous love life—or family life, for that matter. It's about my best friend. If my fragility is going to be tested now, I'll keep my shit together and put up the hardest defense I can. I won't crumble. Not today.

The door to Cass' room is ajar, but Sam knocks anyway. "Cass, Mark is here."

"Come in, come in."

Sam steps in first. "Oh? Where's Ivy?"

I release a breath. I knew that 'someone' was her.

"She went out to answer a phone call," Cass says. "I'm sure she'll be back soon."

"Come on, buddy, don't be a stranger now!" Sam cringes at me. He opens the door wide after setting the shopping bags down in the corner of the room.

The bouquet almost covers half of my face as I gather

myself. As soon as I see baby Philip cradled securely in his mother's arms and his father standing guard, it's not hard to let my happiness out. I don't have to put up a wall. The chain reaction that I'm feeling is only that of joy. It lifts me up as I bury my dark thoughts in the deep corner of my heart—one that had been restitched quickly after yesterday's events with Ivy and Noah.

"Hello, beautiful." I give Cass a peck on her cheek after resting the flowers on the bedside table.

She scans the shopping bags and everything else in my hands. "You know how to make a woman's day. Those flowers... they're gorgeous." She's so radiant. I can't blame my friend for not taking his eyes off her. "Meet Philip."

I reach out to caress his rosy cheek.

"With Cass, he only sleeps after he feeds. But when he's with me, he sleeps all the time," Sam gushes.

"Those arms of yours are baby-proof, huh?"

"Oh yeah, brother!" He rubs his bulging biceps.

"Hold him." Cass hands Philip to me.

My trepidation melts away as soon as that tiny form touches my skin. With my palms supporting him, I draw him close to my chest. He feels so vulnerable that I swear I'll protect this little man come what may, just like how I protected his big sister. "Hello, buddy," I whisper. Philip stays asleep peacefully, oblivious to everything around him.

While I'm admiring the miracle of life in my arms, Cass takes the time to rummage into the shopping bags while sipping the coffee I brought her. "Oh, you're a star, Mark!" she exclaims when she finds the hand lotion and lip balm that Sam asked me to buy.

"You're welcome," I say, perhaps too loud, and Philip stirs. I rock him, and he bats his eyelids open for half a second, then closes them. I get weak. I swear he was looking at me.

"Is there anything you want to tell me?" Sam keenly studies me. "You're so ready to be a dad!"

That's exactly 'the half of me' that my best friend doesn't know.

I plant a light kiss on Philip's forehead, and he wakes. Alas, this time, he follows it up with a loud cry. "Oh, sorry, buddy." He cries even harder. "Okay, okay, you want Mommy or Daddy?"

Smiling, Sam scoots to my side, taking over Philip.

"After all, I may not be ready," I concede.

"What is it, little guy?" Sam cradles his son. "That was Mark. Did he scare you?" He then glances at me.

I know what that glance means. Back in the day, I used to make little kids cry. Apparently, I was lacking 'kiddie empathy'—which Sam has plenty of. But I'm sure I'm past that stage. These days I fancy myself as a child whisperer. My mastery may not extend to babies yet, though.

"Hey, those are from Ben." Cass nods at a box full of cake slices.

Now that's proof that good things happen to good people. Ben Winter's carrot cake is to die for. But beyond my hungry belly, I'm reminded of something, and it's got nothing to do with his baking skills.

"How's your brother doing with his Taekwondo school?" I casually ask Cass. Ben has been on my recruitment radar, but so far, no bite.

"He's doing all right, I think. But between you and me, his entrepreneurial skills have a lot to be desired."

There's something about Ben Winter that I can't ignore. Despite his gigantic physique, the Taekwondo master knows something about kids that perhaps none of the current Red Mark men do. As a teacher, he's an expert in balancing discipline and care. Much as I'd want to claim that I'm Grace's favorite uncle, there's no denying the bond between her and Ben. In the absence of a father, prior to Sam coming into her life, Grace had relied on Ben to fill the void.

"You know our door is always open." I leave Cass with a reminder.

"I'll tell him," she responds.

After a few minutes, Philip decides neither of the men in the room has what he wants.

"I'll get him." Cass extends her arms to Sam as the baby bawls. "I think he's still hungry."

Sam stoops beside his wife. "Finish your coffee. I'll try another trick."

"No, it's fine. Go and have coffee with Mark. I'm sure you need another one." She indicates the empty cup in the trash. Sam has finished that in no time.

"Okay, sweetheart." Sam kisses her crown. He then caresses Philip's head, and his wide palm overlaps with Cass's hand. "Be good," he whispers.

"Sam, while you're there, can you buy me a chocolate chip cookie?"

"Of course."

"Two?"

"I'll get three," he decides, then ushers me to the corridor.

"I can't believe you did it, Sam."

Sam puts an arm around my shoulders. "You know, there's a degree of truth in the saying that a man is no good alone. It's just inherently in us, Mark, that we need a partner and perhaps a family. How well you squash that need will determine your path, I guess. But speaking from experience, it's almost impossible to do. You may do it once, but it'll surface when you least expect it."

"Maybe. But then again, something profound might

happen in your life where you simply have no choice but to squash that need."

"True. True. But for you, my friend, it's not too late, you know." His gaze penetrates my defenseless state.

"You believe that?" I deadpan.

"Of course." Confidence is all over him. "You know I don't do bullshit. You're not that special, you know?" He elbows my shoulder while tossing me a wicked grin.

Not that special?

Sam carries on, "Men get wounded, men heal. You can too."

"No, I'm not that special, Sam. But everything happens for a reason."

"Like your doomed wedding to Rena?"

"Yeah, like my doomed wedding."

We take the elevator down to the café, but he stops as soon as we step out to the floor. "Mark, what happened between you and Rena? The part that you told me I only knew half of?"

The possibility of a new relationship has been pushed from my mind. He knows it. A lot of people know it. And I've always used my disastrous wedding as my reason. But there is a much deeper wound that never heals. The pain is constant, but I've never shown it. Not to anybody.

"Well, actually." Sam assesses me. "Don't tell it to me. Tell it to *her*."

My damn life!

There she is—in the middle of the queue of people trying to get their caffeine fix. Perhaps hearing us or sensing us, she angles her head and leaves the line.

She strides toward Sam and me with a wide smile. "Hey, guys."

Sam peeks at his phone. "Oh, look, Cass needs me. I'd better get back. Why don't you talk to Mark?"

"What about her cookies?" I yell as my best friend runs to catch the elevator.

"She'll change her mind." Sam waves at me.

"Ivy."

"Mark."

As always, she's impeccably dressed. But today I notice a few stains on her shirt.

"Ah, it's baby Phil's," she cackles.

She has a different look. She's not AG Cavanagh. She's not the tense Ivy I'm used to. I imagine she would've cradled Philip for a while, giving Cass a break. She might've shed a tear or two. Whatever it was, there's a kind of happiness I haven't seen on her.

And that takes me back to the question I asked on the first day I met her—when she answered, 'One. Just one.' There was confusion, anger, and regret in her tone as she put her veil up. Maybe she was desperate to have another child, and she couldn't?

"I was hoping to see you here," she confesses.

"Is everything okay?"

"Yeah. Any news from the Helena PD?"

"Forensics found a few strands of hair. They match Noah's classmates' DNAs, including Dylan's. They also found something on the pellets. They're still processing it."

"Okay. Keep me in the loop, please. I kinda don't want to deal with Zander at the moment."

"Why?"

"You know this isn't the first time someone kidnapped my son. I feel like the worst mother when I'm with him. And the press, too, for that matter."

"The important people know who you are. Other people who make you crazy, well, it's their job. You're their attorney general."

That extracts a smile from her.

"Mark, I need to go to Missoula."

"Your mother?"

"Yeah. She's dying."

"I'm sorry to hear."

"Don't be. You know I call her 'mother' just because I don't have another acceptable word that doesn't make me sound nasty like her." The remark doesn't surprise me. "Noah and Jones will come along, but I would feel a lot better if you came with us."

"Of course I'll come with you."

"Thanks." She gulps. "It's been a hard day. Perhaps harder than yesterday, and I need all the help I can get."

"I'm here." I take a step closer to her. The incident with Noah, her confession about Deuce's message, my moment with baby Phil, and now her distraught face are triggering another kind of chain reaction. The need to comfort her takes over.

I square my chest, opening to her. I want her to lean on me —and more.

She comes to me but stops short of falling all the way. She simply places her cheek on my pec and rests a hand on my hip. Her bony shoulder pokes at my ribs, making me realize how thin she is. I'll get to the bottom of that when the time is right.

"Are you sure you're okay?"

She nods slightly.

"Your blood pressure under control?"

"Yeah. I took my meds just now."

"Good. You know I'm here for you."

"Thanks, Mark." She withdraws, straightening herself.

"When do you want to leave?"

"Now?"

"You won't give me time to change?"

She appraises my long-sleeved tee. "You look fine."

"Let's say goodbye to baby Philip first."

She beams at the mention of the name. "Good idea."

We go in two different directions, even though we're heading to the same floor. Ivy loathes elevators. I should've remembered.

"Ivy," I call, extending my hand as I hold the elevator.

Ivy looks at me. That fear...I know it's the work of her mother.

"For old time's sake?" I try to convince her.

Tentatively she abandons the emergency door. She takes my hand—icy cold but familiar. Something sparks in me, knowing I still have her trust.

The elevator doors rattle as they slide shut, and so do her fingers. I withdraw my hand so I can slip my arm around her waist. Her palm meets mine, completing the loop like a belt, locking my hold. With that, I let her lean on me. This is how Ivy Cavanagh survives confined spaces.

"You okay?" I whisper, slanting my face so it touches her hair.

"Maybe."

"Where's Jones?"

"He's with Noah at home. So we'll need to pick them up before heading to Missoula."

"Tell me. Does he ever take the elevator with you?"

She releases a small chuckle. "Sometimes. When it's big and steady enough."

Back in the day, Ivy would choose elevators over stairs—but only when she was with me. Jones will never replace me. I hope no other man will.

I glance at the stains on her shirt, once again imagining

baby Philip in her arms. What the hell am I dealing with? The chain reaction I'm trying to contain isn't just about emotions. It's a vision. Part of me wants to believe that Sam was right—that it is not too late for me.

7

———

IVY

We're taking two cars to Missoula, so when we get to the hospice, Mark can take Noah somewhere more cheerful while I stay with Jones in that grim place.

Keeping thoughts about my dying mother at bay and stopping myself from speculating what she's going to say about the secret, I'm absorbing all good vibes from my handsome driver in his brand-new Jeep Grand Wagoneer.

My fingers trail the smooth walnut finish along the dashboard. "The touch of luxury," I quip.

"I thought it was time to treat myself to a new land yacht. Not that my other one is bad," he replies with a sideway smile.

He's been called cute, baby-faced, forever young, a pin-up boy. Those calls aren't entirely wrong. Sometimes his eyes look dreamy. Or his light brown hair may appear boyish. But those soft qualities are complemented by defined cheeks and jawline. Especially when he's thinking or when he's in Red Mark mode. Then, his strength and determination are easily recognizable. He has earned his badge of courage—in the military and as a civilian. He took a bullet for Sam's adopted daughter and nearly died. That's the kind of courage Mark possesses.

Besides his reputation as a children's rescue specialist, people nickname him 'the last best man of the last best place.' But he's a lone tree and never appears to crave company. Even when Miss Montana tried to bend his heart, he simply said, 'I'm sure you're amazing, and I appreciate your interest. But I just don't feel the same.'

So I heard that and wondered if it was his standard line for every woman who pursued him. Fortunately, he hasn't said it to me.

He and Sam have been tight-lipped about what happened between him and his last love. Surely, no breakup should break a man that bad. Not Mark. And that makes him, in my book, the last great mystery of mankind.

"Turn on the massage if you like," he gushes.

"This seat is already comfortable. And I don't want to fall asleep." Hell no. Much as I dread our destination, I don't want to miss his presence even by a second.

Mark then checks on Noah through the rearview mirror.

"You're all good there, buddy?"

"Yeah." The boy is unusually chilled this afternoon. Perhaps the change of scenery agrees with him.

Mark glances at the side-view mirror.

"He's not going anywhere," I remark. Jones is driving my car, following right behind us.

"He's good. He's jealous of me, but he's good," Mark teases me.

"Why should he be jealous of you?"

"He hasn't cracked the elevator pitch yet."

I acknowledge him with a chuckle. No one else ever will.

We're entering Missoula, and the smell of Mark's Grand Wagoneer fresh leather is slowly taken over by my imagined scent of the hospice. At the same time, a sudden move behind me grabs my attention.

"What is it, Noah?" I check the boy.

"Nothing."

Through the side-view mirror, I catch someone in a hooded jacket lingering on the sidewalk. My teeth grit, blatantly looking back to observe the young man. He's too tall to be The Painter. But Noah's reaction unnerves me. Is he looking out for him? Missing him, even?

I focus on the street once again, and I feel a touch on my hand. My index knuckle rises and falls against it.

"Hey, relax." Mark flattens his palm, squashing my fidgeting finger.

"I saw that!" Noah exclaims, half-grinning.

I scoff. "What did you see?"

"Mom does that a lot, and it drives me nuts," he reveals.

I bite a lip. I thought his comment was for Mark holding my hand. But my son knows about my scratching habit.

"What do you want to see in Missoula?" Mark checks in with Noah.

"Well, I don't know. I'll do anything, I guess. With you." My son seems happy to leave everything in Mark's hands.

"Let's swap here," I tell Mark. The hospice is just around the corner, but I don't want Noah to catch even a glimpse of it.

"All right." Mark pulls over. Jones stops right behind us.

I join Noah in the backseat before I leave. "I won't be long. Listen to Mark, okay? Listen to *everything* he says."

Noah looks at me. It's not his trouble-seeking look. It's a curious one. "Can I see her?"

His question takes me by surprise.

I put my arm around his shoulders. "Look, Noah. My mother is not like Grandma Dorothy." I mention his favorite nanna, Darren's mother—his only nanna. "Grandma Dorothy is kind. She loves you. She cooks your favorite food when you visit her in San Fran, right?"

Noah nods.

"My mother is different. I'll explain it to you when the time comes. For now, you go with Mark." I kiss his forehead and hop out. Then I turn to the man who's about to be my son's guardian once more. "I'll meet you when I'm done."

"Sure. We won't be far. Call me when you need me." He turns to Noah. "Come on, buddy. You wanna see some puppies?"

"For real?"

"Yeah. Let's go."

Noah's and Mark's voices fade as I join Jones inside my car.

The sight of the dull, weathered building stirs my gut and messes with my vision like I'd been swallowing too many painkillers.

"I'm here to see Eloise Cavanagh." Even saying her name feels toxic.

"This way, Ms. Cavanagh." A nurse guides me to my mother's room.

I linger in the doorway, looking at the frail form lying on the bed, covered with a white blanket. Her hands are at her sides.

"Take your time, Ms. Cavanagh." The nurse squeezes past me and leaves the room.

I step in, approaching the bed while the door closes behind me.

Mother's face hasn't changed. Even at this age, you can see she's a beautiful woman. But those hands of hers... Never mind her slaps. The thing I remember most about those hands is them holding a lock and key.

My ears sting, hearing an imaginary click—the dreadful click when she punished me inside that cage.

With that thought, I see her hand twitch.

"Mother, it's me. Ivy."

She remains asleep.

I touch the top of her palm. It feels scaly, like a snake shedding its skin for the last time. She's dying, but she's been dead to me for a long time.

Still, what she did has never left me.

That fucking basement cage—her weapon of choice to so-called 'straighten me up.' I could be left there for hours with only a bottle of water, sometimes all day until I'd wet myself. There were holes in the cage doors, and through them, I saw those hands pressing the lock and turning the key. They were lady's hands, but even then, I'd already seen witch's wrinkles on them.

A lot of parents treat their children's wandering minds like a disease. Some ignorantly call it ADHD. Being a lawyer now, people probably wouldn't believe that I had trouble focusing at school—or on anything that my parents ordered me to. My imagination was my best friend. And that was exactly how I survived Mother's torture.

My fantasy.

Yes. Once upon a time, I dreamed about someone rescuing me. It started with vague visions like a policeman or firefighter, his faces hidden behind their headgear. But as the punishments went on, the vision cleared up. My fantasy became vivid. It was a handsome boy, gentle, his voice reassuring. Since my mother stopped putting me in that cage, though, no one has ever made me go inside a confined space. Because I knew that boy had never existed.

Until Mark.

He was my security, but it wasn't only his body. He had the kind of energy that calmed me. Still does, and the witch's spell is slowly dissipating. Maybe when she's really dead, I'll be able to get out of her clutches. But for now, I need her to be alive.

"Ivy?"

"I'm here, Mother."

She catches my hand feebly, but her eyes stay closed.

"Don't you want to look at me?"

"You're here. I know," she croaks.

"Mother, what did you do to my baby?"

Her shoulders shift. She clearly wants to push herself up, but she can't. In the end, she gives up, huffing, "He died, dear."

"You've been lying to me."

"We buried him, don't you remember?" Tears fall from her closed lids. For what, I don't know.

"But I never saw him."

This time, Mother forces herself to open her eyes. Her pupils are cloudy, their strength completely gone.

"What did you do to my baby, Mother? If I can call you that."

"He died, and I saved you."

I shake my head. "What's his name?"

"He never had a name."

I squeeze her hand, a threatening pressure.

"Where is he?"

Her lids slowly fall shut as her breathing grows coarse. I don't know where it's coming from, but her voice comes out loud and clear, "I'm going to see your father now."

"You're still not going to tell me?" I raise my voice.

Her mouth gapes, releasing a series of wheezes. Her fingers wrap around my palm, shivering.

"Don't you dare go!"

But the tension in her jaws slacks as if her spirit has dissipated into thin air.

"Where is my baby?" I shake her.

Deuce's messages flash in front of me like a vision. It shocks me that I'm believing a dangerous man whose face I don't even know over my own mother.

Is my judgment skewed?

Perhaps.

But I'd deem Deuce more credible, even though my mother nor he has any credibility.

A breath escapes Eloise's shrinking lips. "Arthur..."

"You go and see that man," I whisper. "You deserve each other."

8

___

MARK

The Missoula animal shelter is having an open house. Apparently, they've been overrun with surrendered pets following the jump in the adoption during the Christmas period. A lot of people have this idea that pets make perfect gifts—unfortunately, upon ignorance or impulse.

"Oh, look! That dog has wheels attached to him." Noah points at a black Labrador coming out of the vet's office.

"Yeah. His hind legs are injured. That's why they put him in a doggy wheelchair."

"I want to pet Jasper again," Noah requests. Jasper, the gray and white Great Dane puppy, seems to be his favorite.

"Okay. Let's go back to Jasper."

We walk back to the 'large dogs' area of the shelter.

"You're back." One of the shelter staff smiles at Noah as we approach Jasper's cage. "Would you like to play with him again?"

Noah nods, and the lady lets Jasper out into a cordoned space so we can interact with him away from other dogs. Apparently, Jasper hasn't mastered the art of canine socializing yet.

"Here, you can give him some treats," the lady adds.

"Thanks." Noah tries to calm the jumping mutt. "Easy, boy. Sit. Good puppy!"

While the boy is busy trying to get the dog to do tricks, I ask, "Noah, when you were with that guy yesterday, what did you talk about?"

Noah rests his cheek on Jasper's head, not answering.

"What's his name?" I probe further.

He shrugs, then responds, "I don't know. He said to call him 'bro.'"

"Did he call you that, too?

"No. He called me Noah." He kisses the puppy's head, smiling to himself. "I love you, boy."

A lot of friends call each other 'bro,' and perhaps The Painter was simply trying to cozy up to his victim to gain his trust. But something on Noah's face tells me there was fondness behind the call. "He sounded like a cool guy."

"Yeah, he's cool."

"Do you think if Dylan was there, he would've asked him to call him 'bro' too?" I put his best friend in the scenario, testing him.

"No," Noah answers adamantly.

"You must be special then," I comment, and he simply kisses Jasper again. "Did you see his face?"

"Yeah. We played."

"What did he look like?"

"Well, you're not going to find him." Noah tries to escape my stare.

"Right. Does he go to school too?"

"I don't know."

"How old do you think he is?"

"I don't know."

"Can you guess?"

Noah gives Jasper a treat without the dog doing anything this time. "Old. Like, high-school old."

"I see."

I observe Noah playing tug-of-war with Jasper while still keeping watch on our surroundings. A man in a suit, wearing sunglasses, is loitering around the puppy play area. He's away from us, but his gaze is on Noah.

I crouch closer to my little protectee, wrapping him from behind while giving Jasper a vigorous belly rub. That man is not going to get to Noah without going through me.

"He likes it!" Noah squeals, amused by the wriggling puppy.

While tickling Jasper's belly, my other hand is on the handle of my gun concealed behind my baggy tee. I keep showing my back to the man, who's starting to circle the area.

Then he stops, smiling at a woman coming out of the vet's office. "There you are!" he calls, and the two kiss.

I release a relieved breath. Just a man waiting for his girlfriend or wife.

Still, the atmosphere has changed. Something is unsettling me. It's time to go.

While Noah is busy trying to repel Jasper's licking, I call Jones. "Stay at the hospice. I'm coming to you. Wait at the lobby."

"What? We're going?" Noah protests upon hearing my conversation.

"One last pet, and we'll go and see Mom."

"I thought she'd meet us here."

"Nah. Let's give her a surprise."

"With Jasper?" The boy passes me a cheeky grin.

"Yeah, right! Your mom would kill me."

I slip two hundred dollars into the donation box on our way out. A couple of cars exit the complex at the same time, but they look to be families, and they go the other way. No one seems to be tailing me.

We meet Ivy at the hospice, showing off our 'I hugged a puppy' stickers on our shirts.

"Nice one," she muses, trying to hide her wretched face.

"Noah, stay with Jones for a bit, okay?" I gesture to the bodyguard to take the boy to my car.

"She's gone, Mark," Ivy mutters when we're alone in the lobby.

I know not to say, 'I'm sorry.' I simply take her hand. "How are you feeling?"

"Nothing, really."

With how tight she's holding me now, I don't believe her, but I let it slide. "I know a place where we can have lunch. You'll love it."

She shakes her head tentatively. "Nice idea, but I don't feel like sitting at a restaurant."

"We'll get it to go."

"Okay then."

We stop on the way to get some mac and cheese before we hit the highway.

"I knew you'd like it," I comment as Ivy devours her generously creamy lunch.

She tosses me a smile—a cheesy one—and I wipe her lips. They stay parted in a smile as if asking me to do it again. A dangerous invitation, which I leave alone.

"How's yours, buddy?" I ask Noah.

"Good. Good," he answers through a mouthful.

An hour away from home, Noah falls asleep. I take the opportunity to talk to Ivy alone.

"I'm glad you enjoyed the mac and cheese."

She hitches a shoulder up, and her smile is one of happiness and contentment. "I can't remember the last time I had it before today."

"It's the ultimate comfort food. Can't argue with that."

"You know how to comfort me." She glances at me sweetly.

I acknowledge her with a playful smile. Then I ask, "Did Noah tell you anything about The Painter?"

"No. And I haven't really wanted to ask again—after he refused to say anything last night."

"I understand."

She ponders. "How are your parents, by the way?"

That's her way of changing the conversation. "They're doing well. Striding into their seventies in style."

"They're still in New York?"

"Yeah. They're going on a twenty-day cruise to northern Europe."

"That is style," she comments. "What is it like, to have great parents?"

I look at her, trying to find the right way to answer. "You can ask Noah."

She sniggers. "Darren and I are hardly model parents. We're divorced, for God's sake!"

"It doesn't mean you're not good parents."

"I guess we'll see when he's grown up." She leans back, apparently reflecting. "One good thing I learned from my parents is their love of this state. Look at what we've got here, Mark."

We gaze into the setting sun in front of us for a while. There's a reason why Montana is called Big Sky Country. The heavens here are like nothing else in the world.

"I can't disagree."

"It's worth everything you've got. To protect it. If only I could say I learned more than that from them."

"Every family has its disaster. Yours is an extreme example, and you never deserved it."

Arthur and Eloise Cavanagh were prominent Montanan politicians. Strict, conservative, and according to what Ivy had told me, monstrous. The estranged relationship between her and her mother had become apparent not long after she signed up with Red Mark. Eloise came up in our conversations every now and then. Her father died when Ivy was seventeen, but apparently, he was just as vicious.

"I'm surprised I hadn't ended up in youth detention or something," she gripes.

"You're lovely."

She guffaws. "Lovely?"

I feel silly but honest at the same time. I didn't give it much thought, but it was the first word that came to mind, and I don't know why.

"Well... maybe that's not the best word to describe you, but... you're a good person, Ivy."

"You really mean that?" Her eyes beg me to say more.

"Yes. I'll never lie to you."

Her eyes smile with her. The brown in her irises lightens, sparkling like amber. There, the kindness in her comes to the surface. She's full of appreciation and humility as if no one had ever told her that.

She then asks, "So, what was your family disaster?"

"It wasn't so much a disaster, looking back now. I was a spoiled child, if you must know."

She cringes. "Well, that would've been a disaster!"

Ivy Cavanagh wouldn't have even looked at me had I stayed that way, that's for sure.

I continue. "Being the only child, my parents almost never said no to me. But I grew up okay. I did well at school, and one day I decided to join the Army."

"And they made you a man."

"Perhaps. My mother cried for days when I told her. At the time, I felt unsupported, misunderstood, and all that. But my dad was cool. And my mom got over it eventually."

"She was sure glad you retired a healthy, still-full-of-life, Special Forces Major Connor?"

"She was, indeed."

"Me too," she says.

I take in her statement along with her gaze. While Sam doesn't know half of my story, she doesn't know any of it, although no doubt she's been speculating. However, when she looks like that with the Montana sunlight caressing her flawless complexion, she is truly *lovely*.

9

IVY

"Home sweet home," Mark murmurs to me, so soft I can imagine that's how his bedroom voice would sound.

"Noah, you awake?" I hop out, slinking myself into the backseat. He's still asleep. Perhaps that's why Mark is putting his 'bedroom voice' on.

Despite not getting anything from my dead mother this afternoon, I don't regret the trip. But now that we're home, I can't help feeling like I'm walking out of a theatre in the middle of a romantic movie. Because it's the end of the journey. It's the end of Mark being next to me.

Jones has checked the house and given us the all-clear.

"Noah, we're home." I nudge him.

"Jasper! Come back..."

My heart thumps behind my ribcage. I don't recognize that name. "Is he calling The Painter?" I swivel to Mark, who's standing behind me.

His mouth hooks a calm smile—and those dimples. "No. That's his favorite puppy at the shelter."

"Oh..."

Noah finally wakes, dragging his feet as we head inside.

"You go and have a shower, okay?" I tell my son, ushering him upstairs.

"I'm fine by myself, Mom," he complains, fully alert now. He slips ahead of me.

Jones follows him upstairs while I stay on the landing.

"All windows are shut?" I feel that I needed to ask.

"Yes, ma'am."

I watch Noah plodding into the bathroom, pajamas draping off his arm. "Don't forget to turn on the fan."

"Okay, Mom." He shuts the door.

"Stay with him," I instruct Jones.

I rejoin Mark downstairs. He's waiting for me with a pot of tea and two cups. From the smell, I know he has chosen hibiscus.

"Trying to recreate our first meeting?" I speculate.

He reaches out his arm, gesturing to me to sit down. "I was going to pour us some wine. But then, I thought it wasn't a good idea."

"Tea is fine." I mimic myself replying to him that fateful afternoon in Townsend when he apologized for not having other beverages at his office.

He gets it and smiles shyly. Mark and shy don't go together, but there he is, no doubt reminiscing the awkward moment I saw him for the first time—before the tea was served. I arrived at the location of Red Mark's original office, wondering if I was at the right place. There was no sign, and the front room was full of boxes, impossible to see anything—including a door which I accidentally pushed open, revealing a magnificent body of a man, wearing only his underwear, hissing, 'Jesus Christ!'

"Why did you choose us?"

I glance at him, controlling myself so I don't unleash an x-ray exam on his body under his long-sleeve tee.

"Because you were cheap," I respond, and he cackles. "The state had no budget for security. I mean, they do for the governor, but not me. So everything had to come out of my pocket," I defend my statement.

"You trusted the new and cheap guys?"

"If an oil tycoon worth billions had trusted you, there wouldn't be any reason for me not to."

Sam and Mark were experienced bodyguards in their native New York, but I was their first Montanan client when I became attorney general. Despite that, I had no qualms about signing them up. Never mind that they're the most gorgeous men I'd ever met. Sam is a real-life Hercules with human emotions. And Mark? He makes brooding sexy, he turns listening to desire, and he allows Ivy Cavanagh to be herself. But it was the fact that *they listened* that convinced me they were who I needed.

I sip my tea. He knows how to make it just right. "Thanks for today. I really appreciate it."

"Does that mean you're not going to pay me?"

I laugh, letting myself fall back onto the pile of cushions behind me. Fatigue seems to have caught up with me, but I don't want the night to end.

"Tell me, Mark. If you could change anything, what would you change?"

He sighs, following me in and leaning back. "Not a lot. But there are probably a couple of things."

"What are they?"

He scoffs. "I won't tell you."

"Fair enough." I give in without insisting. If he won't tell me, he won't tell me. "There are a lot of things I would change," I admit. Since I received Deuce's messages, I have been wishing I'd stayed awake when they wheeled me into the Missoula Birth Center.

"Tell me one," Mark prods.

I close my eyes. If he looks into them too long, he'll see it. I don't want him even to get a whiff of that part of my past. So I face him, telling him silently that it's him that I wish I could change. Something that I'm sure he already knows. "I'm not sure if I'll ever graduate from the school of letting go."

"What does that really mean, Ivy?"

"I hold onto things, Mark."

"At some point in life, you'll run out of space. And may I say, perhaps you're close to it."

I sit up straight, scooting myself forward, staring at the small hibiscus leaves dancing in my cup. "I wish I knew the future. I want to know what'll happen to me tomorrow, next week. Next month, next year. So I can plan how much room I will need."

"No, you don't."

"I do."

"You hold onto things that you cherish, not things you hate."

"Do you?" I challenge him. Surely, he's been doing the same.

"I can live in the dark, Ivy. It's not everyone's cup of tea, but I'm telling you this because I care about you. I don't want you to dwell in your dark past."

My dark past is someone's life—one that I created. One that was in me for the whole nine months. I can't dwell in it. It dwells in me.

He adds, "You're strong, but I never want to see you snap."

"Do you remember what you said the first time I had to step into an elevator with you?" I remind him.

"We were in the mine, near the Canadian border," he answers matter-of-factly.

I still remember that moment as clear as yesterday. I was

assisting the EPA settle a dispute there, and we were invited down into one of the shafts.

Mark shifts his sitting position, facing me. "Didn't I tell you that when you're with me, you're allowed to be afraid?"

I complete him, "Because it's your job to turn it around and make me feel safe."

That mine shaft was the first time I confronted my claustrophobia. I was partly driven by pride. I stepped into the wooden elevator, refusing to be the laughingstock of the miners and officials present in the negotiation. But it was because of Mark's hold and the assurance that he was standing behind me no matter what that I managed to stay, allowing the doors to be closed. Even though I was shitting myself inside, I survived. Because of Mark.

"Mom, I'm going to bed now," Noah calls from upstairs.

I get up, about to say goodnight. But my world flips, and my body falls back almost horizontally. This time I'm not going to land on any cushion.

10

______

MARK

"Ivy!"

I catch her mid-fall.

"Mom!" Noah calls out from the gallery upstairs.

"She's fine, Noah. She's just tired." I eyeball Jones to take Noah to his room.

"Ivy." I tap her cheek while maintaining my grip on her body. She's always been slim, and I can still feel her curves, but she's worryingly light.

"Mark," she sighs painfully as I take her upstairs. She lifts her arm, resting it on my shoulder.

"I'm here."

She slants her face toward my chest. I can hold her like this forever. I'm doing what I do best—making her feel safe. But the circumstance is plain wrong.

I lay her on her bed, pulling the covers over her.

"Mom..." Noah enters.

Ivy's head lifts. "Hey, I'm okay. I just got dizzy."

Noah places both of his hands on her arms, massaging her lightly. "Is that good?"

This is the first time I've witnessed the softer side of Noah.

Despite the shenanigans he sometimes creates, it seems the boy knows how to comfort his mother.

"Yeah. It feels good." She holds her son's hand. "It's late. Why don't you go to bed?"

"You want water?"

"Thanks, Noah. Mark will get it for me."

"Okay. Night, Mom." He kisses her and then joins Jones, who's waiting just outside Ivy's room.

I shut the door.

"I guess the tea was a bad idea." I recall that she fainted at Red Mark's Townsend office that afternoon, too, after the tea I served.

"Don't be ridiculous. I have it regularly and I'm usually fine." She shifts herself so her head falls right in the middle of the oversized pillow.

Dismissing that tea was the culprit, I get her a glass of water. Then I crouch next to her. "Look, Ivy. I'm saying this respectfully from a place of care. You've lost weight, and this— this is more than just your low blood pressure."

She draws a breath. "Mark, please."

"Anything you want to tell me?"

"Was this why you fed me mac and cheese this afternoon?"

I chuckle. "Partly, yes."

"Damn you," she flirts. "Well, I haven't been on a diet, or drugs, or anything stupid. I had surgery to remove a kidney stone about a month ago."

"Oh, gee. Are you okay now?"

"It was minor surgery. But, yeah, I've fully recovered."

It wasn't good, but I'm glad the reason was medical, and it has been resolved. "I bet you didn't take a break afterward?"

"What do you think?" She shoots a glare. "But I'm okay. And thank you for asking."

"You go and rest. I'll check on Noah."

"Will you stay the night?" She keeps her voice low as if wanting to let me know she's giving me a real choice, not pushing for a 'yes.'

"Sure, if that's what you want."

She blinks, waiting for my next move.

"Good night." I brush her hand, then plod away.

She's now lying on her side, pulling the covers up to her chin. Just as I'm about to open the door, she murmurs, "Mark."

"Yes?"

"I'm scared."

She has never said it before. Even when she was terrified out of her mind being inside that mine's elevator. Even after a group had pranked her on her second visit. When they covered a shallow void, waiting for her to trip into it. It might've been a joke for them, but I knew it wasn't a laughing matter for her.

I caught her one-handed as soon as I heard her stepping onto a hollow spot. The plywood disguise crumbled into a pile of mud below, but she was secure in my arm while my other hand was drawing my gun, ready to teach anyone a lesson if they ever came near her. She shivered in my embrace then, but she *never* said she was scared.

I take a couple of steps away from the door but I'm unable to bring myself to her. Being in the same room while she's in bed, needing me, has awakened my need to accommodate her. And it'll be anything but professional.

"What are you afraid of, Ivy?"

She doesn't respond, and somehow her silence draws me in. Little by little, I erase the distance between us. She's still in the same position on her side. Only her head is visible, looking ahead. Somehow I don't want to be in her line of sight. I sense that she'll feel safer if she doesn't see me. So I settle behind her, kneeling next to the bed.

"Myself."

Whatever she's scared of, it is my job to turn it around.

"Stay with me, Mark," she implores.

She's never begged for me before. Not like this.

Maybe I'm the one who feels safer that her gaze isn't on me. Because the urge to touch her is uncontainable, and if I revealed everything at once, it would surely ruin the moment.

I land a fingertip on the side of her head, feeling her soft hair. My other fingers follow, and in the end, I caress the whole length of her sleek brunette strands. She wants me to stay. So even though it goes against my instinct, I edge the covers off her slightly, climbing in, cocooning her.

My arm tightens around her waist. God forgive me. It feels damn good to hold her like this. Not just because of our closeness but because I feel her softening, releasing her fear.

In a gentle move, my hand coasts to her midriff. Her blouse is thin, and it may well be her skin that I'm touching. She's got firm abs, and when I brush her belly button, she contracts.

A soft giggle.

She clearly likes it.

Then I feel her hands move. She's unbuttoning her blouse, giving me a chance to have unrestricted contact, and without hesitation, I accept her invitation.

I could move up or down. Either direction will feel divine, but I choose up. She's still wearing a bra, and I stop just below a cup.

Ivy places her hand on top of mine, driving it further. My palm is now cupping her breast. Her nipple is hardening against the lacy fabric, and I can feel my own hard-on wedged between my pelvis and her buttocks. She moves her backside, massaging my shaft.

I've forgotten how good a woman can feel. How comforting. How satisfying. And after depriving myself of it for so long, the intensity of each touch, each stroke, is doubled. Everywhere is a sensitive spot right now, and the sensation prompts me to place my lips on the side of her neck. A peck, that's all it is. But she hums erotically, sending my cock to pulse.

She tries to curtail her hips from bucking and swaying when I rub her nipple harder, but there's no hiding it. I never thought I'd do this, but I'm turning her on like a man ready to make love to her.

In between my breaths, as I try to weigh up the wrongs and rights of our contact, she rolls over to face me, her knees bent, touching the front of my thighs. Then with a hopeful gaze, she mutters, "Is it too much to ask you to love me?"

It's almost inaudible, maybe because I'm still wrapped in a cloud of my newfound pleasure. But it hits me like lightning.

Love.

What happened between Rena and me has taught me to loathe that word. To avoid it at all costs. I've heard Sam telling me many times that Ivy loves me. But to hear it from her? While her gaze is giving me nowhere to hide?

I haven't forgotten how quickly good can turn to hurt in the name of love. Like pretty candles with their flames snuffed out.

"Ivy." I pull myself an inch away from her. "I'll make you feel safe. I'll give you protection. I'll give you my life. But—"

I close my eyes, resting my forehead on her shoulder helplessly. Then I let her go, withdrawing altogether.

Ivy shoots me a bitter look. "Who was she?" Her gaze tears through me. "Who was the woman who turned your heart into stone?"

I keep my stance. "My heart has always been like this."

"Bullshit!"

The lightning has cracked into thunder. She's provoking me, and I'm responding. My fists clench, trying to contain the fight within myself. I've never been challenged the way this woman is now. Not even Sam the SEAL had dared to hit me head-on like this.

And my combat instincts kick in.

"You want to know? You want to know, Ivy?" I exclaim, getting close to her, looking down as I tower over the bed.

She sits up, letting the covers slide down to her lap. "I dare you!" She's just as charged, as if she's looking to settle an old score.

It's all storm in my sky, and Ivy is ready to unleash rain from the clouds. I'm losing all control. Mark the stoic is no more.

"Her name is Rena," I blurt, and my voice trembles along with the quake behind my ribcage. "Rena Bunton. We were together for ten goddamn years. I proposed to her—down on one knee, over a romantic dinner by the lake. She cried over the huge diamond ring I'd gotten her. At that point, I thought nothing could go wrong. But you know what happened, Ivy?"

She keeps looking at me. "No, I don't."

"She stood me up at the altar." I rush my sentence, can't wait to get it over with. "She fucking stood me up! Standing there in front of people like a fool."

"I'm sorry, Mark."

"Me, too. But you know what?" I tremble harder. "That wasn't the worst of it. A month later, I learned she'd had an abortion."

She cringes in pain.

"Yes, Ivy. She was pregnant with my child, and she discarded him or her because *I* was their father."

She reaches out her hand to me, but I refuse it.

"You wanna know her excuse?" My lips flatten in disgust.

"She said I would never be hers because I would always be married to my job. That she didn't love me after all—that she'd gotten it all wrong like she'd had some kind of epiphany. She wanted her future child to have a better father—not an absent father."

"And you fell for those accusations? And you hang on to them?"

"That's the darkness I was referring to, Ivy."

"Mark, your heart turned to stone because of her poison!"

"It's her, all right. I mean, what kind of woman hurts another human being like that? Or kills an innocent soul like it's garbage?" I argue. It almost feels like I'm mourning again. "But then there's me. Because, in the end, she married another man merely months after that abortion. She and her husband are still happily together, with two kids."

"Mark..."

"That *other man* deserves to be a dad. I'm not. An unborn child died because his or her father was me. *Me.*" I thump a fist against my chest.

"First, she poisoned you. Then, she made you poison yourself. You know I'm not her."

"I never believed Rena was who she was. But after ten goddamn years, I was still wrong. What is time when it cheats you like that?"

"You and I, we haven't known each other that long. But you know in your heart."

I whip my head forward as if bowing down to Ivy, shedding my hurt in front of her. She's not Rena, but what is she capable of? A woman with a secret is a woman who'll break your heart. I believe that's the truth.

"Get out of that dark space, Mark. I'm here for you. Even if you don't love me, let me help you out."

"Ivy." I hold her hands. I don't doubt her intention. And I

know she could stand by me, setting aside her love, and give me all the help I need. But I've arrived at a point where I can't be with her because I'm falling hard.

Sensing she's giving me space to let it all out, I place my hands on her cheeks, pleading for her to understand. "You're the most precious thing I have in my life. The last thing I want is to hurt you. Because God forbid, you have no idea what kind of rage I had for Rena. I still do."

She shakes her head. Her lips quiver without saying anything.

I hiss out my hopelessness and finally let her go.

Standing in the doorway, I say, "I'll stay in the spare room. I'll get Tyler Hunt to come over first thing in the morning. He's good. Trust me. He's good. He's better than me."

"No one's better than you, Mark."

"He is. Because he's not distracted."

She leaves the bed, gingerly stepping toward me. "You've got to forgive her. She's a monster, but you've got to," she asserts. "Then you forgive yourself. Whatever it is that you feel guilty about. Get out of that dark place, Mark."

Her eyes strip me bare.

"Before you try to read me, I dare you." I don't know why I'm attacking her. Perhaps because I never want to be defenseless, especially in front of Ivy. "I dare you to confess."

"Confess what, Mark? About Deuce's cryptic message?"

"You can deal with Zander for that. Right now, I don't give a damn about Deuce. Tell me, do you know who The Painter is?"

"No."

"But you have some idea."

"No." Her voice fades.

"Why do you think he asked Noah to call him 'bro'?"

She frowns angrily. "He told you that?"

"Why are you so surprised?"

"Are you saying my son trusts you more than me?"

"Even a child knows when you're lying."

Her face flushes in anger. "I'm not like my mother!"

I sigh, regretting where my provocation has led to. "That's not what I meant. It's not about trust. I asked him at the time if he was willing to open up. But really, Ivy, why did he call him 'bro'? Don't tell me because they're just kids trying to sound cool."

She remains tight-lipped. But I wait.

After a long moment, I conclude, "I didn't think you'd say. And you want me to love you?"

I spin around, can't wait to get out of this room.

"Am I just your duty, Mark?" she asks while I keep walking. "Someone you can set and forget?"

Marching on, I leave her to answer her own questions. I pass the closed door of Noah's bedroom. Jones is sitting close by, nodding at me. It looks like the man has taken the guest room in front of Noah's. I walk on, heading into the spare room, which once upon a time used to be my room.

I press my face against the pillow.

God, it hurts. Even my own blood burns me as if it's turned into boiling lava. No goddamn bullets or blades would ever hurt like this.

I told her *everything*. I never thought I'd ever do that as long as I was breathing. Yet I did. And even though she didn't reciprocate my honesty, somehow, I understand her. My wound isn't as old as hers. For me to confess to her tonight—it was quick. Whatever hers is, she has buried it for a very long time. I can see it. And it will take her more than the span of time we've known each other to open up.

Tonight has been a mix of revelation, confrontation, and realization. I'm not the same person. For the better or worse remains to be seen. But one thing is sure. She's the one. She's the only one who will understand me.

I trail some damp spots on the pillow, exactly where my eyes were.

After all these years, Ivy Wren Cavanagh has finally drawn tears out of me.

11

IVY

After twelve hours of juggling state business and the police's investigation on Noah's kidnapping, fronting the media—and forcing myself to stay diplomatic amongst the glances of sympathy and condemnation alike—I can't wait to go home, kick off my heels, and have a long shower.

My phone beeps. Noah. He's just sent me a picture of his funny face, with his new bodyguard laughing in the background.

Five days without seeing Mark, hearing his voice, feeling him, is like learning how to walk again.

That night was the closest I got to him. Lying next to the safety of his body, warmed by his breath, secured by his hold —that was how I imagined it would be like to be loved by him. For it to be cut short, it broke me like I'd fallen off a horse I'd been riding with my knight in shining armor.

But for someone that beautiful, I will drag my ass back in the saddle no matter how many of my bones are broken. I have no regrets about asking him to love me. Because at that moment, I tore his walls down. He let me feel the hurt in him and see the darkness he has been trying to defend.

With that, I finally heard her name. The Medusa who had robbed him of his happiness. Perhaps she didn't have a heart, so when she saw one in Mark—a big one, too—she just had to petrify it. After ten years together, for her to perform such cruelty is unfathomable. She may have had her reasons. I'll never know. But she destroyed an innocent child—and Mark. That upsets me more than anything.

I understand it all, and I swear this isn't the end of me and him. He's the kind of good that deserves every last dollop of fight I have in me.

Mark isn't paradise. I've never seen him that way. He's the reality I've been craving ever since my mother started locking me up in that basement cage. To be rescued by him, to be cared for, to be protected. What I know now about Mark hasn't changed my feelings for him. Not even a single atom in my body is willing to let him go.

"Come in," I say to whoever's knocking on my door.

"You're packing up already?" It's my campaign manager. Eight o'clock at night, and she's still looking fresh thanks to her impeccable bob hair and sleek tweed suit.

"I'm hoping I can catch Noah before he goes to bed."

She nods her head. "How is he?"

"He's coping." I shut my laptop lid. "You have something for me?"

"Have you looked at my proposal?"

"I'll look at it tonight."

"Time is running out, Ivy. The polls are getting tight."

She's not wrong. Less than three months to the primary elections, the worm has been going up and down for me—erratic, vulnerable. Not a good sign.

"I'll look at it tonight," I repeat.

"Look, I have four kids. All teenagers. Like other parents in this state, I want to protect them. But there's more than just fentanyl that we have to fight against," the seasoned political campaigner says. "You've done great work outside the state's drug problems in your tenure. People have got to be reminded of that. There's the environment, sexual assaults, minors abuse—"

"Of course. Our campaign isn't just about fentanyl."

"But it hell sounds like that," she persists.

I sigh. "Illicit drug abusers and traffickers are getting younger and younger. I just want to protect those kids."

"Sure. That may be your angle—protecting our youth."

"Okay." I take my bag and start making my way out. Jones is already waiting for me.

"And?" My campaign manager keeps at it.

"And what?"

"What's going to be your action?"

"Resources, resources, resources," I answer. "Boost law enforcement funding, strengthen coordination between agencies, and more money for education and mental health. And I'll think of more tonight."

"Good." She grins, satisfied.

We go our separate ways. I'm sure she's going to wordsmith my ideas, and by the time I turn on my laptop again tonight, she'll have a new proposal for me.

"Going straight home, ma'am?" Jones opens the car door for me.

I pull my coat tight. We're in the middle of spring, but tonight is unusually cold. "Yes, please."

My feet are aching, and my eyes are twitching. The first thing I'll do after getting my son to bed is have a shower.

"Hey, Noah. I'm home!" I'm expecting him to be upstairs, perhaps getting ready for bed, but he's in the dining room with his bodyguard.

Tyler Hunt gets along with everyone—but especially Jones.

Nanny Linda adores him, too. I mean, she adored Mark, but there's something about Tyler that keeps her smiling. Most importantly, Noah himself approved of the twenty-eight-year-old former SEAL on day one. In the beginning, I used to call Tyler several times a day, but by the third day, having proven that he always has things under control, I only called once or twice a day.

A man with an impressive resume—nine years in the Navy, five of those as a SEAL sharpshooter—Tyler has been a godsend. But I'm still hoping that he will be Mark's *interim* replacement.

"Hey, Mom!"

"You're playing chess now? Do you even know how?" I tease Noah.

"Not really," he admits. "I just want Ty's horses."

"Knights, Noah, knights," Tyler corrects.

"Oh, yeah. Knights." He stares at a piece.

I observe my son from behind, recalling how close I was to losing him.

The Helena PD had arrested two suspects, both of them related to the company hired by Noah's school to upgrade their sports facilities. But none of them could've been The Painter, so they have been released. So far, the police don't believe the kidnapping was linked to my declaration of war against fentanyl.

"How do I get your knight?" Noah huffs out in frustration.

Tyler gives him time to think. His chunky hands clasp together. I've never seen so many protruding veins on one's arms. I can't imagine what kind of weights he would be lifting in his fitness regime.

Noah leans back, and I steal a kiss on his crown.

"Mom! I'm trying to think!" he protests.

I smile silently. I've been warned by other mothers that

children will grow up in a blink of an eye, and before you know it, it'll be time to let them go. I don't know how I'll feel when the time comes for Noah to leave home and get on with his own life. But the thing that frightens me the most is, what kind of mother will he remember me as?

He opened up to Mark about The Painter while shrugging and shaking his head when I asked the questions. Mark said it wasn't about trust, but I think it was. My son trusted his watch-bear more than he did me. Have I disciplined him the wrong way, and my son now loathes me? Or even worse, fears me? Why did The Painter appeal to him? I'm sure it wasn't just because he was willing to play shooting with him. And Noah called him 'bro'?

"I don't know!" Noah finally gives up on his effort to take down Tyler's knight.

The big man slowly shifts his focus to the right side of the board.

Noah sits up straight. "Oh! Of course!" He then moves his bishop and claims his opponent's knight. "Take that, Tyler boy!"

I giggle. Boy? That man could hoist Noah up with just a pinch of his two fingers!

"All right, it's late." Tyler packs up the chessboard.

"You've done your homework?" I ask.

"Of course. It was an easy one today. We even had time to play cowboy earlier. It was way fun."

I throw a glance at Tyler.

"No guns, ma'am. We were herding cows. Pillow cows."

I restrain my laugh.

"And we cleaned the room. Right, Noah?"

"Yes. We put everything back."

"Good boy. Or boys," I praise. "All right, Noah. Bedtime."

"Fine," Noah drawls, then pleads to his bodyguard. "Play again tomorrow?"

"Sure can."

"Night, Mom," Noah kisses me. It's his routine, but somehow tonight feels special. Perhaps because it's been a long day for me. But really, tonight feels different.

Noah scoots upstairs, where Nanny Linda is waiting for him.

"He's a smart boy," Tyler comments.

"He is," I beam. "You have kids?"

"No. Not yet." He throws me a smile, a story-filled smile. "If I'm honest, it's really hard for me to keep a steady relationship. I mean, I'm hardly home and all that. Work has been keeping me busy."

"You mean Noah and I?"

"Oh, don't get me wrong, Ms. Cavanagh. You guys are keeping me busy in a good way." He passes me a big grin as if a small one wouldn't convince me he means it. "It's the nature of my job. I just haven't found the right woman, I guess."

"I understand." I help him put the chess set on the shelf. "How's Mark?"

"He, um, he's been training the newbies in Bozeman." His face gets animated as if reminiscing his own experience.

I wonder, can boot camp be that much fun?

"What kind of training is it? You seem... amused."

"Well, it's not so much about the training itself, ma'am. I mean, those guys are all ex-military. Probably a little cocky, with a know-it-all attitude. Boy... I bet they didn't know what they were in for. Well, I was one of them." He chuckles to himself but then clarifies, "Honestly though, ma'am, I wasn't that bad."

"Ty, you're a down-to-earth guy, I can tell you."

"You know us men. We always have to deal with egos—whether our own or someone else's."

"I understand. Still, so far, I haven't seen a sign of ego in you. Mark said you're good. And I agree with him."

"Thank you, ma'am." He smirks, then restarts. "Red Mark training isn't about who's the sharpest shooter or the fastest runner. Mr. Connor—he spots your weakness like an eagle. Not so much your tactics or physique, but here." He points at his temple. "He always knows. And he's okay with weaknesses—everyone's got one. If you stick around long enough, he'll teach you how to use it to your advantage. That's how good he is."

Ty's explanation reopens a debate in my head that I thought had been settled. I've decided that Mark shouldn't ever find out about my baby—but maybe, just maybe…

"You know, Ms. Cavanagh. Whether those boys make it to the end or not, they should consider themselves lucky to have Mr. Connor as their trainer. Anyway, Mr. Connor should be back tonight." He looks at me with a hint of guilt as if realizing he'd been rambling. "If you want me to swap back with him—"

"Oh, no. No. You've been wonderful. I'd like you to stay if you want to continue your assignment here."

"Of course, ma'am."

"Good night, Ty."

He nods at me gentlemanly.

In my room, I kick off my heels and fall onto my bed with a long sigh, contemplating what Ty had told me about Mark. *He's okay with weaknesses.*

But not so with secrets.

A message on my phone cuts short my deliberation.

"Fuck…"

It's not what I was hoping for, but I'm not surprised. I

contacted a friend in the FBI to trace Deuce's first message. As expected, the call came from a burner phone. It wasn't even a day old before it was destroyed.

That means the second message was sent from a different phone. Likely it has been destroyed too.

I still remember every word.

They told you he remained nameless. But trust me, AG Cavanagh, he has a name.

My thumb is on the call button, and Mark's number is selected. No one knows about the second message, but it's time to tell him.

Or not.

My temples start pulsing.

After all, I need to have my long shower first, then my meds. If I am to reveal everything to Mark, I'll need to be sober, or the discussion may go astray because of my lack of sensibility.

I keep the water temperature lukewarm even though I'm dying for hot streams of water to pound my aching body. Hot water and low blood pressure don't mix, and I'm not planning to play with fire tonight.

I must've spent about fifteen minutes in the shower and missed a couple of calls in the process. But as if on cue, my phone rings again.

"Ivy Cavanagh," I answer, looking at the No Caller ID on the screen.

"AG Cavanagh."

My neck tightens. His voice is so deep. Unfamiliar. Either he's The Painter or Deuce. But it's got to be the latter. I don't know for sure how old The Painter is, but he can't be older than eighteen. This voice talking to me belongs to a man. It's how I imagined Deuce's voice would sound.

He continues, "You know who I am. Yet you never bothered to ask what I wanted from those messages."

"Deuce."

"Good to talk to you, Attorney General. You're a busy woman."

"You're getting desperate."

"You've failed to track me."

"I haven't even tried," I mock. "Nevertheless, now that we're talking. What do you want?"

"You'll know my demands soon."

The call ends. Before I can dial Mark's number, a figure lunges at me from behind. Quiet like a cat, powerful like a leopard. He snatches my phone and then destroys it under his boot. I can't see him, but I can feel him. He's skinny, his breathing light.

"Keep quiet." He presses the blade of a knife on my throat.

And now I hear him. A young voice. Could it be him? I know it's The Painter—but could it be *him*? The reason why he asked Noah to call him 'bro'?

After all, he is connected to the elusive fentanyl overlord, and I can't afford to let emotions overcome me.

"Deuce sent a teenager to get me? What an insult!"

He tightens his grip. "I'm the best he's got, but don't flatter yourself. Walk!"

"At least let me get dressed."

The lapels of my bathrobe are tight in his fist as he shoves me forward. "Be quick about it. And don't abuse my trust. It doesn't go that far."

He angles his face away as I disrobe, seemingly happy for me to do whatever I want behind his back. He knows I won't go anywhere without my clothes on, even in my own house. Besides, there's nothing in this bedroom that I can use to retaliate against him. A bedside lamp, perhaps, but he would've apprehended me by the time I managed to deal with the cable and all.

At the same time, I don't feel the need to fight him. My gut says he won't harm me if I play along.

"You've got one minute." He looks at his watch, his back to me.

I keep an eye on him while rushing to put on my underwear, pants, and blouse. His ski mask prevents me from seeing his face. He's wearing a form-fitting top and pants, no doubt to allow him to move freely and quickly.

"Who are you?" I brace myself to ask him. "Why did you let Noah go that day?"

"Hurry up!"

He's still looking away, but he apparently senses that I'm done. Just as quick as he took me the first time, he pounces at me, spins me around, and the knife is back at my throat.

"Who are you?" I insist.

"Walk!" he orders. "And keep your mouth shut."

As soon as I open the door, I see Jones lying on the floor, bloody. The door to Noah's room is ajar.

"No—"

The Painter puts a hand over my mouth.

"Shut the fuck up!" he whisper-shouts, pulling me back a step. "The last thing you want now is to call your son's name!"

My eyes wander to scan my house as much as I can. The second level is where the bedrooms are, and there is a gallery that allows me to see downstairs. From where I am, I detect at least two other men in the living room below. And ironically, being in The Painter's clutches feels like the safest place right now. Not because he's a boy—compared to those bulky, adult-like soldiers—but there's a small voice telling me I shouldn't be afraid of him. Is it my voice or even *his* voice I'm hearing?

The Painter drags me behind a wall. He clearly doesn't

want the others to see us. "Look, I have every intention of taking you to Deuce, but I'm not here to take Noah. When you're asked where he is, say he's with his father in California. Got that?"

So he knows that Noah sees my ex regularly.

Slowly he releases his hand from my mouth.

"What have you done to him?"

"He's safe. Walk!"

And we're moving again.

Should I believe him? All I can go by is the fact that he returned Noah safely when he 'abducted' him. But that small voice in my head persists.

We pass another man standing on the same level as us. The Painter signals to him with a bob of his head as if indicating that he's got me.

Where the hell is Tyler? Where the hell is Linda?

We then head downstairs, joining the two men stationed in the living room. They're all wearing the same thing—black outfits with black ski masks. In fact, there are five of them here. I don't know how many more that I can't see.

A man who seems to be in charge approaches me. "Good evening, AG Cavanagh."

I squint, trying to trace the eyes behind the narrow holes in the ski mask.

"No, I'm not Deuce. But I can assure you, you'll meet him soon." He then turns to The Painter, who's still gripping me like he will never let go. "Where's the boy?"

"He's not here," The Painter answers, his voice hissing past my ear as if reminding me to stick to the plan. "His room is empty."

"What do you mean?" The man in charge then steps closer to us. Now his face is right in front of me. "Where's Noah, Ms. Cavanagh?"

The Painter tightens his grip around my neck. I can feel the coldness of the blade. Perhaps it has even left a cut.

"Where's the boy?"

I tremble. "He's with his father."

"Where?"

"Far away."

"Where?"

"California."

The man in charge orders one of his troops to go upstairs, no doubt to check Noah's room, perhaps for the second time. A few minutes later, the soldier returns. "The boy's not here."

Suddenly shots are fired from the gallery.

Tyler!

He's crawling, one hand on his side while the other keeps shooting. Every man in black I can see mounts an attack on him. Clearly, they're highly trained and organized. All of them use silencers, so there's no hope of anyone hearing us. I certainly heard nothing from my bedroom at the time when Jones was brought down and when Tyler was initially hit.

Tyler manages to avoid the bullets, killing two of the soldiers. The man in charge gives a signal to The Painter. The young man spins me, using me as a shield, and then takes me across the room like we were flying. In a split second he switches his knife to his gun. His agility and speed astonish me—but it's devastating. With one shot, he brings Tyler down.

The leader grumbles, yelling to everybody who's still moving to kill the lights and leave.

In the dark, The Painter gags my mouth and blindfolds me. Then I'm dragged out without mercy.

I'm sure I've been pushed into the back seat of a car, but this time The Painter is no longer handling me. I feel weight at my left and right—I think two big men are flanking me now.

The car moves, and I feel exposed for the first time in this attack.

The Painter captured me. He shot Tyler. Yet he's on my side—or at least he's on Noah's. And with my heart bursting with emotions, my head filled with yearning voices, I'm sure he's my long-lost son. But...

Where is he?

12

MARK

"So? Whose heart did you break today?" Lisa, Cass' colleague at the Thirsty Fox, sets another bottle of Fallen Angel on the bar for me.

I toss her a lopsided smile, taking the last bite of my chicken burger before sipping the ale.

She then comments, "Late dinner, huh? I haven't seen you in the past few days." Lisa is also Cass' best friend, and while Cass is on maternity leave, she's taking over her managerial duties at the Fox.

"I was in Bozeman."

"Bozeman, huh? So, who's *she*?" She's not about to let me go.

"You know I don't break hearts."

"Tell that to Miss Montana," she quips.

I raise my eyebrows. Miss Montana. That's who Lisa's alluding to. I respectfully said no to the beauty queen's persistent requests to have a private dinner with me. She's a world-class socialite, so there was no way my rejection would even dent her heart.

"I guess these walls talk?" My eyes wander around the bar. Like at any watering hole, gossip flies like flights from JFK.

"You betcha!" she winks. "Nice scarf, by the way." She steps aside to serve the gentleman next to me.

I lick the last drops of the burger's tangy sauce, then continue drenching my throat with the Fallen Angel. Just what I need after the intense multi-day personnel training in Bozeman. Three out of the four candidates made it—although they're still on probation—while one bailed out, unable to deal with the pressure.

As I'm about to have another sip of my ale, my back cops a smack. I'm almost knocked off my seat while the culprit himself is off balance. I shake my hand, getting rid of the ale dripping off my fingers.

"I'm so sorry!" He stares at me ruefully. "So sorry! That guy just shoved me out of the blue!" His thumb points to the bar entrance.

Never mind my scarf that's turning sticky and smelly. Something tells me the movement behind the fretting man is worth noticing.

Shit!

It's him!

The Painter.

"Hey!" I yell, leaping out of my seat, running in pursuit as he slips out of the bar.

Outside, I can see him turning a corner, and as my chase gets close, I hear a revving motorbike. He speeds off on it while I'm scrambling to get to my car. I start the engine, and a piece of paper falls out of my jacket pocket.

Get Noah at home.

"Fuck!" I slap the steering wheel. I've got no choice but to let him go. I've got to get to Noah.

"Pick up, pick up, pick up!"

But neither Ivy, Jones, nor Tyler answers my calls—like they'd been swallowed into the earth. My chest is filled with foreboding flutters, and when I approach her house, those flutters turn to foulness. The house is dark and the gates are closed as if everyone had gone on vacation.

I park on the other side of the street, leaving with a Glock in my hand.

Ivy's house is surrounded by large gardens. Even outside the premises, there are a lot of large trees growing along the street.

"Noah? You here?" I whisper, moving under the shadows of the vegetation around me.

A branch above me shakes. I direct my gun upwards. And a bird flies off, likely a nighthawk.

I continue moving toward Ivy's house.

The hedges on my right suddenly rattle, then part, and a small figure squeezes out of the gap.

"Mark!" Noah runs to me, ramming himself against my side, grasping me with all his might like he's about to be sucked in by a powerful force. Another figure follows—Linda, his nanny.

"Mark...what's happening?" Noah cries.

"Where's your mother?"

"I don't know."

I look at Linda.

"He was in the house. That young man who took Noah," the nanny says as she picks up Noah's teddy bear from the ground. I recognize that toy—his favorite since I knew him as a four-year-old. He must've dropped it when he was hugging me.

"Get in the car!"

I start the engine.

"Mom may still be inside," Noah begs.

He's right. And my heart is roaring at me, instructing me to march in and find her. And Ty, and Jones. But crisis and tough decisions go hand-in-hand. It's not my heart I should follow. Right now, my priority is Noah. Enemies, or traps, could be waiting inside. Even out here, someone may be watching, waiting for the right moment to release an ambush, and none of us would come out alive.

I reverse. The last thing I want is for us to be sitting ducks.

"I'll get to your mom, I promise. But right now, we've gotta go."

I drive around, away from the house but keep to the neighborhood so I can return as soon as I've got back up. I call Zander. "Get your men to Cavanagh's house. Bring in the SWAT team too."

"What the hell is going on, Connor?"

"I've got Noah and his nanny. They only saw The Painter entering the house—and he let them go. But I don't know what's happened to Ivy. The house is dark."

"Fuck. I'm on my way! Where are you?"

"Moving, but close by."

"Stay in touch, Connor!"

I look at Noah through the rearview mirror. "Noah, was it 'bro' who got you out?"

It takes him a while to answer, but he admits, "Yes."

"Did he tell you anything?"

Noah keeps his head down in silence. Linda explains, "That man was in Noah's room when I checked on him. He was wearing a ski mask, so I couldn't see his face. He... um... helped us, I guess, get out of the house through the balcony off Noah's room."

"Is Mom okay?" Noah trembles, clutching his teddy. It looks like the man even let Noah take his toy.

"Yes, she's okay. We've just got to find her. The police are on their way."

"Mark..."

"Yes, Noah?"

"I let him in."

"Noah!" Linda exclaims in disbelief.

"He knocked on my bedroom window, and I opened it. I'm sorry. I didn't mean to cause all this..." The boy starts to cry.

"Shh... shh. Noah, it's okay." I reach back, extending my arm to calm him. "I think Bro wanted you safe, and you letting him in has nothing to do with whatever happened tonight. Okay?"

Noah doesn't say anything, although still sobbing hard.

Sirens wail—that's Zander's men closing in. This time I call Cora-Lee Rancic, Red Mark's ever-reliable head of tech. "Cee, I know it's late. But I want you to go into the office and try to get anything from Ty's radio or video feed, if it was ever on." For client privacy, he shouldn't have had any of it on, but perhaps he did when the attack happened.

"Yes, sir. Is everything okay?"

"Something happened at AG Cavanagh's house."

"God. Okay. I'm leaving now. I'll let you know what I find."

"And Cee, who do we have available in Helena? And I don't mean Sam."

"I'm afraid none. Ty was the only one."

Red Mark really needs to recruit more men. But tonight, there's only one option left.

"Ben," I call Ben Winter, Sam's brother-in-law, the man who's been on my radar. "We can discuss things later. But right now, you've got to meet me at the attorney general's house."

"Connor? The fuck!"

"Ben, get your ass over there!"

"Fine! I'll see you in fifteen."

I circle back to Ivy's house, stopping a few yards away. Zander's men and, as I advised, the SWAT team are already there.

"Will they find Mom?" Noah says.

"I hope so. If she's not there, I'll find her. I promise." This time I open the back door and talk to Noah face to face. "Who's Bro, Noah? Did he say his name? Did you look at his face?"

"I swear I don't know his name. But I did see his face when we met at school," he confesses. "It's weird, but I thought... I thought he looked like me."

I nod, trying to piece together whatever I've learned about Ivy with this new information. I pat Noah's shoulder. "Thanks for being honest with me."

"Connor!" the voice of Ben Winter arrives behind me.

I take a deep breath. It will soon be revealed if my instincts about this giant of a man is right. That he has something special when it comes to handling kids.

"Thanks for coming. Meet Noah." I step aside to let the boy see Ben.

"Hi, Noah," Ben greets him. With warmth and cheers, he's turned into an uncle every kid would wish for. The way he looks at Noah is just the same as he looks at his niece Grace.

"You're so tall!" Noah mutters.

"Yeah. When you're with me, no one can get to you. I promise." He offers Noah his fist, and the two soon do a fist bump.

I leave the two of them doing their express bonding while calling Zander.

"Connor, where are you?"

"Outside. Have you found Ivy?"

"I'm afraid not. Jones and your guy Hunt are badly injured."

I release a grunt, trying to keep my emotions at bay. "I'm going to get Ben Winter to take Noah to my place. Get your men to escort them."

"Consider it done."

I return to Ben, who's sharing a few cookies and a flask of milk with Noah. I wasn't wrong about him.

I say to Noah, "You and Linda stay with Ben, okay?" I help him get out of my car, settling into Ben's car. Then I tell the big man, "Take them to my place. Memorize the code—12051974."

"It's not your birthday, is it?"

"Come on. I'm not that old!"

He smirks.

"Zander's men will escort you. Call me if you need anything."

"Okay."

"You guard that boy with your life, do you understand?" I tell him.

"You don't even have to say it."

That's a Red Mark man.

"I owe you," I slap his shoulder and go behind the police line to join Zander.

Paramedics are wheeling Jones out. He's really messed up. I'm not sure if he's going to make it.

"Where's Tyler Hunt?" I finally find Zander among the sea of police and SWAT personnel.

"There!" The captain points me to a corner.

My man isn't looking any better. "What are his injuries?" I ask the paramedics.

"Bullet wounds on the leg, right side, and shoulder."

"Goddamn it!" I follow the stretcher, holding his hand. "Hang in there, pal."

Ty squeezes my hand, then slowly removes his oxygen mask. "Noah?"

"He's safe. I found him."

He breathes out, "Deuce."

He's behind all this? And he's connected to The Painter?

"Did he take Ivy?"

He blinks once, then falls into unconsciousness. A paramedic puts the mask back on him. "Sir, let us through."

Deuce.

He's gonna pay for this!

13

IVY

My head feels like a courthouse clock tower—ringing at the hour, vibrating, and being pounded from the inside repeatedly. After being taken to this warehouse, the knock to my head has me lying on my side. I squeal at the burn in my shoulders—my arms stretch behind my back, halted by my bound wrists.

Someone taps my cheek. "Get up!"

I'm no longer blindfolded or gagged. Even so, when I open my eyes, all I can see is haze.

Soon, I feel water poured all over me.

"Fuck!" I yell and instantly wake.

"Feeling refreshed?" the masked man who earlier introduced himself as Deuce mocks at me.

Two men force me to kneel on the floor.

"Now, where were we?" Deuce bellows.

I survey the room. Where is he? The teenager captured me at home, then he disappeared, but I thought I saw him again briefly before that knock to my head—though it could've been someone else's shadow.

A scoff flies out Deuce's mouth. "Ah, you saw *him* just

now." The Mosaic boss hasn't revealed himself, but now I've heard him enough, and I will remember that sandy voice until the day he's behind bars—or six feet underground.

I gulp, still dealing with the excruciating blow to the side of my head and trying to control my shivering. My hair and blouse are drenched in what feels like ice water.

"You weren't seeing things. He was here." Deuce looks back behind him. The space is dim, and with Deuce's almost choreographed move, it truly looks like a stage with only one light shining on him. "He's still here. In fact, he's got his friends with him." He motions for whoever is hiding in the backdrop to walk forward.

Six figures, all of the same height and build, walk out of the shadow in unison. They're all wearing the same thing—all black, faces hidden behind ski masks.

"They're all my loyal men, AG Cavanagh," Deuce announces proudly. "I wanted them when no one else did. I've shaped and loved them—the way I know how."

"Loved them?" I frown.

An evil laugh escapes his mouth. "It may be different from how you love your own child. Or should I say...children?"

I release quick breaths, trying to compensate for my racing heartbeat.

"Well, Ms. Cavanagh, I know for a fact that one of these boys is your son."

Being with Deuce is a nightmare, but knowing he has my son, whom I thought had been dead, is like walking through a forest, anticipating it will eventually open up to a beautiful meadow. Everything in me cries out for him, yet I keep silent.

"I could've done some DNA tests, but I thought, why not ask the mother herself?" Deuce walks in front of the lineup as if inspecting a troop. "You see, politics and scandals go together, but your scandal is the kind that will ruin your career no matter how you try to salvage it."

"You think I will release that criminal—whoever he is—just because I'm afraid of my reputation being tarnished? You don't know me at all, Deuce."

"You'd rather serve the people of Montana than save your own ass. Admirable, Attorney General." He pauses as if giving me time to read between the lines. "But family is different, isn't it? That's the card I'm playing here."

"You may call yourself 'Deuce,' but don't play games with me!"

"Oh, I will. Let's call it the 'Who's The Cavanagh Bastard' game."

His words hit me like a hatchet. "If he's my son, he's my son. He's no bastard."

"I see. A mother always has it in her. That maternal instinct. So tell me, which one of these boys is your son?" Deuce presents the group to me as if it was a circus. "They're all seventeen years old."

Among the wild emotions, my brain is trying to figure out how this man knows about it—while I, the one who's in the middle of it all, didn't have a single clue.

Had my baby survived, he would've been seventeen. But whoever they are, they don't belong here. They're boys, and they have lives ahead of them. More than just counting money and getting high.

"Pick one, AG Cavanagh. Or I'll start shooting them."

My teeth grit. "Fuck you, Deuce."

"Pick one!"

Desperation clogs my throat. I have no friggin' clue which one of them is The Painter, or Noah's 'bro'—his real brother.

Deuce cocks his gun.

"Second from the right!" I blurt, shivering from the cold

and the prospect that one, if not all, of these young boys might die because of me.

Deuce motions to the boy I picked to step forward, and he rips the ski mask off him.

I stare at that young face.

I feel nothing. Those yearning voices in my head, induced by The Painter's close presence when he took me, are nowhere to be found.

Deuce chuckles. "Look at you. Like a barren woman in an orphanage." He then strides toward the boy, arms crossed behind his back. "Who's your mother?"

"She's dead," the boy answers.

His voice is robotic, yet it hurts. If that's really my son, I don't blame him.

I notice he's wearing a gold chain with a 'W' pendant. Perhaps his name starts with it. I still don't recognize him. Well, I shouldn't be able to recognize my seventeen-year-old son I didn't even know I gave birth to alive. But truly, there is no stir of emotion in me. Not like when The Painter was with me.

"No. That's not your son," Deuce snarls. "His mother's name was Cynthia. Maybe not as beautiful as 'Ivy,' but my point is—you've lost your motherly instinct, Ms. Cavanagh."

He pushes the boy aside while I examine the remaining five boys.

"If you're not sure, why don't you call his name?" his sandy voice penetrates me.

My lips shake.

"Ah..." Deuce taunts. "You don't even know his name, do you?"

I bow my head.

"Last try!" Deuce extends his arm, aiming the gun at the line-up.

Probably nervous themselves, the boys move—except one, and he's exhibiting a familiar posture. That boy wraps his shoulders forward just like how The Painter walked in the CCTV footage.

"The last one on my right."

Deuce glances at me, then he does the same, revealing the boy's face.

Those round eyes. It's like staring into myself. Water is still dripping from my hair, and there's barely enough light in here, but I see him clearly.

He's *my son*. The son my mother had told me was dead. The son my mother had told me was nameless.

I furiously blink, giving him silent cues about how much I want to hug him and apologize. But he stares at me with contempt, like I'm the worst sinner in the world.

Deuce points his gun at the boy's head.

"No! No!" I get up, ready to slide myself between him and my son.

Two men pull me back to my kneeling place while the boy stands like a martyr, ready to be slaughtered.

"Let's keep this 'free the prisoner' business to just the two of us!" I quiver. "Give me his name!"

"You'll release him?"

I force myself to answer. "Yes."

Deuce withdraws his gun and laughs. "Your son's my best mule. I won't kill him." The disgusting man then rounds his arm over my son's shoulders. "This secret child of yours...you don't even know the father, do you?"

I remember nothing about that night except bodies taking turns piling on top of me. And sweat... lots of sweat.

"I'm so sorry," I beg my son as I'm finally able to speak to him. I want to call him by his name, but like Deuce said, I don't even know it.

"Are you, Mother?" my son suddenly utters. Cold. Colder than the water drenching me.

"I don't know who your father is."

"He's mine," Deuce croaks.

My blood stops flowing. My brain freezes.

And Deuce guffaws. "Look at your fucking face!" He keeps laughing, and he almost chokes. "Not literally. God, no!"

Everyone in the room is laughing with him, although my son remains stone-cold.

"Puberty might've made me desperate back then. But fucking the daughter of two conservatives? God, no! Even if she's as bitchy hot as you were back in the day." He mocks, and he rummages into his jacket pocket. "Look at this. Another part of your past, which will come to light if you don't do as I demand."

He tosses a cut-up magazine page to the floor in front of me.

I close my eyes, refusing to see it.

"You were very young here. Probably around the time when my grandfather could still jerk himself off."

Laughter echoes around me once again.

He admires the page. "They said they were promoting this brand-new shampoo. Well, yeah, what the hell does *We Love Candy* have to do with shampoo? Why would men care about menstruating girls' hair products? They just wanted to have sex with your hair. I mean, if they could. And look at those long legs, bare and wet. Not to mention..." He clicks his tongue.

Without continuing his description, he shoves the magazine page to my face. "If I dig harder, I'm sure this is not the only one."

His words shake my guts as if I've been tossed inside a running washing machine. And I'm soaked in worthlessness, ignominy, and guilt. How could he do this in front of my son?

Deuce strides back to him. "Your mother was hot, huh? Boys or men would've thrown themselves at her. She could've had a different life. But look where she is now. The most powerful woman in Montana. Do you know how she got there? By lying, by burying her past. By abandoning you!"

I shed my cloak of humiliation, yelling as loud as I can. "That's not true! I was lied to. My mother lied to me—" Once again, I'm desperate to call his name. "She told me you died, and she took you away from me."

His expression remains unchanged.

Deuce mocks me. "You can spin your story all you want. You're a lawyer, a master of flipping the truth. "

"What I'm telling you *is* the truth!" I insist.

Deuce pats my son's shoulder. "You see, your mother comes from a long line of liars. Do you believe her? Or do you believe me?"

"I believe you, Deuce," he asserts.

My head hangs down helplessly.

A conquering smirk paints Deuce's face. "See, he looks up to *me*. He's *mine*."

"You don't own anyone, Deuce!" I snarl. Then I beg the boy. "I'm so sorry. You can blame me. But you can't believe this man."

Deuce puts a hand on him. "You're done here, son." He motions for everybody to leave us.

I know the man said he wouldn't kill my boy. I believe him. He still needs him. But it won't be long before someone else comes along. And my son's time will be up.

"Now, let's get down to business." He spins around, his arms crossed behind his back. "They say a lawyer will never forget their first case."

"My first case was petty theft by a twenty-year-old. He didn't even go to jail."

"That's just a saying. What I meant, AG Cavanagh, I'm sure you remember the first man you successfully prosecuted as deputy county attorney. Missoula, seven years ago."

My chest rises, sucking in air. "You want me to release him?"

"Ah, I thought you'd remember."

JJ Marcusso. He killed a whole family of four by burning their home while they were asleep. All because of an unpaid debt. He was a violent man, but I never knew of any connection between him and the fentanyl industry—or any drug business.

"You want him out? You could've saved yourself the trouble and told me over the phone. If you wanted to humiliate me, you could've announced whatever you know about me to the world. Why all this? Why the game?"

"I wanted to teach you a lesson about family."

In the absence of facial expression, I rely on his tone of voice. Could JJ Marcusso be related to Deuce?

"So, you want me to release JJ Marcusso, or 'Stumpy' as the police called him?" I scorn. After killing a police officer during arrest, the criminal got his left leg shattered thanks to his failed attempt to jump over a building.

I hear a grunt. "Either you or your successor will get him out."

"I will release him. With that, you keep your hands off Noah and... my older son."

"Whose name you don't even know. I believe you, Ms. Cavanagh."

"Why Marcusso?"

"Took his name out of a hat."

"I thought you would've forwarded the name of someone

more powerful. But really, JJ 'Stumpy' Marcusso? Didn't one of the inmates in Montana State Prison bust one of his balls? Now, I can't call him 'Ballsy,' can I?"

Deuce forces me down so I'm back to kneeling.

There it is. JJ Marcusso must mean something to Deuce.

Without mercy, he pulls my hair until I look up at him, knife firmly in his grip. He looms over me as he swings the blade. I stare at him—the man who claimed he has shaped and loved my son. No, he hasn't. Even if he kills me now, I know my son will never be his.

14

MARK

Zander and I head to Ivy's bedroom while crime scene investigators are taking photos and scanning for fingerprints around us.

"Those men disabled the CCTV. We found Cavanagh's phone in her bedroom, smashed," Zander says. "Hopefully, the lab can recover the content."

I survey Ivy's bedroom. Apart from her broken phone, nothing suggests there has been a struggle.

Noah's revelation about what The Painter looks like is playing in my head. What prompted him to think they look alike? Everyone knows Noah takes after Ivy more than his dad.

My thought goes back to Townsend. Her answer when I asked how many children she had—'One, just one'—is attacking my brain, as if it was the answer I've been looking for among this crazy chaos.

"How many men were here?" I ask the captain.

"At least five. Two were definitely injured or dead. We found blood on the living room floor, and it couldn't have belonged to any of the bodyguards, as they were both upstairs."

"What do you know about Deuce?"

Zander looks at me. "You know about him? Do you think he's behind this?"

"He is behind this, Zander. My man told me."

"We did put him as the prime suspect, although recently, we haven't got any indication of a threat or attack from his organization. It's only days ago that we found trails to him, confirming he's the man controlling the Mosaic. Unfortunately, we don't know his real name yet, and what he looks like is only speculation at this stage."

"You have sketches?"

"Yes."

"Send them to me."

Zander narrows his gaze, pondering.

"Hey, finding Ivy is as important to me as it is to you, Zander. If not more. You know she's more than just a client to me."

"Fine. I trust your discretion, Connor. I'll get my detectives to send the sketches to you."

Suddenly one of the investigators approaches us. "Captain, AG Cavanagh received a call at 9.13 p.m. We suspect it was just before her phone was destroyed."

"Location?" Zander asks.

"Helena Valley."

I leave Zander and scurry to my car, heading north toward the valley. I soon get a call from Cora-Lee.

"Mr. Connor, Ty did turn on the video for a few minutes before he was shot—well, shot the last time, I mean."

"Send it to me."

"Already did."

I pull over to watch the video. My gut wrenches seeing Ty's camera almost at the floor level. He's clearly crawling. His hand flashes into view—bloodied. This is the first time Red

Mark has suffered casualties. He's fighting for his life, yet he keeps going, giving everything he has to stop those mongrels.

Then the camera pans to his right, and he's looking down below. His P.O.V shows Ivy, held by—I'm sure it's The Painter. There were at least six other men down there with them.

Ty opens fire, taking out two of the men.

The next segment sends chills to my bone. The Painter moves like he's a trained assassin. He points his gun at my man, and everything stops. Ty's head seems to have hit the floor, and the camera is stuck, pointing at the balustrade of the second-floor gallery.

"Fuck!" I yell.

I replay the video a couple of times. Everything happens so quickly, but...

"What the..."

Did that son of a bitch change his aim? I zoom in, replaying the last five seconds of the clip again and again. The Painter is going for Ty's head, then in a tenth of a second, he appears to change his mind, shooting his shoulder instead.

That kid had let Ty live.

I continue driving, and I see Ben's name flashing on my phone. What now?

"Don't tell me you screwed up already."

"You don't mean that, Connor!" Ben complains, almost threatening. "Noah wants to speak to you."

"Okay."

"Mark?" Noah says tentatively.

"What is it, buddy?"

"Have you found Mom?"

"Not yet. But I'm close."

"When you find her, tell her that I love her?"

My heart cracks a little. "Of course. I'll tell her that. I'm sure it'll mean a lot to her."

"I'm sorry I let Bro in."

"Noah, it's not your fault. I think Bro is really on our side."

"But you will still protect Mom, right?"

"Of course."

"And do everything you can to keep her safe?"

It sounds like an order, and I'm only too happy to oblige.

"I'll protect her with my life, Noah."

"Thank you, Mark."

I see that Cora-Lee is calling me again.

"Hey, I've got to go. You stay close to Ben, okay? Is he good?"

"Yeah. He's good. Like Ty."

"Cool. I'll talk to you later."

I hang up and answer Cora-Lee.

"Sir, I investigated Ms. Cavanagh's number again. There were two text messages sent to her phone from around Helena Valley. Three weeks ago, then six days ago. I don't know if they're related, but it's odd that both numbers don't exist anymore. I'm sending you the locations."

"Got them. Relay them to Zander."

"On it, sir."

I drive around the northwest area of Helena Valley, checking the locations Cora-Lee sent me. "Cee, anything in the areas jump out at you? An abandoned building? Ownerships that don't make sense? A property that just changed hands?"

"Let me check."

"I'm on the Mountain Highway." It's a long road, and there's not much around me.

"Most of the properties there are farms. But there's a warehouse, sir. Toward the top end of the highway. It's about two thousand square feet, quite a big one, but I can't see a company name attached to it."

"I trust your instinct, Cee."

"Give me a second, and I'll see who owns it. It's just been purchased by a Daemon Drury. Does that name ring a bell?"

Two D's?

Deuce?

It may be a long shot, but it's currently my only shot.

"You're a lifesaver, Cee." I speed toward the top of the highway.

15

IVY

I refuse to look at the floor. It's just the icing on the cake for Deuce, but that's my pride scattering in front of me. I don't even know how much hair is left on my head.

My scalp is burning from his pulling earlier, and I'm sure my neck has taken some slicing when he used his blade to cut what used to be my waist-length hair. This is more than Deuce trying to make a point about his threatened empire. This is another level of humiliation.

To add to my shame, Deuce has called everyone back, including my son. But no one says anything.

I lift my head. Soon I learn that I won't get any sympathy from my son, either. The boy only stands there watching.

Deuce squats, only to enjoy my defeated face. "Tonight is nothing compared to what I could do to you in a week, a month, a year."

I spit at him, and another slap assaults my cheek.

Suddenly another man enters, whispering something in Deuce's ear.

Deuce slowly rises, telling me, "I'll leave you to think about it."

He then strides to my son. "She'll still be here when we come back, won't she? I'd like to keep her one more day so she doesn't forget her promise."

"Yes," my son replies.

Deuce taps his cheek with his palm. "Show me where your loyalty lies. Remember, I saved you. She abandoned you."

"You can count on me," my son affirms.

"You, you stay with them," Deuce orders another man. Then he commands the rest of the group. "Come on. We've got business to take care of."

When most of the men are gone, my shoulders relax—just a little. My son is standing behind me while the other man that Deuce tasked as a chaperone is manning the front door.

"What's your name?" I ask.

"Which mother doesn't know the name of his own son? Her firstborn?" He kicks the *We Love Candy* magazine page to the corner of the room. "You know, ever since I fired a gun, I told myself if I ever found my real parents, I'd destroy their lives." He tightens the rope on my wrists.

"Is that what that man taught you?"

"No. I taught myself."

"I didn't even have a chance to name you because I was unconscious when I gave birth to you. My mother took you away from me," I plead. "Please, tell me your name."

"I don't care about your excuses."

"You don't have to come back to me. You don't have to love me or even care about me." I suck a breath.

"You know who I am now, and you know that I won't harm my brother." For the first time, I hear emotions in his voice. "I won't hurt my brother because I know how much it hurts to be your son. But I *will* hurt you if I must."

"Just tell me your name, and then go. Go far. I can help you get a new identity, protection, whatever! Just get away from Deuce."

Both our attention lands on the front door. The chaperone has opened it to talk to his friends on the other side. Breeze intrudes the room ferociously, and I start shivering again.

"Deuce wants you!" the man says to my son.

My son walks to the door, stepping out.

When the door is shut behind him, the chaperone watches me, sucking on his cigarette. It's too dark to see his eyes behind his ski mask, but with my blouse all wet and me cowering hopelessly like a slave, it doesn't take long for him to start rubbing his crotch.

He comes closer, presenting his bulge to me. I whip my head away in disgust.

"I can be your warmth tonight." He touches the collars of my blouse.

"Hands off me, you fucker!" I jerk away.

My resistance only heightens his excitement. He rips my blouse and starts groping my breasts. He then pins me down, leaving my bound hands crushed under my own ass.

"Fuck you!" I keep gyrating.

It sounds awfully quiet outside. I'm wondering if Deuce has decided to take my son with him to whatever business he has to sort out.

"No!" I scream when the foul chaperone puts his hand between my thighs.

"No one will hear you in this dump of a place, AG Cavanagh."

Just as he's about to unzip his pants, another door bursts open. It's at the other end of the room, about ten yards away from us.

My assailant spins around. Realizing the man joining us is a foe, he fires. But the filthy prick is no match to the man I know will stop at nothing to protect me. He's dead even before he can open the fly of his pants.

"Ivy!"

"Mark!" I try to get up.

But his stride is cut short by a figure flying across the room, tackling me from the side. Mark is charging as the boy gets a hold of me. He drags me, my back to Mark. I feel the tension between the two people trying to claim me. But I willingly put myself in front of my son.

"Release her!" Mark roars as my son pushes me to stand up straight, covering himself.

"Mark, don't—"

My son swiftly grips my mouth, and I'm unable to speak anymore. I'm facing Mark this time, shivering at the sight of his gun. I don't know how much of us he can see in this dim place, let alone know what's going on.

While watching Mark, my son grouches to my ear, "I didn't know you two are on a first-name term."

"Drop the gun!" Mark orders.

"Your secret boyfriend?" my son whispers some more. "Do you have another secret child with him? Or is Noah his?" He's completely behind me, and at this stage, it's impossible for Mark to shoot him unless he shoots me.

And that's how I want it to be right now. What I should've done seventeen years ago—to be my son's line of protection.

Mark maintains his stance. I know he's thinking hard— perhaps trying to make out what my muffled voice is saying.

My son takes one step back, Mark forward.

Both guns cock.

Mark steps into the light—the only light in this warehouse-like space.

My heart stops, almost not recognizing him. His thinker face turns lethal. His youthful features transform—they tighten and sharpen, filled with fury. He's not a 'watchbear.' He's a dragon, ready to burn anything in his path to get to me.

I spread myself wide. While I'm sure my son is adequately shielded, I also know that Mark never misses.

On the other hand, behind me is a boy who's been trained and brainwashed by one of the most dangerous men in the country. He shot Ty with precision. Chances are, this time, he won't miss either.

16

MARK

The state of her hurts me. She's shivering. Her wet blouse is barely clinging to her shoulders. Clumps of hair scatter on the floor—it must be hers. It's her dignity that whoever this bastard is attacking, but my priority is still Ivy herself.

The only lamp illuminating the space is high up, and its beam spreads meagerly. I can see Ivy because of her bright-colored blouse reflecting the light, but her captor is blending in with the darkness. I don't think the man I've shot dead was Deuce. But this man trying to claim Ivy, could it be him?

"Release her, you son of a bitch!" I command.

Ivy is trying to tell me something behind the man's gagging hand. As both of them move, gaps start appearing, and I assess which one I'm going to exploit. But the inadequate lighting concerns me, and to make matters worse, Ivy keeps wriggling as if knowing where I'm aiming and wanting to keep those gaps sealed.

"I have an order to keep her here, Mr. Connor." A cocky voice. "You can choose to leave quietly, or in a body bag."

This guy isn't Deuce, but he has nerve. And I'm going to

exploit his cockiness. I will take him down sooner rather than later.

I stride closer and step in a puddle of water. Wet drips hit the top of my head.

This time Ivy pulls hard, escaping the hand that has been gagging her.

"Mark! No! He's my son."

My heart stops along with my steps.

I've had my suspicion about The Painter. But to hear it from her—and to realize it's her own flesh and blood I'm trying to take out—my brain twists, trying to accept the reality. I'll do anything to save Ivy, but Jesus! I didn't sign up for this.

Ignoring the boiling emotions inside me, I keep pressuring him. "Release her, or I'll kill you!" He can't be older than eighteen. My warning is a bluff because I will never shoot dead a fucking teenager. But he's a threat, and I swear I will hurt him if he does something to Ivy.

"Don't, Mark," she begs.

I slowly lower my gun, hoping the boy will do the same.

He does, but he's still using Ivy as a shield while he does something behind her back.

He's just cut her hands loose.

Smart move on his part.

Because now Ivy is standing wide, arms covering him. This boy knows his mother will do that. He's skinny, and although taller than Ivy, he only needs to crouch a little, and the whole of him, including his legs and feet, are behind her.

I watch him. I called him 'son of a bitch' earlier—what should I call him now? He's Ivy's son, but that doesn't change the fact that I won't ever let anyone—*anyone*—harm Ivy.

The boy is now pointing his gun at her nape, forcing me to raise my Glock again. There are two inches of him exposed—

right beside the curve of her neck. I can exploit it, but there's no way on earth I can pull the trigger now.

"Let. Her. Go." I bark as I whisper to myself *don't do anything stupid, boy*. I don't want to think of what I'll do against my instincts if the boy shoots his mother.

Unexpectedly, the boy throws Ivy forward toward me, and at the same time, he shoots at the only light in this room.

In total darkness, Ivy crashes against me as she falls. I catch her, hold her trembling body, and drag her toward the door where I came in from. But she quickly whips around, trying to free herself.

The air has changed. I turn on my flashlight. It's only the two of us in this room now—if not the whole warehouse.

"We've got to find him! They'll kill him," she begs, pulling me in the direction of where the boy has disappeared to.

I follow her. My flashlight shines on the wall where I last saw him. There must be a hidden door somewhere. But before I can start searching, shots are fired—outside in the distance.

I halt her. Discreet steps are closing in.

"Change of plan!" I whisper.

"They'll kill him!"

"Ivy, they won't," I counter, feeling her resistance.

They're right on the doorstep now. Deuce clearly believes in power in numbers—he sent at least eight men to take Ivy from her house. Here, I'm sure he won't hesitate to bolster that number. I've been trained for situations like this, but with Ivy next to me, I'm not about to test how many I'm up against. It's not that she's the type who's easily overcome by panic and ends up putting others in danger—she's simply in distress, exhausted, and I'm sure her son is all she has on her mind right now.

I take off my scarf, toss it on the ground and step on it.

"What are you doing?" she asks, watching me using my

scarf as a foot mat.

I'd stepped in a puddle. The last thing I want is for those men to follow my wet footsteps. It's too far for us to reach the door from which I entered the warehouse. Someone might even be there waiting on the other side. Until I can figure out another way out, we have to hide.

Her feet are wet, and I have a feeling she's going to keep pulling me toward where her son has escaped to. Not giving any warning, I scoop her up with one arm while my Glock is still in my other hand. Before the boy killed the light, I'd seen a series of equipment cages. Whether she likes it or not, we're heading there.

I run, open the first cage I can reach, enter, and close it.

Ivy whimpers, clinging to me with all her might as she shivers uncontrollably.

"Stay with me, Ivy." I tighten my grip as I take us behind what looks to be a pallet truck. "You can do this." I crouch and cover us with a tarp.

She stays silent, but she's convulsing. I know this is more than a battle for her. I wrap one arm around her waist, the other over her shoulder. Her body rattles against my chest, and her wet blouse soaks my shirt. I'd absorb the fear from her if I could.

I stroke the back of her neck as if comforting a child. I know this cage, the re-enacted torture her mother subjected her to when she was a child, is getting to her like a silent killer. But she's mounting a fight against it. She's still the defiant Ivy that I know.

Her anxious breaths caress my ear.

"Shh... I'm here." I place my lips on her crown, kissing it.

There must be at least half a dozen men searching near our hiding place. No doubt, many more are coming or patrolling outside.

"They're not here, sir," one closest to us says. "Fig is dead. I think the boy shot him and left with his mother. Or he might've let her go."

Boots keep treading the concrete floor around us, and flashlights shine all over the place.

"What are your orders, sir?... Right away."

The men trudge on, abandoning the room altogether.

I move first, making sure no one is around, then I guide Ivy out of the cage.

"Let's go," I release her slowly. My flashlight is back on.

"We've got to save him!" She tugs me toward the spot where we last saw the boy.

"No. We've got to go."

She grunts. She's still trying to gather her energy, but I know we're not going in the same direction.

No time to wait for her stubbornness to manifest itself, I bend down and seize her. I take the gamble and return to where I entered this warehouse. It's small, so if someone is guarding it, I'm confident I'll be able to take him out.

"Mark! Let me down!" she whispers, annoyed.

"Nah." I keep my course. As I run closer to the door, from the corner of my eye, I notice an object on the floor—out of place yet recognizable. It's a magazine page showing a girl emerging out of a swimming pool, topless, her long hair barely covering her breasts.

Ivy...

"Mark, please, he's my son," she begs, unaware of the object that caught my attention.

I press her head against my chest so she can't see what my other hand is doing—snatching that piece of paper and shoving it into my jacket pocket. Without saying anything, I charge ahead.

Our escape goes unchallenged. We arrive at an overgrown paddock where I had parked my car.

The cold air sends her to shiver again. As soon as she's inside, I lock the passenger door. Then I rush to the driver's side, cranking up the heater as I remove her wet blouse and put my suit jacket on her.

"You okay? You're warming up?" I rub her back, giving her all the help her body needs to get warm.

She nods, although she's still shaking.

I start the car without the headlights, and two shots ring out, further in the distance this time. Not at us, but at someone they're trying to bring down. Ignoring the noise, I make a U-turn, then zoom into the dark.

"Mark! Did you hear that? Deuce's men have found him. We've got to save him."

"Yes, we've gotta," I say. "But not tonight."

"I'm gonna do this with or without your help!" She flicks the door latch. But knowing she's stuck, she curses, "If he dies, it'll be on you!"

"Ivy, trust me. We leave here now, and the three of us will stay alive. If we were running after your son, all of us would be dead."

"You heard what my son said. He's got orders to keep me in that warehouse. And that man on the radio, he told Deuce my son had let me go. Deuce will kill him, perhaps even torture him first." She growls, pounding her fist on the leather surface of the passenger door. "It'll be on you! Do you hear me?"

"It will be on me, Ivy. I hear you loud and clear. But I've also got orders to protect you with my life."

"You only answer to me. And that's not my order!"

"Not yours. Noah's."

She huffs in helplessness.

"So I'll do that first, then we'll find your other son," I resolve.

She places a hand over her eyes, sighing, "Is Noah okay?"

"Yes. He's safe. He and Linda are with Ben at my place," I assure her. She knows my house is fitted with security not even Deuce can breach.

"Ben, Cass' brother?"

"Yes."

She acknowledges me, perhaps with a silent thank you from her eyes. Then she stares at her own lap.

I take time to appraise her, clearing the fringe off her face. If it weren't so dark, I'd see her pasty-white face, but even in the dark, I can see the fire in her eyes dimming.

I soften my tone. "Look, I'm not asking you to choose between your two sons. I'm just asking you to be patient. That boy is well-trained. He had a head start, and it's wilderness out there. Your son will find a hiding place, and no one will find him. Not tonight."

"He protected Noah." Her calm voice returns. "Deuce's other men were going to get Noah too, but 'Bro' hid him and Linda that they gave up searching and left with just me."

We're entering the outer rim of the city of Helena. The streetlights shining into the car make me notice stains on the cuff of my sleeves. It's blood. I'm not hurt, so it's got to be hers!

"Ivy..." I feel her neck, startling her. It's wet, and that's blood on my fingertips. Something must've happened when that bastard cut her hair. "I'm taking you to the hospital."

"No! Don't you dare!" Her eyes flare.

"You're hurt."

"Of course I'm fucking hurt, Mark!" she barks. "But not this." She points at the back of her neck. Then she slumps forward, explaining, "It's just a scratch. The blade scraped the back of my neck when Deuce—"

I stop the car. This time she lets me inspect her. I part her uneven hair to expose the skin of her neck. It's more than a scratch, but it's not a big wound. I decide to drive on.

She takes a few harsh breaths, then says, "I told you it would be on you if my son died."

"Yes, Ivy," I accept. "You don't have to remind me. But he's not a fool. He knows how to defend himself. He shot Ty, for God's sake!"

I don't know how that fact didn't interfere with my state of mind when I aimed at that boy. I guess after all these years, my training is still in me. We're trained to read people. I read him, and I didn't see a killer.

"What I was saying... Mark, I'm sorry. I didn't mean it. My son is not your responsibility. And I'm sorry about Tyler."

I breathe out, digesting her statement. "I think Ty will be fine." I stay positive for the both of us even though I have no reassurance whatsoever about how my man is doing.

She nods, then looks ahead, and I focus back on the road.

I feel a sudden chill spreading on top of my hand. Her palm seems to have some way to go in warming up.

"I'm sorry," she murmurs.

I flip my palm up and squeeze her hand. "It's fine, Ivy. We're good."

She slowly leans against my shoulder. "He's only seventeen. How could he be so vicious?"

So this is her secret. Her first son. I don't know how the hell Deuce got hold of that information—and I'm not sure how that prick intends to exploit those old magazine shoots of her. But by all accounts, she had hidden her secret well.

I take time to look at her profile. Her long hair used to touch her cheeks, framing her complexion. Now, I can see her clearly, even in the dark of night. I see her beyond just that beautiful face, beyond that veil that she had put up since my first question about her children. Now I know why it took her a moment to answer, 'One. Just one.' I still haven't got a clue how she and her first son got separated, but this is the Ivy Wren I've been longing to see. Not that I'm relishing her anguish, but I see a woman I'm willing to surrender to unconditionally.

"Are the police at my place?" she asks.

"Yes."

"And so are the press, I'm guessing?"

"Most probably, yes. But you're not going home. You're going to my place."

She looks around. She knows we're close. "Of course. You said Noah is there?"

"Yes."

"With Ben?"

"Yes. And Zander and a few of his men may be there, too."

"And perhaps the press would've figured out that I may be with you?"

"Possibly."

She sits tall despite her clear agitation as she feels the jagged ends of her hair. "No one can see me like this." Her breaths shake. "At least for tonight."

Seeing herself in the mirror, her defiance crumbles. She tilts toward me, resting her forehead on my shoulder.

Strong or weak, she's still the feisty Ivy Wren Cavanagh. However she wears her hair, it doesn't change how I see her or how I feel about her. On the other hand, I understand how hard she's been tested. Her hair is her dignity—and right now, it keeps reminding her of everything that went wrong tonight.

I turn my face to her, and between her wet strands, I breathe into her crown. "No one else will see. I promise."

"Only you."

I reassure her with a slow dip of my head. "Only me."

17

———

IVY

Mark pulls over next to a park, and my heart jolts to a halt.

"Why are we stopping? Is someone following us?"

He taps my hand—*I've got this*—then takes a pair of night-vision binoculars out of the glovebox. "I just want to check the welcoming party."

Now the spot he has chosen to stop at makes sense. We're able to see the street where he lives, yet trees obscure us.

"Any sign of the press?"

"No. It's quiet apart from Zander's men guarding the gate," he describes. "Let me call Ben."

He jumps out, heading to the cargo space of his Jeep, phone pressed to his ear. He takes out something while speaking to Ben Winter. The call is brief, and he's soon back next to me, a windbreaker in his hand.

"What did Ben say?"

"Noah is asleep. Linda is keeping watch."

"Zander?"

"Yeah, he's with them. Here, wear this."

He helps me cover myself up. Wearing his windbreaker feels like I'm cloaked under an oversized poncho, reminding me of how big this man is, even though he never appears hulky.

"I'll be your shield," he emphasizes, pulling the hood down. "No one will see you as long as you stay close to me."

He doesn't have to tell me that. Staying close to him is second nature for me. But after how erratic I've been tonight, I guess he had to spell it out.

"Ready?" He restarts the car.

"Yeah."

"Lie here." He invites me to rest on his lap, so I'm out of view.

That night before he told me everything about his ex, we had been in bed, lying so close, blanketed by unresolved desire. But now, inside his car, lying with my cheek resting on the buckle of his belt, it all feels more intimate. But most of all, I've never felt this protected.

"Mr. Connor." I'm sure it's one of the officers guarding his gate. "Is everything okay? Is the Attorney General all right?"

"She's fine." I feel Mark's hand securing me. "Anything suspicious?"

"It's been quiet, sir."

"Thanks for staying. Good night," Mark replies and drives on. I feel comforting strokes across my back. "Come on. We're here."

Like a bundle of garments, I roll out of the car into the arms of my protector.

"Connor!" Zander yells from the porch.

Mark nudges me behind him. Our bodies overlap. And as if that's not enough, he reaches back to put his arm around me as I bury my face between his taut traps. He meant it when he said *no one* would see me like this.

"Ivy, are you okay?"

"She's fine. Just let us through," Mark orders.

Mark has shielded me numerous times, but never like this. When he was my bodyguard, ironically, I had never been in real danger. Maybe because I had him and his partner Sam for 'just in case' situations. Or perhaps because they were around, that danger stayed away. The worst was probably the mine prank when I almost fell inside a shallow shaft. That was the first time I felt what it was like to be saved by him. Swift. Secure. And that was with just one of his arms.

Tonight has been different. Even though Deuce didn't intend to kill me, I'm in much worse shape—probably the worst I've ever been in my life. And right now, despite no longer being in imminent danger, Mark knows how much it means to me to stay hidden.

With a solid wall of muscle obscuring me, I can only watch my feet moving one in front of the other along a wooden floor. I've never been to Mark's house before, but I know we're in his bedroom.

I pull back my hood but keep his windbreaker on me. I instantly feel naked, exposed, and not myself. Thank goodness there's no mirror in here.

But I'm comforted by his presence.

Someone is outside the door. "Mark, you okay?" That's the voice of Ben Winter, Cass's brother.

"Yeah. Ivy is with me. She's all right. Is Noah okay?" Mark replies, keeping the door shut.

"He's good. He was awake a few times, but he's settled now."

"Miss Cavanagh!" That's Nanny Linda. "Are—"

"She's okay," Ben interrupts her. "Let's leave them be." His voice fades for a moment, then he's back behind the door, telling Mark, "I'll be outside if you need me."

Then it all goes quiet.

Mark walks around the room, checking the windows and

peeking out a few times. He adjusted the curtains that are already drawn close, making sure there are absolutely no gaps.

"You wait here, okay? I'm gonna talk to Ben."

"You'll be back, won't you?" Why am I sensing that he's going to leave me here and sleep on the couch?

"I'll be back. Feel free to take anything from my closet. Have a bath if you want."

"I want to see Noah."

"Of course. You wait here."

I hear chattering outside. I can't make out what the men are talking about, but soon Mark comes back, a first aid kit in his hand.

"Let me see your neck."

I lift my hair. It's so light—there's really not much of it left.

He gently touches my wound, and I should be wincing in pain. But the contact trumps the hurt and humiliation I've been feeling all night.

"You're right. It's just a scratch." His voice is soothing. "Hold still." He takes time cleaning the sore spot. Judging by the pile of blood-stained cotton balls he used, I think it's more than just a scratch. But it doesn't hurt as bad, especially after he spreads some ointment and puts a Band-Aid over it.

"Thanks."

"Are you hurt anywhere else?"

"No. I'm fine."

"Okay. I've told them not to bother you." His eyes are still assessing me. "You wanna see Noah now?"

"Please."

He slowly puts the hood of his windbreaker back over my head. I glue myself behind him, exactly like how I arrived here.

No one seems to be lingering in the rooms that we're passing. Mark keeps guiding me until we arrive at another bedroom where Noah is sleeping.

I sit at the edge of the bed, observing my son—my youngest son. Without me touching him, he mutters, "Mom?"

"I'm here, Noah." My voice trembles.

His lips curve into a small smile, but his eyes remain closed.

It'll be a long night ahead for me. I may not even sleep at all. But hearing him calling me 'mom' and knowing he's safe, I feel a little peace.

Then he turns to his side, his back to me. He puts a hand on his teddy. "Mark…"

"What is it, buddy?" He brushes Noah's arm.

My boy stays unstirred, no doubt sleeping soundly because he knows his 'watchbear' has carried out his order to protect his mother.

I TAKE a shower in Mark's ensuite, with lukewarm water as usual. There's a bathrobe folded on the shelf, but I choose to wear the one that's hanging up. It smells like him, feels like him.

I rest my hands on the vanity, still refusing to look in the mirror. Instead, I study the items placed neatly at its base—his toothbrush, comb, razor, and cologne. When was the last time I saw toiletries belonging to a man?

My head pulses, still recovering from Deuce's nasty hair work. But it doesn't hurt as much as the realization that I've missed seventeen years of my oldest son's life. My firstborn. And I don't know if I'll ever see him again—dead or alive.

I bend down to reach the pile of my dirty clothes and rummage through my pants pocket in case he left me a note or some kind of sign. It's empty. But something *is* inside Mark's jacket—not his windbreaker, but the suit jacket he put on me as soon as we were out of that warehouse.

Just when I thought nothing else would go wrong tonight...

Siren at play.

He saw this? Why the hell did he take it with him? To use it as an excuse that I'm not worthy of his love?

I scrunch the piece of paper, toss it into the trash, and stare at it. My shoulders heave up and down. Whatever stupid thought I have, my hand reaches in, retrieving it. I spread and flatten the *We Love Candy* magazine page, laying it on the vanity. There were at least three more pages of me in that special edition—as raunchy, if not dirtier, than that shot.

The past is a bitch. Dismally, my present is the mother of all bitches.

I brace myself to confront my own reflection in the mirror. *Who's that?*

I touch my hair, feeling it from roots to tips. Am I that different now from that girl coming out of the swimming pool?

I exhale as if I can get rid of the filth out of my system.

Damn it! I'm not going to cry just because a man has cut my hair.

But it's not that. The hurt isn't coming from tonight. It's coming from far away—way back. And here I am, wishing that Mark would love me.

I toss the page once again and kick the waste basket.

"Ivy?" The noise must've flicked his switch. It sounds like he's back in alert mode.

"I'm okay, Mark."

"Can I come in?"

My eyes involuntary shut, preparing myself. "Yes."

Mark steps in. "What's going on?"

"Don't look at me like that."

"Like what?" He stands beside me, placing his hand on the small of my back as if giving me strength. He has a lot of it—a *lot*—but I don't know if he can stop me from falling to pieces now.

"Like I was a beauty queen who had lost her crown."

"No. Never."

"Don't say it'll grow back."

"No, I won't."

I'm dying to fall apart in front of him, but he notices what's in the trash.

"Why did you take it, Mark?"

He holds my shoulders, asking me to look at him. "So nobody else would find it. The police will tear that warehouse apart."

Truly, this man doesn't judge. I shouldn't even have considered that he had any bad intentions. I'm relieved, but I haven't found my peace. Now I want him to help me find it.

"She was pretty, wasn't she?" I recall that old chapter that will forever haunt me.

"Ivy ..." Mark calls me softly. "It's your past."

"It has become my present, Mark."

"Our past will be part of our present. But that—" He points at the crumpled page in the trash. "That piece of paper is your past that'll stop with me, so it doesn't become your future."

I bow my head. "It's too late. Deuce would've found a way to let the world know about it."

"The world isn't your concern. It's here, Ivy." He places a hand on my heart. "Your past stops with me—in here. So you can handle whatever the world is going to throw at you."

My eyes give him quiet gratefulness. But with him near, I can't stay quiet for long. He has to know the truth.

"That photo was taken a few days before my eighteenth birthday." The shame, the guilt, the regret, they're all crawling to the surface. "You know how my parents were. They never let me see any boy. When a model scout asked me if I'd be interested in posing for their magazine, I was flattered—or perhaps normal, like a teen who's finally been accepted by society.

"When that photoshoot happened, I was on top of the world. Men—young and old—couldn't get enough of looking at me. Like I was some kind of rare diamond in the rough. They gawked at me, leered at me. And guess what? That made me feel beautiful and appreciated. Sick as it was."

His hold doesn't relent. There's no speck of condemnation or disgust in his gaze. It's not his stoicism on display. It's love.

"The day I turned eighteen, my parents threw me a party as if I was twelve. After dinner, when my parents apparently had to sort out some urgent business, I sneaked out of the house, feeling like an adult." I sigh sourly, recalling the feeling of freedom when I managed to run to the bar without anyone stopping me. "I joined the magazine staff who had their Friday night drinks. They were my people, my safety."

I frown, anticipating a regretful look to rise on his face. But that love is still there as if I could touch it.

"You don't have to explain, Ivy Wren."

The way he says my name is always special, whether it's Ivy or AG Cavanagh. But this is the first time he mentions my middle name—so naturally, as if he'd called me that forever. And that makes me adamant that I have to explain everything to him.

"I do, Mark. I have to."

"Go on." His voice is even gentler than his touch.

I close my eyes, drawing strength from within me, only to realize he's already given it.

"I slept with several men that night. Men twice my age, men I have no hope of remembering who. I don't even know how many. I was so drunk," I explain. "So I'll never know who the father was. As soon as I found out I was pregnant, abortion crossed my mind. I feared what my mother would do if she found out. But I couldn't bring myself to do it. I couldn't." I shake my head repeatedly.

Mark draws me close, letting me lean on him entirely. Safe, comforting, freeing. "It's your past, Ivy. I accept it, and so should you."

"Pregnancy for a teenage girl should feel like a nightmare. But you know, Mark? When I saw the test results, I felt... joy. I can't explain why or how. I just felt that, finally, I'd have someone on my side. Who would smile at me or cry with me," I recount, feeling the joy bubbling in my belly even now. "But then it all ended. I was in labor, my blood pressure got danger-ously low, and I fainted. When I woke up, my mother told me the baby didn't make it. Little did I know, what my mother eventually did went beyond what I feared could've happened."

He caresses my cheek with the back of his hand, sighing as if feeling my pain.

"But what I still can't understand," I continue. "At the hospital and in the days that followed, I felt nothing. *Nothing.*" I stare at the vanity as if I was back in that small room inside that maternity clinic. "I saw the Certificate of Stillbirth, but I didn't even read it. There wasn't anything in me that wanted to challenge what my mother told me. Or ask questions. I just accepted it and moved on. What kind of a mother was I?"

I withdraw from his embrace, looking him in the eye as if telling him this is his chance to condemn me.

"Ivy..."

"You grieved for your child. You grieved until your heart bled. I know you did, Mark."

"I did." He nods, blinking furiously as if being reminded of the day he received the news. "It still hurts."

I reciprocate his nod. "Now here I am, telling you I felt nothing when I lost mine."

"Ivy, don't be too hard on yourself. We all grieve differently."

I shake my head. "I moved on. Went to law school, got into politics, got married, had Noah, and became the Attorney General of Montana. And I still questioned nothing about that day at the Missoula Birth Center. When Deuce's first message arrived, I didn't even think it could be about that part of my past. Because in my head, my baby died. It was fact—indisputable."

His hand on my cheek turns from soft to reassuring. "Look, maybe you didn't grieve. Maybe you didn't move on, either. Instead, you died. You died with him."

Tears stream down my face. I've never cried. Not since my mother put me in that basement cage for the first time. But the tears he invokes fulfill me. I cry for all that he has given me.

"Now, the question is, Ivy Wren, do you want to *live* with me?"

I sob in his arms, unable to answer. His formidable body softens, and his manliness mollifies me. He's now protecting my heart and all the pain that comes with it.

"Tell me this isn't too good to be true?" my whisper trembles.

"We're not too good to be true. We're just too slow at being true to ourselves. But we're here now. We're the truth."

My whole body loses its strength, and I let it. Knowing an indelible force is supporting me, I collapse into him. My heart pounds against his chest, only to slow down as I take the first step to start living. My dark past will stop with him—he's that steady.

I moan in comfort as I feel the raging muscles on his arms snake around me, reaching my back to grant me slow, deliberate strokes. He draws his thick palm so he cups my chin.

We lock eyes.

"Don't say I still look beautiful," I speculate about what he's thinking.

"You're always beautiful, but that's not what I'm going to say."

"Then what are you going to say?"

He shakes his head, watching tears rolling down my face. I can't even stop them, as if I'd only learned how to cry just now.

"Is it too much to ask you to love me?" I pose the same question as I did the night he left me in my bed.

"Ivy, I've been keeping a distance so I will never break you." He thumbs some stubborn tears from my eyes. "We're so close now, but if I'm completely honest with you, I'm still terrified. If something ever happens between us, I don't want to be the one who wrecks you."

"Four goddamn years." I shake my head, forcing him to take accountability. "If it's the only way to taste your love, then wreck me. You have my permission."

"Ivy..."

"Do it."

The challenge prompts him to look at me as if analyzing what's behind my eyes. "No. Love shouldn't hurt," he hums, low and intense. It may well be the sound of him shedding his last shield. "Well, maybe a little. But it shouldn't wreck you."

He's full of resolve, laying it bare for me.

His hand gentle on my chin, he whispers, "I'm yours, and I'm not going to destroy you. How could I?" After all this time, his heart is now out in the open.

He's the same man who served me hibiscus tea, caught me fainting, and the only one who can keep me alive even when

I'm coiled in a dark cage. He never stops fighting for my safety and dignity. But he's not the same Mark Connor I fell in love with four years ago—*he's mine now.*

"Then let me see you," I demand.

Without question, he takes off his shirt. In the name of God, how have I been able to live in close proximity to him without ransacking those perfectly-carved abs?

I raise my eyes to him as my fingers trail his collarbone across to his shoulders. I crisscross my way down, stalling at a spot on his left rib.

I kiss it.

"It's just a scar," he dismisses.

"It's not a scar," I counter. "It's devotion." I know it's where the bullet had hit him—the bullet he took for Grace, Sam's adopted daughter.

I go on to rub his pecs. "I've seen you like this," I provoke, hinting at our first meeting.

His lips curve. "What the hell were you doing barging in while I was changing?"

"You liked it," I deadpan.

"After being stuck for days with dozens of boxes and a work husband named Sam, hell yeah."

"Now I want more."

He undoes his belt and pulls down his pants, revealing his underwear-clad pelvis.

"I've seen you like this, too."

"Oh, I don't think so." He slams my hand on his bulging dick.

With that, his lips crash onto mine, like an enormous thirst has made him do it. Mark doesn't operate on impulse. Perhaps he had planned our first kiss—if ever—to be soulful, tender, affectionate. But hell, whatever kind of kiss it is, as long as it's his, it'll be the best first kiss I've ever had.

I raise the stakes, nipping at his lips, pushing my tongue into his mouth.

"I want to see all of you," I keep demanding, our lips still searing each other.

His impatience heightens. Clearly, he can't wait to show it to me so he pulls down his underwear completely, letting his dick jut out. Serenaded by my own moans, my body dances against his, my belly rubbing the length of him. He's a beautiful man, and he's responding to me, but I don't think he's fully hard yet.

Despite the temptation to go all-out, I start from the beginning—trailing his well-sculpted shoulders down to his arms. Firm curves arise as his muscles tighten. He doesn't need to prove to me what those arms can do. I already know. I plant kisses on the top of his palms, thanking him for his protection tonight.

"That feels so good," he murmurs. He gazes at me as if my kisses were touching gestures he'd never experienced before.

"Oh, there's more." I move on to hand-paint his pecs and abs, telling him I appreciate *all* of him.

A coarse huff sails out of his throat as if replying that he accepts.

My hands coast down to reach below his belly. Seeing his enjoyment, I slide them down even lower, getting tickled by his generous pubic hair in the process. I wrap my fingers around his thick dick, my other hand cupping his sac.

"God, Ivy..."

I relish in his masculinity, rubbing his hardening shaft. I've worshipped him in silence for so long. For him to give me access like this, I feel humbled, liberated, aroused, and blessed at the same time.

"Now let me see you," he requests, encircling his fingers around my wrists so I stop.

I let his dick go with a long caress. Then I untie the belt of his bathrobe I'm wearing.

Resting his palms on my waist, he hisses as the robe falls at my feet. He pulls me toward him, pressing himself against my breasts. Panting, he maintains, "When I told you that night that you're the most precious thing I have. I meant it."

He takes half a step back, ducking to kiss my chest, trailing his lips until he finds my nipple. He sucks it deep as if trying to prove his point.

I fling my head back, absorbing the sheer ecstasy. Mark then reaches the back of my neck, but feeling the bandaged wound, he shifts his hand down. I'm sure it's so he doesn't hurt me. After a brief pause, he kisses his way to my other breast, cupping it, then latching his mouth to suck my aching nipple.

"And you taste so good," he sighs.

I release a series of soft moans, then conclude them with a statement, "Because that's my love you're tasting."

He eases his nibbling, then lets go of my nipple slowly.

"And I'll give you mine. I swear," he resolves.

Unrequited love? What unrequited love!

Finally, my secret love is my love—no adjective needed.

I'm now as impatient as he was, if not more, and he responds by lifting me by the ass and taking us into the shower. I feel his biceps flex against my side while our lips lock again. I extend my hand, flicking the tap on, and dial it closer to 'hot.' He's with me. There's no way my body will falter.

Mark lathers my breasts under the fall of water, smiling at the bubbles sliding down the mounds. But soon, he draws me close, growling as if the distance between us is unbearable. His lips are back on mine, his tongue ravaging my palate. As we grow breathless, we break the kiss, staring at each other like we're soulmates that have been reunited.

My love has been put on trial. It might've taken the long, painful way, but never once, *never once,* did I feel wrong.

I spin him around so he's right under the shower—my chance to feel his magnificent body—rubbing it, massaging it. I slow when I arrive at his bullet scar, and he notices. Taking my hand without shifting its position, he says, "I'll do it for you too and for Noah." His eyes meet mine. "And for your oldest son. That's my devotion to *you.*"

And he seals it with a kiss.

I don't doubt his promise. But I truly hope it won't take a bullet to prove that his devotion will stretch that far.

As steam rises around us, I glide down, my chest skin wiping his wet body. A hand pushes my elbow up as if not allowing me to get all the way down. But I challenge him—I'm dying to do this, for him as much as myself.

He lets me be as my mouth meets the tip of his dick. His precum mixes with warm water. I lick it to get a taste. It's divine, and I let him know by shooting him a rapacious gaze.

His thick pubic hair caresses my cheeks as I position myself to suck him in deeper. His hips rise, and his legs shudder as I take him in all the way. The head of his cock arrives at the back of my throat, and I tease it with a grinding movement. My open hands press at his taut ass cheeks, at times playing along his crack, swiping his perineum.

"God, Ivy..." The first time he calls my name in a raw, feral way. The back of his head hits the shower pane behind him, and his gaping mouth is pounded by the droplets of water showering above us.

I love how he feels inside my mouth. How the crown of his dick oozes out precum, giving it away that he's getting closer and closer. I give it some reprieve, only to take his balls in my mouth. He can't even moan as his head jerks back—damn, he's sensitive everywhere!

This time I'm back to tending to his dick. His hips prance, and the air is filled with his erotic groans. He caresses my shoulders, only to grip them so he can stay upright. His flesh swells inside my throat, and for once, he can't help his weakening body.

"Wait... Ivy, wait." He pulls his shaft out, not letting me continue. I've never seen a man looking so guilty after being given a blowjob.

He then gently grabs my armpits, motioning me to stand up. Face to face, he lets his head falls forward, the tip of his nose touching mine.

I whisper, "If you want to come, I'll take you."

"No. I want to please you first."

Longing to be with a man doesn't always mean longing to have him in me. That's how I survived all these years without it. Truly, I'll *gladly* take him and get lost in the scent and the taste of him.

"Mark," I complain. Doesn't he know that it turns me on to watch him squirm when I suck him? Not to mention hearing his animalistic groans. But he puts his index finger up, sealing my lips shut.

"Out there, I'll be the first to face danger for you. In here, *you* come first."

Can a woman argue with that?

Having known Mark, having felt him, I don't have to imagine what this man is capable of—in battle or in bed. Whatever he's going to do to me, 'ladies first' sounds fucking appealing.

18

MARK

She has given me something that I'd forgotten possible and more. Her touch is what every man's dreams are made of. It's the fruit of her passion. Yet, with every caress, she responds to my cues—learning how I like it and giving it to me. She's pleased me like she would've died in vain if she hadn't done it. All that while kneeling in front of me.

Now it's my turn to surrender to her.

Ivy relaxes, seemingly content to shift her attention from my cock to herself as I lick water off her skin. I stop the shower from running so I can keep going without having to constantly wipe my face. She doesn't seem to mind the cool air that's slowly crawling over our skin.

Crouching, I drag my tongue down until I reach her soft folds while my hands haven't stopped fondling her ample breasts. I push her thighs wide, dipping my head so I can lick her. Her skin tastes like heaven, but this... This is the reason men kneel.

"Mark... don't stop." Her moans are compelling yet wild. I know I've hit her most sensitive spot. So she's now begging —*begging*—for me to make it last.

I keep teasing her with the tip of my tongue—sometimes a hard poke, sometimes a gentle brush. Her pussy is engorged. Its coral shade deepens like it has turned into a precious ruby. She shudders, unable to contain herself, squeezing her thighs and then falling back, sliding down the glass pane. Her back erases a wide layer of fog, while on her left and right, her handprints are all over.

That's my girl... that's her first.

I pick her up, and she can barely cling to me. I pat a towel to dry her as much as I can, then carry her to my bed.

She releases a couple of shivers as she lands on the cool sheet. But I won't leave her exposed for long. I spread myself on top of her like a blanket, then I press myself against her, lips first. Once steady, I sink my tongue into her mouth. Our lips spin against each other, puckering, sucking, nibbling. Then, I feel her legs part under me.

I ready myself, but I break the kiss, confessing, "I don't keep condoms here."

She smiles. "With you, I'm always protected."

So this is real. I'm going to make love to her all the way. Actually, this isn't making love. It's giving love. Years of being penned in by betrayal haven't erased who I really am. After all, I'm not the frigid, love-resistant man I've foolishly labeled myself as. The urge to give more to her is overwhelming. And that's exactly what I'm going to do.

I grab her leg from under her knee, lifting it so I can enter her. Her folds curve away as I glide, letting my length travel at will. My erection is raging, and it's stopping at nothing to tease her core, luring pleasure out of her.

Ivy moans painfully as she bucks. The sensation drives her to squeeze out a few teardrops. I pause to assess what kind of pain I'm giving her. Her fingers dig into my ass cheeks as if cautioning *don't you dare stop*. It must be a good pain, then. So I grind my cock harder.

We pant as we stare at each other. Whether I'm going to have a child with her, or children, remain to be seen. I hope we do. But whatever the future holds, I know the void within me has been filled. I'm home, and so is she. We belong to each other, and no one and nothing can ever dispute that. Not even ourselves.

I palm her buttock with one hand, lifting it—a cue that I'm going to roll her over. She smiles, agreeing. I'd want her to control how deep she wants me to be, so she's got to be on top. My other intention is to have a hand ready—between her legs, within touching distance of her bud.

She rides me, then she gasps. Sensuality swirls in her eyes. Startling amber hues spark into their hazel shade. God, she's so beautiful like that. How the hell was I able to wait this long?

"Mark, I'm close…"

Her distended breasts rub against my chest as she bends down to reach me. While her entrance accommodates me, I've been pressing her clit, flicking it, circling it.

"Come all over me, Ivy," I moan.

She moves her core. It's tight against my cock, yet her juice lubricates me. But I want more than her wetness.

"All of you," I hint.

Yes. I want all of her—every part that shudders and stretches from gratification beyond what her body can take.

I put a hand on her back, nudging her down. She gets it. She laminates her body over mine—completely—and I kiss her ferociously as soon as her mouth closes in.

There's something deep in me that connects to her. And my heart bursts. It may be bleeding, but it's a kind of destruction that, until tonight, I didn't know I needed. Sometimes you just have to start from the beginning. Like her—to die first.

Now that she's going to start a new life with me, I vow to do the same with her.

Tonight revealed how far her enemy was willing to go to hurt her. Tonight revealed how far Ivy would go to protect her son. And now it reveals that there is no boundary between us. I took responsibility for her agonizing wait. But I don't regret it. True love doesn't have room for doubt, and that's what I have in my hand. Now I can give all of me to her without inhibitions.

Ivy rises up and sinks into me one last time, and I hold my shaft, releasing into her with steady pulses. She collapses onto me. There's no scene more beautiful than to witness Ivy drenched in her own sweat, filled with wild pleasure that I've imposed on her. As I absorb my own pleasure, I, too, capitulate.

"My God, Mark... what the hell..." She rolls herself over to my side.

I chuckle. "Worth the wait?"

She climbs over me, resting on my chest, and gives me a dissatisfied smile. "I waited too long!"

My belly shakes in laughter, taking her body up and down with it.

"Actually, when I look back now, the time I spent with you was the best time I had," she admits. "Even without sex or your adequate attention."

"Hey! I've always paid attention to you."

She hums. "I know."

I kiss her forehead, gently rubbing her arm. She looks up, serious this time.

"What is it?"

She releases a deep breath. "Whatever tomorrow brings, I won't be able to do it without you." She takes my hand into hers. Her grip is that of 'I need you.' And I don't know why it feels like something I'd had before but lost.

I remember that night at the hospital after I was shot. I wasn't seeing the light or anything, but I was in pain even though I was supposed to be sedated. And that hold comforted me. There were two people in that room that day. And I'm glad it was her holding me, not my goddamn work husband!

"What?" she says in amusement.

"Thank you for never giving up on me. You must've thought I was a cold son of a bitch."

"At times, yes," she giggles. "But, if you love someone, you keep them in your heart. Whether it's hot or cold. Because when the night gets even colder, that love will always warm you."

I don't think we need extra warmth tonight, but I pull up the covers over her anyway. Then I kiss her goodnight. "Do you think you'll be able to sleep?"

"I don't know."

"I'll still be here tomorrow." I run my fingers through her hair, and she lets me. It's exactly how I thought it would feel— long or short. And even though she doesn't want me to say it, she's as beautiful as ever. "I'll be right here when you wake up."

"Promise?"

"Promise," I whisper. "So close your eyes."

She rises, putting her hand on my cheek, then kisses me. "I will then."

Years of memories flutter inside me like a pile of autumn leaves blowing in the wind. One becomes clearer than the rest. Me, the luckiest groom standing in a New York church, only to face cruel rejection from a woman who was supposed to be my forever. Then she killed me when her cruelty turned into savageness. *I did it because it was best for it*—her words that have held me ransom. She even referred to the baby as 'it.'

Yet, those memories are withering, replaced by an abundance of evergreens. The bright, hardy leaves from seeds Ivy has planted deep in my soul.

"I love you, Ivy Wren."

"I love you, too, Mark Connor."

Her eyes gradually fall shut, and a naughty smile plasters her face as if she's already dreaming of our next sex. How could I ever wreck her? Even if someday we have to part—which I hope is never—I will always love her.

I put my hand on top of hers, one that's still perching on my chest as if asking her to find my wounded heart. Her fingers twitch under my palm. I think she's saying that she can't find it. Because I have a new, stronger heart where the loss and defeat from my past no longer hurts, not even feels bitter.

19

IVY

I roll my body lazily. My arm is aching, having been folded under my shoulder all night. My intention is to lie flat on my back to relieve the pressure, but I hit a wall of... something.

I grope behind me. It's a man. Definitely a man, because—

"Good morning."

I spring into awareness, making sense of where I am and, more importantly, the man sleeping in my bed.

Turning to face him, I grin. I'm not in my bed—it's his bed, which almost feels like *our* bed. And as he promised, he's with me when I wake up.

"I must've done something right last night," he quips.

"Hm?"

"Because one, you slept soundly. And two—" He nods at where my hand is.

On top of his morning wood.

"You're clearly awake." I abandon his crotch and kiss him.

"Bodyguards always wake up before their protectees."

It occurred to me last night that I'd wake up before he did so I could watch him sleep. The first and last time I saw Mark in his slumber was when he was Noah's full-time bodyguard.

Suffering from PTSD after his first kidnapping, Noah couldn't sleep for weeks. One night, I found the former Green Beret lying on the couch with him, falling asleep together in the middle of *The Incredibles 2*. I couldn't bring myself to wake them, so I covered them both with a quilt, hoping they'd go on till morning. Mark woke up then, but Noah didn't even stir.

I sit up, and only now do I realize I've taken two-thirds of the bed. "Sorry. It must've been uncomfortable for you."

"Uncomfortable? You almost banished me out of my own bed!"

I laugh. "Blame me. I haven't slept with a man since... I don't know..."

I do know. It was since my ex-husband decided that my nanny was more sexually attractive than I was.

"Sorry," I repeat.

Mark plants a kiss on my lips. "It didn't bother me. *You* come first."

That seriously wakes up my appetite. But before I can initiate anything, his phone buzzes with a text message.

"Everything okay?" I ask.

"It's the hospital. Ty."

"How is he?"

"He's awake. Doctors say he'll make a full recovery."

"Oh, thank God! Anything on Jones?"

"He's still in an induced coma. But doctors are hopeful."

"I really hope he'll be okay."

Mark holds my hand. "Yeah. He's good."

"He is." I huff. "Mark, was I a good client to you?"

"Initially, I thought you'd be the type who didn't want to be protected, giving us a hard time. But you weren't. You're a good client and a good person."

"I hope Jones and Ty think so too." Good people have

gotten physically hurt because of me—that's something that I haven't fronted before.

"I'm sure they do."

I lie back down, my head on his abs. "Mark, do you really believe my son is still alive?"

"Yes."

"How do we find him?"

"Now that we know what he looks like, we can sketch it out and try to find a match with facial recognition." He holds my shoulder. "May I say he looks like you?"

"I thought so too."

"Noah actually told me that 'Bro' looked like him."

"Oh, Noah..." My thought flashes back to the day he walked away with 'The Painter.' It turned out he was just playing with his older brother.

"Ivy, it's okay if you don't know, but I've got to ask. Do you remember his date of birth?"

I shake my head drearily. I have no memory of it, which reinforces what Mark said—that I had died with my baby. "I'm sorry, Mark."

"Hey, it's okay." He pats my arm. "We'll find a way, I promise."

"Deuce lined up six boys, forcing me to pick which one of them was my son. They were all seventeen. That man also showed video footage of a bunch of kids, probably as young as fourteen, working in his—I don't know—maybe his factory. I know drug problems in this state are dire, but seeing that... how on earth can I ever fight him? And the others?"

"One step at a time, Ivy. For now, we have to find your son and Deuce."

I've got no choice, but how do you prioritize when everyone you're trying to protect means just as much?

"Did you see Deuce's face?"

"No. He was wearing a white mask. I told myself it was like the mask of Phantom of The Opera, but a full one. He was about six-two, stocky, and his voice was sandy."

"That's a start."

"And he was going through puberty at the time I gave birth to my first son." I'm not sure if I want to elaborate to Mark why Deuce said that. "I don't know if it was just a silly remark, or it could be the truth."

"So he's maybe five or six years younger than you? So, thirtyish?" Mark seems to take the information seriously. "I guess that narrows it down a bit. The warehouse you were taken to was purchased by a man named Daemon Drury. Let's see if he's about that age."

"You think... DD—Deuce?" I frown. "It's silly, but I can't imagine that man is a Daemon Drury."

"Well, Zander is investigating him," Mark says. "So far, none of the sketches of what Deuce might look like match him. You're probably right."

"Gimme your laptop." I do a quick search. Daemon Drury, a farmer who owns that warehouse, is a fifty-year-old man, and according to the record, he's five-foot-five. "No. This man can't be Deuce."

"There we go then. I'll let Zander know it's not him, but he may be connected." Mark sends a text.

"Do you keep the sketches here?"

"Yeah. Let me bring them up for you."

I peruse the six sketches the police supposedly gathered from eyewitnesses and tip-offs. They vary wildly. "I guess these two could be him. Long, narrow face. I can't point out anything else."

"It's okay. I'll let Zander know."

"Did he find anything in that warehouse?"

"No. I think Deuce prepared that place just to take you."

And to perform a show I'd never forget.

Mark then asks, "Did Deuce say what he wanted?"

"Well, he wanted to scare me, humiliate me, and bully me into releasing a prisoner. Perhaps more than bully because my son's life is in his hands."

"Which prisoner?"

"JJ Marcusso. He killed a family of four."

"Did you have anything to do with that criminal?"

"He's been rotting in Montana State Prison for seven years. I put him there." I ponder hard. "But I can't immediately find any connection between him and whatever Deuce is into."

"Leave Deuce to Zander, and let me find your son. You know I'm good at it. You know I will find him."

"I'm not ready to share my past with the world."

"Just like I protected you last night, no one will know for now. But you're well aware that in the end, you'll have to come clean."

"All right." I try to picture what that moment will look like, but it's currently a jumble of shit that is far from clean. "How the hell a fentanyl boss got hold of information that wasn't supposed to exist? My parents were powerful politicians. They must've buried the records very deep."

"Perhaps not deep enough."

I lean on a pillow. "Deuce said he went through all the trouble to take me, to teach me a lesson about family. Of course it was about my oldest son, whom I didn't even know I gave birth to alive. But there was something else. He was pissed, absolutely pissed, when I described JJ Marcusso—that one of his balls was busted by another inmate."

Guilty amusement rises on his face. "So he may be Deuce's family?"

"Maybe. I have to dig into Marcusso's files."

"You do that. And I'll find your son. Are you okay with Ben guarding you? Along with Zander's men?"

I shake my head. Something else has taken over my thought. "What time is it?"

"Six thirty."

"Noah will wake up soon." I touch my hair, and I feel reality tugging me back into the despair zone. "I hope I don't scare him."

"Hey, of course not." He shakes my shoulder gently. "You're the same woman I knew four years ago, last week, and yesterday. I'm sure you are, too, in his eyes."

"If I had to lose my long hair so I could find my long-lost son, so be it," I settle. Then I give him a begging smile. "Tell me I'm still beautiful."

"You're always beautiful."

"Tell me it'll grow back."

He smiles sweetly. "It'll grow back."

I kiss him. "As soon as the police are done with my place, I want to have a press conference there."

"Ivy, don't rush it."

"I have to."

"I know you're—"

I sense where he's going. "This isn't about re-election, Mark. It's about reassuring the public and setting an example. I don't want speculation. I want to show the state that I'm alive and well, and that I won't bow down to threats."

"If you're sure."

"Will you be beside me?"

"You don't even have to ask, Ivy Wren." He then fiddles with my hair. "May I?"

"Yeah." Whatever he's about to do.

He tucks my hair behind my ears. "Perhaps you could comb it back. Like... Trinity."

"Carrie-Ann Moss?"

"Yeah. Like that."

I chuckle. "Not a bad idea. Although I won't wear black."

"What are you going to wear?"

"Blue, navy blue. The color of power."

"Good choice. And I'll stick with my charcoal wool suit."

"Charcoal? Not black?"

"No, charcoal."

With that answer, I'm reminded of his precision. There's a difference between black and charcoal. However, his handsomeness will go well with either color. "I'm looking forward to it."

"Just like old times."

God, I can't wait to see him in that formal suit, standing behind me, watching out for me.

"Fuck my hair. I always look good when you're by my side."

He rolls on top of me, kissing me as he looks at the clock. Hell, yeah. We've got time.

20

MARK

Attorney General Defiant After Kidnapping Ordeal.

That was the headline we woke up to this morning following her press conference late last night.

Ivy and Noah have gone back to their house after the Helena PD concluded their crime scene investigation. The boy was surprised by his mother's hair, but he didn't seem bothered. The first morning he saw her, he simply said, 'You look all right, Mom. Although I prefer your hair long.'

If I'm honest, I do too. It's a guy thing, I guess. But truly, it hasn't changed anything for me.

Ivy and I know this is just the beginning, and her defiance continues today as we head into her office.

"Good to see you, Ms. Cavanagh," her assistant says. "I... I'm sorry I didn't expect you back till tomorrow. I've taken the liberty of postponing your meetings."

"It's okay, Zoe. But if you can, I'd like to keep my meeting with the sheriff this afternoon."

"Certainly, ma'am. Oh, also, there is some urgent paperwork for you to sign. It's all in your in-tray."

"Thanks." Ivy closes the door. She heads to her desk and peruses a few more newspaper articles on her laptop. "Tortured? They really know how to invoke readers' imagination."

"They weren't wrong," I remark. She was hurt, and she was mentally tortured in that warehouse.

"Since when are you on the press' side?"

I smirk. "I'm always on your side."

She skims the article some more. "I wish they'd put more emphasis on the fact that I thanked Jones, Tyler—as in Red Mark—and the Helena PD."

I stare at her.

She comes to me, her arms rounding my waist, her mouth forming a teasing smirk. "You're my lover. I can't thank you in public."

"Lover?" I exclaim. "Am I just your lover?"

Her smirk widens. "No. You're my partner, my love, my everything. But I hope you don't mind the secrecy for now."

I kiss her. "I understand."

She goes back to her executive chair, staring at her L-shape desk. She has three different monitors, making it look like her own command center.

"Should I let you be? I guess that urgent pile of paperwork won't sign itself." I nod at the left end of her desk where her in-tray is.

She keeps looking, one hand on her mouse, the other obscured under the desk. I approach her. Old habit dies hard. That hand is on her thigh, and I stack mine over it, stopping her from scratching her skirt.

She withdraws. "It'll take a second to sign those. I'll do it this afternoon. Right now, we have to go to Missoula."

I look at her tentatively. "Are you sure you're ready for that?"

She gets up, giving me a light embrace. "Oh, I'm always

ready," she hums, rubbing my ass.

"If we were going to bed, I'd say you are. But, Ivy, we're going to the place where you died."

Her face grows heavy, but she stands tall. "I know, Mark. But I'm ready."

"Okay. We'll go to Missoula. On one condition."

"What?"

"You ride in the backseat."

She huffs, annoyed. "All right! Come on."

After making an excuse that we're going to Missoula to visit her parents' graves, the police reluctantly let us go alone.

As soon as we hop in my car, she moves forward from her seat to reach me. She stretches and plants a kiss on my cheek.

"What's that for?"

"Attorney General thanks her long-time love and body-guard for her safe return."

I glance at her, smiling proudly. She soon reclines into her seat, looking at her phone.

"Come on, stop looking at those."

"Well, this is new," she comments, leaning forward again to show me an article: *AG Cavanagh Before and After*. Some jerk has put up Ivy's photos with different short hairstyles pasted on top of her face.

"Ivy... that's in bad taste."

"Gotta give it to them for creativity, though," she quips, her face playful. Then she blurts out a laugh.

That is a sign her defiance has gone a step further. I know she's gotten over her hair, and we can now focus on finding her son.

The Missoula Birth Center is quiet. It's not a big hospital, and we're hopeful if Ivy's records are there, we will find them quickly.

A young receptionist greets us. "Attorney General? Are... are you okay? I read in the news you were—"

"I'm fine," she says. "Thanks for your concern."

"So, how can I help you?"

"I'm investigating an urgent case that stretches back fifteen to twenty years ago," she continues in a professional yet soft tone. "We need access to some of your patient files within that period."

"Ooo-kay. Um... has this got something to do with your kidnapping?"

"Maybe. We don't know yet."

"Um, okay. Do you have the paperwork?"

"Subpoena is being processed as we speak. It's an urgent case, and I need access now. I will give you the paperwork when it's ready."

"I... um... I'm sorry, Ms. Cavanagh. We will need that subpoena in order to release any kind of patient information. Or would you like to wait and speak to the clinic manager?"

I can see Ivy deciding between pressing on or turning back.

She takes a deep breath. "We'll be back."

I nod at her, agreeing with her decision. She knows not to make a scene and perhaps to avoid involving the senior staff— which may lead to an unwanted investigation by the clinic itself.

"I don't think that woman knows anything," I maintain. "Apart from whatever she read about you in the paper."

"She's too young to know what happened seventeen years ago."

I usher her back into my car. "Let's go to your mother's hospice, see if that car follows," I suggest, watching through the rearview mirror. That car has been on my tail, although keeping a distance.

"Who's that?" She notices.

"Could be reporters, could be Zander's men. Could be Deuce's spies."

We make a slow turn, and she suddenly says, "Mark! Look!" She's pointing at a pharmacy just around the corner from the maternity clinic.

Marcusso Pharmacy.

"Fuck me..." I murmur. "Any relation to JJ Marcusso?"

"Maybe. Let's find out."

"No." I keep driving. That car is still there, but it has pulled over about twenty yards from us.

"Let's go in and test what that car does. This may be our chance to find out what happened to my baby."

"Ivy, no!" I immediately recheck that the central lock is on. I don't trust her not to do anything brash right now.

Another car joins us.

"Mark, please. Isn't this our priority?"

My phone beeps, and I glance at the new text message. "We've got to go back to Helena." I step on the gas while trying not to attract more attention than the two cars already following us.

She growls, shaking her head. As soon as we hit the highway, the two cars seem to give up the chase.

"Ivy, we don't want to hit two birds with one stone today."

She scoffs. "We missed the first bird anyway. I've gotta get that file some other way. My own fucking medical file!"

Her annoyance is apparent, but we've got a more pressing matter. And that medical file may not be needed after all. If it even exists.

"Zander's got something," I say.

Captain Zander from Helena PD is waiting at Ivy's office in the Justice Building.

"We've got further DNA results on those toy pellets we found inside Noah's coat," he says. "There were blood specks on them. They weren't Noah's, so it must've belonged to the man who took him. Perhaps he tried to play too hard and hurt himself."

"So, who is he?" Ivy says.

"A man called Ethan Fulton. A seventeen-year-old from Minnesota."

"Minnesota?" She frowns. "He's a long way away from home."

Zander presents a printout of Ethan's photo to Ivy. It looks to be an older one—he's wearing a pair of glasses, his face a little chubby. The captain doesn't seem to recognize the boy's resemblance to Ivy—not that he would immediately come to that conclusion.

Ivy keeps everything to herself while I remain passive, even though my heart is crying out to me to hold her.

Zander explains, "He was adopted by Terry and Vera Fulton when he was a baby. The adoption papers were a mess. We don't really know where that boy was born, when, or anything else about him."

"Did you talk to the Fultons?" she asks, gripping the printout. I can imagine she's dying to trail a finger on the boy's face.

"Not yet. Vera Fulton passed away three days ago, and her husband is inconsolable, not ready to talk."

"Suspicious death?"

"No. She'd been battling bowel cancer for years."

Ivy accepts the statement with a blink.

"Here's what's interesting, though," Zander says. "The DNA is a partial match to Noah's. Twenty-five percent."

"What does that mean?" she grits out.

"He could be a relative. Or—"

She responds to him with a straight gaze. "He's my son, Zander."

"Ivy?" Zander gawks at her.

"Yes. The Painter, that boy, he's my son. He was the one who took me."

Zander releases a deep breath. "Jesus…"

"I got pregnant when I was eighteen. My mother told me the baby didn't make it. But she lied."

The captain stays speechless.

Ivy adds, "I want you to focus on Deuce. Leave my son to Mark. Please."

Zander leans back as if still trying to process the revelation. "So The Painter is connected to Deuce?"

"Yes. He's one of Deuce's troops. One of his best."

"I'm so sorry, Ivy," Zander's voice almost falters. He and Ivy have been close. They've got each other's back in a professional way, but this is the first time I see deep affection on his face. "I'll do everything I can."

"I know you will," she says. "Look, Deuce gave me his demand. He wants me to release a prisoner."

"Who?"

"JJ Marcusso."

"Marcusso? That mass murderer and cop killer?"

"Yes."

"Never in a million years, Ivy."

"I made a promise to him, but no. I don't intend to keep it," she resolves. "Just now in Missoula, we saw a pharmacy called Marcusso Pharmacy. Not far from the clinic where I gave birth to my first son. And we were followed. On the drive back here, I found the pharmacy is owned by JJ's sister, Sandra Marcusso."

Now I know she's ready to reveal everything to Zander, and

suddenly something clicks in me. "Ivy, you told me then that Sandra was a nurse before she became a pharmacist?"

"Yes."

"Which hospital?" I probe.

She soon takes her laptop and punches the keyboard like mad. "Shit..."

I cock a brow. "Missoula Birth Center?"

"Fuck," she sighs.

"What's going on?" Zander says.

I explain, "Sandra is in her fifties. If she used to work at the clinic, chances are, she was there when Ivy gave birth to her first son. She must be connected to Mosaic. Perhaps with information so important that she managed to bargain with Deuce to get her brother's freedom."

"That makes sense," Ivy says, but something is weighing on her mind. "Deuce said he took me that night to teach a lesson about family."

Zander frowns. "You think JJ Marcusso is his family?"

"Maybe. There's just something about him. Deuce behaved differently when he was talking about him."

"Well, JJ Marcusso is old enough to be his father, but the man never had a child," Zander reveals.

"Look into it anyway," she says. "You might find something else. Because—"

I look at Ivy, encouraging her.

"Because Deuce did this after I mocked Marcusso." She points at her hair.

Zander holds her shoulder. "We'll get to the bottom of this."

"Okay. But leave my son to Mark. Please."

"Fine," Zander agrees after a long thought. Before he leaves the office, he turns to us. "By the way... are you two?"

Ivy smiles, taking my hand into hers. "Yes. We're together."

"About friggin' time!" he says and leaves.

Ivy is back on her laptop, loading a social media account under Ethan Fulton. "That's him, Mark."

It is, indeed.

"So his name is Ethan." Her eyes glisten. "Ethan. It's a nice name."

"It is."

"He looks a bit different here.... Just like a normal kid... Although he was a lot younger. His last post was a couple of years ago." She keeps scrolling, smiling, and chuckling. The posts go back as far as four years. "Look how cute he was..."

I hold her hand as she finally lets go of her laptop, breathing into me as I stroke her back. "We'll find him, and you will have your mother-son talk, I promise."

She nods. Then she composes herself. "I need to sign that paperwork now. Will you be my patient boyfriend and bodyguard?"

"Of course," I affirm. "By the way, I got an update on Tyler earlier. He's recovering well, and he can't wait to be home. He'll probably be discharged by the end of the week."

"That's excellent news."

"And he can't wait to get back to work. Can you believe it!"

"You'll do the same, won't you?"

"Hmm..." I ponder. Last week, maybe. But today? If I'd gotten hurt, I would've wanted to spend a few quiet days with her.

"I heard from Jones, too. He's out of the ICU. His wife is by his side. He has a long recovery ahead, and he decided to retire."

"He did well to delay the attack. I think he was one of the reasons The Painter, or Ethan, managed to smuggle Noah and Linda out of the house."

"I'll talk to his wife later. I'll need to think about how I can give him ongoing support."

Of course she will. Her compassion shines yet again. Sometimes I wonder where she got it from—definitely not from her parents. I think it's from her own experience. She's the type who can turn tragedy into valuable lessons and... well, compassion.

Suddenly her assistant comes in.

"Ms. Cavanagh... um... the press is outside. I don't know if you've noticed..."

She loads the Montana News website. This time, she slumps helplessly.

"If you're heading out, you might want to take the back way," her assistant warns.

I give her a look to leave us be.

"Fuck. Mark..."

The topless and even nude photos of her are all over the news. Her breasts and pelvis are blacked out, but I have no doubt the cheap and raunchy sites will show everything. From the look on her face, I know the magnitude of the exposure takes her by surprise.

"You can't let this stop you."

"No. Even if I have to crawl in shit, I won't stop finding my son, and I won't stop hunting Deuce! This scandal may be raging out of control, but I've got to do what I've got to do. I know they'll still be everywhere. But I'll stop those whom I can stop, sue whoever I can sue."

Her bitterness shows as she peruses a copy. "I was the state's hero this morning. How fast was that? I'm now the whore of the west."

I close the lid of her laptop.

"Sign that paperwork, and have your meeting with the

sheriff. I know you can do this. That's your past, and you'll find a way to respond to it. Those nasty articles mean nothing to those who love you. I guarantee it."

She puts a palm on my cheek then draws a determined breath.

21

IVY

I take the media grilling on the chin after issuing an apology for the indecent photoshoot, citing an error of judgment. Public opinions seem to split—one camp acknowledging I was a child then, another highlighting my lack of moral values, calling me 'dynamite waiting to explode.'

The polls look dire, and my campaign manager is in damage control. She was quick to convince me to use the debacle to my advantage—creating what she called a 'sub-angle' that would make young women feel empowered. 'Everybody makes mistakes, and they can turn their lives around no matter how big the mistake is.' But politicizing my sexuality would be wrong on so many levels. I do have moral values, and they don't allow me to do it. So I fired her.

However, all that flies past my ears like meaningless noise. Because finally, I know my son's name.

Ethan.

Speaking it gives me the same joy as the moment I held Noah for the first time, calling him by his name. A wave of emotions washes through me, but I stem the tide before I'm completely engulfed by it. Seventeen years—that's a lot of days, a lot of hours, where the ups and downs of being Ethan's mother have been taken away from me.

But Mark's words keep me on course. I want to *live* with him, not reconstruct the past. I will take back what I've lost. And with that man by my side, no one can stop me.

From what I gather, the Fultons are a good family. They live in Minneapolis. Father Terry is a textile manufacturer, while his wife Vera was the company's in-house designer. I can only hope Ethan was loved.

Ethan doesn't have any siblings. It's not surprising to me. And that explains a lot about how he treated Noah.

Meanwhile, I've spent the afternoon keeping tabs on the latest drug bust led by the Helena PD.

"Come on, Zander!" I mutter to myself, waiting for my phone to ring.

Mark is watching me pacing the room like a caged-in lion.

A week after the joined task force between the sheriff's department and the Helena PD started operating, we yield results. Significant results.

Zander and his men raided the Marcusso Pharmacy and discovered that owner Sandra Marcusso is indeed connected to the Mosaic. Her secret supply chain has grown exponentially since she started business with Deuce.

More importantly, she was one of the nurses present when I gave birth to Ethan. She had sold the information about me to Deuce two years ago, resulting in two things. One, to get herself on Mosaic's preferred suppliers' list. And two, to allow Deuce to recruit Ethan into the Mosaic, train him, and threaten me.

Still, JJ 'Stumpy' Marcusso is the odd one out in this revelation.

Why him?

So far, Sandra Marcusso has not mentioned anything about her brother, let alone a demand for his release.

That question will have to be answered, but not now. Following Sandra Marcusso's arrest, the Helena PD is conducting a raid on a house northeast of Helena. Most likely the one that I saw in the video the bastard showed me that night.

I stare at my phone placed in the middle of my office desk.

After waiting for almost an hour, a call comes through, and I immediately put it on speaker.

"We've got 'em, guys!" Zander announces.

"Hell, yes!" I slap Sandra Marcusso's case folder against my desk.

"Two of the boys we found were missing children, registered two and three years ago. This is huge!" Zander continues.

Mark nods, tilting his face to me with pride. Sandra Marcusso gave us a clue, but it was Mark who prompted Zander to look into old, unsolved cases of missing children around the area. And one name led to the exact house they're raiding. It's amazing how half a piece of a puzzle can create a domino effect.

"Any sign of Deuce?" I ask.

"Unfortunately not. But he can't hide forever, Attorney General. He'll run out of places to hide and allies to hide him."

"At least we've crippled a chunk of Mosaic's supply and disrupted one of his distribution hubs. People like Deuce are trying to make fentanyl production cheap. We'll make it expensive and, in time, unsustainable. That son of a bitch can lick his mange-covered ass," I gripe. "So, what about JJ Marcusso? Any progress?"

"Hmm... I did want to talk to you about that," Zander replies. "Two of our detectives paid him a visit in Montana

State Prison. By the way, it was true that his ball was busted."

I know Mark is itching to say something, but he simply shrugs.

"And?" I say impatiently.

"He won't say anything."

"Well, force him to! Your detectives are trained to do that, are they not? Or perhaps ask the DOC to give him a little carrot."

"He wants to talk to you. Alone."

"No! Absolutely not!" Mark yells into my phone as if Zander wouldn't get it. He stands up, warning me with his eyes. "It may be a trap."

As if I can feel his heartbeat, mine goes up in a sprint. I don't want to go against his advice, but this is an opportunity. "I think it's a risk worth taking."

"Ivy, he's trying to exploit your stubborn nature. He knew you'd do it."

"And I can exploit his eagerness."

"If you go in there, you're gonna be with me."

"Listen to him," Zander backs Mark.

I sit in my executive chair, weighing my desperation against playing it safe. "Time is running out. We have to find Deuce, or at least know who we're actually looking for." I stare at a painting on the wall in front of me as if it will give me clues. I then decide, "You'll be with me, Mark."

"Good," he says, relieved.

"Only not in the same room."

"Ivy!"

"He won't reveal anything if you're in the room with me. It will be secure, and he will be restrained. It's worth the risk."

Mark rubs his chin, growling as he walks to the corner of my office. Yes, I may have become one of those difficult protectees, but I won't let this opportunity slide. Deuce's days are almost over, and I want to make them as short as possible.

"Take me to him," I say to Zander as a lightbulb moment leaves a ping in my head.

Mark stares at me. He'll never agree to this, but he's not surprised at my decision.

I'VE BEEN TOLD that JJ Marcusso will see me with his hands cuffed to the table and his only leg chained to his chair. He usually walks with a prison-issued crutch, but that crutch will be taken away from him for the duration of our talk.

"He's ready," a prison representative says.

"I'll be here," Mark affirms. "The first second you feel threatened—scream and run to the door. Got it?"

"Yeah."

"Don't wait until the last minute. Actually, not when you feel threatened—as soon as he's too close, you do that."

I acknowledge him with a quick blink, then enter the room.

JJ Marcusso smiles at me. His sixty-year-old wrinkles form around his cheeks and jowl. I take a seat in front of him, not giving away much, just like when I was the prosecutor who was about to send him to jail.

"DCA Cavanagh," Marcusso greets me.

Jesus, his voice!

Seeing me speechless, he scoffs, "Oh, my bad. It's been a long time. AG Cavanagh."

I heard his voice when he was arrested. His cursing and swearing continued when he was at the hospital where doctors were treating his leg. Even when he stood in court, he didn't stop. Yet, only now, after hearing Deuce's voice, I can't help comparing the two.

Deuce might've planned to cut my hair for fun at the beginning. But for him to do it with such rage after I mocked Marcusso—it's starting to make sense.

"Short hair suits you," he comments as if reading my mind.

"You wanted to see me."

"Yes. How are my release papers going?"

"Haven't even started."

"I thought you were known for your efficiency."

"I'm sure you're not inviting me here to crack a whip on me. Who is Deuce?"

He laughs.

If I put a white mask on this man, he would laugh like Deuce did in that warehouse.

"Did you start Mosaic?" I provoke.

He laughs again. "Oh no, I'm just an old man. I'm not as smart as him." I notice his little finger lift up. I'm watching his hands, so I know he's not doing anything stupid like trying to set himself free and attack me. That movement may be nothing, but my gaze will surely catch it if he does it again.

"How did you know him?" I ask, more casually this time.

He shrugs.

"Why are you inviting me here, Mr. Marcusso?"

"I want you to look me in the eye and promise me I will get out of here within twenty-four hours."

"Can't do that. You killed four people."

"And how many have you killed, AG Cavanagh?"

"None."

His eyes turn fiery. "Sh—"

"What is it, Mr. Marcusso? Are you trying to shut me up?" Then I think for a second. "No. *She.* Who's she?"

He leans forward, trying to whisper to me something. The guard pulls him back, but I raise my hand, asking him to let the man be.

"Look, someone is out to get me. Give me protective custody, and I'll tell you what I can," he bargains.

"I can arrange for that." I lean back with my arms crossed. "But you tell me what you can first."

"It doesn't work like that," he negates as if trying to assert his authority. "I'll tell you when I'm in some obscure hotel room, draining the state's money on room service and porn."

"You've been watching the wrong crime shows, Mr. Marcusso. The best I can do is to protect you from other inmates."

His face grows bitter as if he's been reminded of the attack on his groin. In the end, he says, "You have my demand."

"What's your relationship with Deuce?"

His little finger lifts again. "Nothing. It was all Sandra."

"You killed people. That's what you did. But illicit drugs?"

"It's a new and upcoming thing, isn't it, fentanyl? But as you said, it's got nothing to do with me."

I lean forward. "You mean a lot to him, I know. Maybe he doesn't mean shit to you, but perhaps his mother did?"

Ah, that finger again.

"You heard about your sister's arrest, didn't you?"

"Say hello to her from me."

"I will. Perhaps when she's ready to tell me who Deuce is. Deuce means money and power to her. But to you—"

This time he forms a fist.

"Mr. Marcusso. You're sixty now. But I know for a fact your marriage didn't last that long. For the last thirty years, give or take, you've been nothing but a miserable single man."

The bitterness on his face cracks into something more sinister.

Deuce told me he was in puberty when I gave birth to Ethan. So if he's thirty now, the timeline fits.

"Or not?" I provoke further. "You left your wife for another woman, didn't you, Mr. Marcusso?"

His jaws tighten. "I want protective custody, starting tonight."

"You begged me for mercy when you were handed that guilty verdict. I must give it to you. Your reason wasn't as selfish or cowardly as I thought."

"You're testing me now?"

"That other woman had a child with you. While you seemed to be an absent father, you kept loving her. That was why you begged—you wanted to keep protecting her from whatever deadly moves she'd made against those gangster friends of hers."

He bangs his fists against the table, shouting, "I want protective custody, or you and I will meet in hell tomorrow!"

The guard restrains him, and Mark barges into the room, putting himself between me and the prisoner. His body drapes me as he rams me out of the room. He's no longer in the military, but there's no mistaking that he's still a powerhouse.

"Hell, Ivy!" my protector grunts. "What did I tell you?" If I must deal with his rage, so be it. But he pants, calming himself down. "Are you okay?"

I smooth my jacket. "Never better."

Mark observes me, looking for any sign of injury. He holds my chin up so he can examine my face as if that bastard could've ruffled me.

"I'm fine, Mark," I contend. "I know who Deuce is. It's time to flush the phantom out of his opera."

22

MARK

We took the last flight to Minneapolis yesterday, and this morning we're off to see Ethan's adoptive father.

"No suit today?" Ivy questions my choice of clothes as we take the lift down to the hotel garage.

I'm wearing a checkered shirt and a pair of semi-formal pants. "Terry Fulton didn't want to talk to Zander's men, so the last thing I want is to look like yet another detective."

"Fair enough."

"Or an insurance salesman." Somehow I blurt the label that Sam used to describe my lack of emotions in front of Ivy.

She chuckles. "I'd buy anything off you, you know?"

"No, you wouldn't," I brush off her remark. That label has expired, but it shows how persistent Sam can be, deliberately or not. As we exit into the garage, I stop her. "Stay here."

I've arranged for a car through my contact, and I checked and double-checked it last night. No tracking devices or explosives. But I can't take any chances.

I survey the car while Ivy is waiting a few yards away. Everything looks clean.

"You're really making sure, aren't you?" Ivy says as I escort her to our vehicle.

"You're a national treasure." I kiss her.

Whatever she did in that Montana State Prison visit room, she found out that Deuce is, in fact, JJ Marcusso's son, with his secret mistress who had connections with a couple of feuding underbelly organizations. She had been protected because no one dared to cross JJ. But once he was incarcerated, she was left exposed and ended up gunned down in her own home barely a week after his conviction.

"And you're my insurance," she says jovially.

"I'd better stay alive, then."

She straightens her spine, glancing as if telling me the 'stay alive' bit actually has the opposite effect on her.

"Hey, relax. You know I'll keep myself safe as much as I do you." It's true—because I want to keep protecting her. Yet it's not because her safety is way more important than mine. "I'm good at what I do. Keep the faith." I tap her hand.

"Let's go. then."

She wriggles in her seat as I start the car.

"Are you comfortable?" I check in on her. "I asked for a standard car, so we're not competing with Mr. Fulton."

"Mark, I love your Jeep, but I'm not a princess. The car's fine."

I smile, wagging my fingers under her chin. "I know. I'm just teasing you."

"You're nervous," she points out.

"Perhaps." This 'meeting the parent' business is surprisingly filling me with trepidation. Ethan Fulton is not just a missing persons case. I mean, when Red Mark is assigned to find a missing child, it's only natural that we put ourselves in their parents' shoes. We operate not only based on clues and instinct, but on empathy too. This time, though, I'm trying to

find the son of the woman I love—and much as I want to separate emotions from actions, it's friggin' impossible.

"I studied Val DeMaria's files last night," she says. "While
you were asleep."

"I knew you were doing something on your laptop. I wasn't
asleep."

"Yes, you were."

"Well, I sleep with one eye open."

Ivy coos as if pitying me for sleep deprivation. Really, I
wasn't asleep.

She moves on. "DeMaria is indeed thirty years old. Before
Mosaic, there really was nothing special about him. Grew up
in Bozeman, his mother raised him on her own. He dropped
out of high school and worked as a hotel clerk and some other
mundane jobs. It was quite a transformation for him to
become Deuce."

"But he wasn't that elusive after all. He was out and about
under everyone's nose. It was just because no one knew his
face that he got away with it."

"A face changed it all," she mutters.

"I don't know how you did it, Ivy."

"It turned out I knew a thing or two about family," she
gushes. "What he did to my hair was personal. Very personal."

"I guess he's blaming you for his mother's death?"

"Yes. I bet. I put her lover in jail, she lost her protection,
and she was murdered."

As the navigation shows that our destination is only
minutes away, Ivy stays silent, breathing in and out like she's
in yoga class.

The Fultons' residence is a complex that looks like a Victo-
rian palace in the affluent neighborhood of Lowry Hill.
Having been an entrepreneur for more than thirty years, the
man seems happy to splurge his cash.

"You'll face him first, okay?" Ivy huffs.

"Of course. Are you okay?" I ask her as we arrive at the gate. She looks like she's about to give a press conference—standing tall, straight-faced. Both her hands are at her sides, no sign of her scratching.

"I'm fine. Let's do this."

I knock on the door.

"Go away, detective!" a voice blares from the inside.

I notice creases appear on Ivy's straight face, just a bit, no doubt hinting my no-suit attire hasn't made a difference.

"Mr. Fulton. My name is Mark Connor. I'm not a police detective. I rang earlier."

Silence.

Then the door is pushed open—faster than I thought it would be.

"Good God!" Terry Fulton doesn't even look at me. He's staring at Ivy instead. "You really are his mother."

"Mr. Fulton, I'm Ivy Cavanagh." She extends her hand.

The man smiles, shaking her hand as if she was a VIP guest. "He looks so much like you." He holds her hand for a few seconds, then continues, "Oh, come on in, please. I'm sorry about earlier." He looks at me and shakes my hand. "Mark Connor, you said?"

"Yes."

"I'm Terry. Are you her husband?"

Among the uncertainty, hearing that question sparks a little cheer inside me. *Her husband.* It sounds so good, so right.

"Mark is my boyfriend," Ivy clarifies.

We sit in the living room. For such a grand house, the room is sparse and rather plain. There are plants and paintings around us, but only a couple of family photos. The photos are small compared to the display cabinet they sit on, and they don't look recent. Ethan must've been six or seven, flanked by Terry and Vera.

Ivy smiles at those photos. There is a glimmer of tears, but she manages to keep everything to herself. From the corner of my eye, I know Terry is observing her closely.

"Let's cut to the chase," Terry suddenly gets jittery. "Are you here to dispute my custody over Ethan?"

"No! Not at all, Mr. Fulton," Ivy says. "I am his mother, but I know, too, that I've been absent throughout his life because of an unforgivable lie my mother had told me. I will make it up to him, but not by taking him away from the family he knows. I'll let Ethan decide what he wants to do."

Terry nods. "Thank you." With that, he relaxes, and his good-host expression is back.

"Do you know my mother?"

"Yes. I was a friend of hers. When she found out you were pregnant, she discussed the possibility of putting up the baby for adoption."

Ivy keeps sitting tall. Her finger twitches, but she quickly puts her hand back on her side. I reach for it, and her fingers respond, wrapping around my palm.

"Did I know you back then?" Ivy asks.

"No. Your mother never allowed me or Vera to meet you. She said it was for the best. That night when Ethan was born, it all happened so quickly. He was ours right after the birth. Everything had been arranged. And we moved to Minneapolis a week after."

Ivy's head bobs up and down. Her finger scratches at my palm, and I let her.

"Mr. Fulton," I say. "When was the last time you saw or spoke to Ethan?"

"Um... I haven't seen him for more than six months. But he had decided to leave home a couple of years ago. Didn't even say goodbye. Didn't even bring his things. He just left a message: *Don't look for me.*"

"Did you ever report him missing?"

"Yes. And a week later, he called, telling me he was in Montana. Well, I thought he'd finally found out about his adoption. But at the time, I don't think so—he never sounded like he had found anything. I guess he just wanted to disappear. What else would a young man like him do in Montana?"

I observe him, and a long silence follows.

Finally, Fulton asks Ivy, "Does he know now? Did you ever talk to him?"

"He knows. I talked to him briefly, but he disappeared."

"That's why we're here," I say. "We thought you might have some information—no matter how small. Anything that can help us find him."

"Is he in danger?"

"Possibly."

His distraught face takes over. "Clearly, I haven't done a great job being his father."

"It's not your fault," I counter.

Terry Fulton's face creases, and he shakes his head again and again. Then he looks at me, his gaze piercing. "Have you ever raised a boy?"

"No."

"Then how do you know, Mr. Connor?" His tone turns condescending.

If that question had come up before I was with Ivy, when I was still married to the job, believing I'd never be a father, it would've knocked me back. But knowing that I have a future with the magnificent woman sitting beside me now—I'm calm.

"It's got nothing to do with me not being a father," I respond. "I rescue children, Mr. Fulton. It's my job, but it's more than that. I've rescued boys who were fourteen, fifteen. About Ethan's age when he left home. Those boys ran away with profound hatred toward their parents. But they were only trying to prove a point—that they were invincible. A point which was ultimately proven wrong. Because parents' love never dies. And those boys felt it when they were at their lowest."

Mr. Fulton gets teary, while next to me, I feel Ivy's hold on my hand tighten.

I add, "Not all missing children's cases are like that. Sometimes their parents are just as messed up as they are, if not more. But I know you're on the good side of the spectrum."

The old man nods. "Ethan moved around. But the last time I spoke to him, he was in Livingston."

"You mean Livingston, Montana?"

"Yes. Yes. Not far from Bozeman, I think he said?"

Ivy nods, but she remains silent.

"When was this?" I query.

"A month ago. Roughly."

"Does he know that your wife passed away?"

"No. Well, I don't know. I called his last known number and left a message. But there was no answer."

"When you two talked, what did you talk about?"

His cheeks lift as if thinking about Ethan fondly. "He'd ask how I was, how his mom was. But he never said anything about himself. Just 'fine.'"

"Did he talk to your wife too?"

"Rarely. Vera wasn't keen on adoption. But there was no other way. I wanted a boy so much," he admits. "But she was lovely, accommodating. It's just that their relationship was cold. Perhaps the boy knew."

I slant my head toward Ivy, observing her quietness. What's going through her mind? Or her heart?

What happened between Rena and me suddenly feels small. It's nothing compared to what she's facing now, even when she was pregnant with Ethan. Right now, she stays composed, unwavering. But I know she must be taming a hurricane inside.

"Did Ethan ever mention a name, a location, or anything?"

"Nothing that I remember."

"Mr. Fulton, can I see his room?" Ivy suddenly requests.

"Of course. Come this way." He escorts us to the west wing of the house. We pass at least four bedrooms before we reach Ethan's.

The room looks like any other teenager's room. Although there are no posters or signs of what the boy was into. Things like rock music, sports, games, or conspiracy theories, for that matter.

"Kids usually want to be astronauts, but Ethan wanted to be an alien," the old man chuckles.

Not even a sign of alien worship in here.

"Did Ethan have any friends he was close to?" I ask as I can't find any photos around.

"Not really. He was a loner, keeping things to himself. He was never in trouble at school, though. And he did well academically." Fulton watches Ivy as she walks around the room. "Well, I'll leave you to it. If you want photos, I'll bring in some albums."

Ivy sits at Ethan's bed, clutching his blanket. She closes her eyes. There're no tears. It's as if she's a mother connecting with her son silently, privately. I stay where I am, giving her space.

After a few minutes, she murmurs, "So this is where he grew up."

I stride next to her. "Yeah."

"I swear I'll make it up to him, Mark."

"He's got the whole life ahead of him. We'll make sure that you're in it." I hug her.

Then Fulton comes in with a photo album. Baby photos.

"Oh... look at him," Ivy murmurs.

"That's my favorite. You can keep it if you want."

"Thank you." Ivy pulls out the photo from its sleeve.

"By the way, I remember from one of our phone conversations. Ethan—well, this may sound silly."

"Nothing is silly, Mr. Fulton."

"Ethan liked to give me a hard time when I was watching *Seinfeld*. He thought it was a stupid show. One night when he called, we talked about it, and he said, 'God, you sound like so-and-so's father'—I can't quite remember who he was talking about, but he did mention a name."

Ivy and I stand.

"Mr. Fulton, please, if you can remember."

"Something with a 'W.' Warren? Wayne? I really can't remember. I'm sorry."

Ivy signals to me that she's ready to leave, and we wrap up our visit.

Just before we hop into the car, she receives a call. At the same time, I get one from Ben.

"Winter, what's up?" I ask.

"Zander has transferred us back to your place. He said there has been a threat coming Ivy's way."

"Is everything okay?"

"Yeah... well, apart from Noah."

"What the hell, Ben?"

"I think he's just being a brat, but um... Linda and I are at the end of our ropes. Zander told us not to send him to school today. So I was playing softball with him this morning, and when I said it was time for him to do his homework, he threw a tantrum. Now he doesn't want to eat. He keeps saying his head hurts, but he spat out his medication. I think he just wants his mom."

"I think she's talking to him now." I glance at Ivy, who's rubbing her forehead.

"Did you find anything?" Ben asks.

"A little bit. But we're heading back now."

"By the way, we almost broke one of your windows. I hit the ball too hard."

I chuckle. There's no way he would've broken any of my windows.

He then asks, "Are they made of bulletproof glass?"

"The best quality polycarbonate, my friend."

"Jesus! And here I am, thinking you're a simple guy living in a simple country house just outside Helena," he rattles on. "When's your birthday?"

"What? August. Why?"

"You're a Leo."

"Didn't think you were into astrology."

"I know just what to buy for your present."

"And what is that?"

"A 22-carat gold placard with 'Fortress Connor' carved on it."

I laugh. Actually not a bad thought. It would've looked good against the wood grain of the gate. "Hey, I've gotta go."

Ivy ends the call at the same time. "Noah is sick."

"He's just missing you. Let's go back to Helena."

We drive off, and suddenly she huffs out a heavy breath.

"Ivy?"

"That was one of the hardest things I've ever had to do in that bedroom," she confesses, pressing her chest.

I don't doubt it, although she's done a great job keeping herself together then. This time I know she needs a comforting touch. So I pull over at the next street. "Come here." I take her into my arms.

She lets go of herself as if giving her life to me. I swear I'll do anything to turn this around. One day soon, she will hold me like this, with a big smile on her face. Because Ethan is hers again.

After a long minute, she suddenly sits up straight as if she's been electrocuted.

"Mark..."

"What is it?"

"That night, I told you Deuce forced me to pick a boy out of a line-up. He was testing my so-called motherly instincts, challenging me if I'd recognize my son without looking at his face. The first boy that I chose—he showed me his face. He was blond, skinny, um... an oblong face with small eyes. And he had a necklace on with a gold 'W' pendant. Could that be Ethan's friend Terry was talking about?"

"Makes sense. Ethan may be hanging with someone his age, in his circle. Or in this case, Deuce's circle."

"Deuce said his mother's name was—argh.." She frowns, thinking hard. "Was... Cynthia! I don't know if he was lying or not."

"Well, it's worth investigating. I'll drop you off so you can be with Noah. Then I'll search for a Warren or a Wayne, who's the son of a deceased woman named Cynthia. Shouldn't be too hard to find in Livingston."

23

IVY

As soon as Mark and I land in Helena, we're greeted by two plain-clothed police officers.

"This is unusual," I comment. "Did Zander send you?"

"Yes, ma'am. We've got intel about Mosaic's movements. We're not taking any chances. Ben has taken Noah back to Mr. Connor's place, too."

I acknowledge him. "Any progress on JJ Marcusso?"

"DOC is preparing for his transfer into protective custody."

"Good. Let's go, then."

Mark puts his arm around my waist, slanting his body so he's covering half of me. He had parked his Jeep in a secure location at the airport, but he still does his usual pre-drive check.

"My lady." He opens the door after he's satisfied everything is in order.

With the police car trailing us, we make our way back to Mark's place.

"Do you know what the governor is gonna say about this?"

"What?"

"'Who's she? POTUS' daughter?'" I mimic the voice of the governor.

"You're more precious than the President of the United States, let alone his children," he claims. "To me, anyway. You deserve this level of security."

We're entering the street where he lives.

"Home sweet home," I sing.

Yes, Mark's house is our home now.

The classic Montana stone home sits on ten acres. The whole area is fenced off, most of it picket-style, but there are privacy panels around the back of the house that act as an extra layer of security. The look and the natural wood color complement the building, so you don't really feel 'fenced in.' We almost always enter via the back gate, allowing the car to go straight into the garage.

"I hope Noah is okay," Mark murmurs as he punches in the code, and the gate slides open. It looks like any other country-home gate, with Western charm and all, but he told me the wood is actually reinforced with steel. 'Good-lookin' and strong,' he'd gushed. 'Just like how I like my woman.'

"He's okay," I assure him. "I think he's just feeling pent up. He's been going to school—well, not today—but he has had things to do and regular contact with other kids. But I know it's different. I mean, he's being watched twenty-four seven. He's got to go home right after school. I think it's taking a toll on him."

"It's not for much longer."

"I hope so."

The huge figure of Ben Winter stands by the door. "Thank God you two are back!" He glances at Noah's closed bedroom. "He was never like this before."

"You're still on probation, Winter. Toughen up!" Mark banters.

Ben scoffs. "I'm not even on your payroll yet!"

"Show me you deserve it," Mark winks and pats his shoulder.

"I'm sorry, Ms. Cavanagh," Nanny Linda says. "It has been a tough day for all of us."

"I bet. Thanks for putting up with him." I smile and head straight to Noah's room.

"Mom!"

The boy looks as bright as day.

"What happened to you?"

"My head feels so bad. So sore."

I feel his forehead. A little warm, but not a fever.

"So you didn't go to school today."

He shakes his head.

"Did you talk to Dylan, though?"

"Yes. He's going away soon with his brother and parents."

"Did he say for how long?"

"A couple of weeks." His head bows. "Mom... when can I see Dad again? He promised we'd go on a helicopter ride. And Nanna Dorothy said she'd make me her special banana split."

"Come here." I pull him into my embrace. "You'll see Dad and Nanna soon. I promise. Now, are you hungry?"

"Yeah," he murmurs tentatively as if he'll get in trouble.

"Okay, then."

I make him M&M pancakes, and before I know it, he's back to being besties with Ben like nothing had happened.

"Now do your homework," I insist when Noah starts to push Ben to play softball with him.

He sulks for a while, feeling his own forehead and putting on his sorry face. But I shake my head, and he knows his spell doesn't work on me.

It's raining outside, so after homework, Ben takes Noah to the open-plan living area. The big man asks Noah to sit on the floor with his legs crossed, and he stands tall like a sensei, demonstrating a few moves. He then invites him to stand up.

"Hold your hand up like this," Ben instructs, then picks up a cushion for Noah to aim his kick at. "Now swing your leg up and kick!"

Noah's leg lifts, and he releases a wild one. Ben moves the cushion to follow the boy's foot which ends up way off target.

"Not bad." The big man gets animated. "Come on. Kick higher! And say '*kaia!*' when you lift your leg."

Noah does, and I can see him giving all he has into his kick.

I leave the two boys be as I plonk myself into the sofa. Mark makes us two cups of hibiscus tea.

"Just what I need," I sigh. "Thanks."

He puts his mobile phone aside after glancing at something on the screen.

"What's there?" I look at him.

"You don't want to see it."

"Let me see!"

My gut twists. I knew this would've happened, but it still sickens me. My nude photos have made an appearance in the media yet again, along with calls for me to resign, labeling me as a disgrace to the state.

I close my eyes. Overwhelmed. "Jesus... if I can't protect myself, I've at least got to make sure Noah never sees these."

"He won't."

"So what's next?" I ask. He appears ready to leave.

Mark rubs my arms. "I should go now."

My chest is stretched in different directions—it's going to rip open soon. This man will stop at nothing to find Ethan or any child. He has proven that with what he's done with Red Mark. But the prospect of him getting hurt terrifies me—or even worse, him getting killed.

I take his hand. "Be careful. Deuce isn't the type who'll cower when cornered."

Mark kisses me. "I'll find him."

"You might want to bring a jacket. It's getting chilly out there."

"Good idea." He gets up, goes to his room, and picks up a puffy jacket to conceal his bulletproof vest.

I wave at him from my seat, unable to bring myself to see him walking out the door.

I go back to Noah, trying to distract myself from the danger Mark may be heading to.

"Can you teach me that rotating kick?" Noah asks Ben.

Ben looks at me, then answers Noah, "Nah. You're not ready. You need to work on your balance first."

"Oh, what?" the boy protests. "Hey, Ben! Can you break wood with your hand?"

"Yeah."

"Show me."

"Let's see if Mark has something to break."

"Geez, Ben. Don't!" I warn. Is he going to destroy Mark's house?

"Doesn't look like it, pal," Ben says. "I've got another trick, though."

Ben takes a vase.

"Ben!" I exclaim. "Mark is gonna kill you!" The tribal-patterned, foot-tall glass vase looks heavy—and expensive.

He laughs at me. "I'm sure he's insured." Then he turns to Noah. "Watch!" He puts the vase on top of his head, then does a spin kick.

"Whoa!" Noah is impressed, while I almost can't watch.

Ben tips his head and catches the vase with one hand. "That's how you do it, buddy."

"Can you teach me?" Noah says.

"Not with that thing!" I point at the vase. Surely, Ben won't.

"Let's use a book," Ben suggests, almost laughing at me. He takes the smallest encyclopedia from one of the many bookshelves Mark has in this place. He puts it on top of Noah's head, then asks him to walk around without dropping it.

"I can't!"

"It takes practice, pal."

While Noah is practicing, Ben and I catch up.

"Heard from your sister?"

"Yes. She's good. Baby Phil is still as hungry as ever, and she's hardly slept. Neither has Sam."

"So, what's the deal with you and Red Mark?"

"As Mark said, I'm still on probation. Well, actually, my status is still 'nanny' as far as I know."

"That's Linda. You're Noah's guardian."

"Guardian? I like that. Is it true that Noah nicknamed Mark 'watchbear'?"

I chuckle. "Yes."

Ben laughs. "Guardian sounds more macho, no?"

"If you say so. Well, you came to our aid at the drop of a hat, and you haven't left since. I guess no one has prepared the paperwork yet."

"It's no big deal, really. I'm happy here. Noah is a good kid. And you're a good... well, boss. Surprising, considering you're a politician."

I toss him a smile. "I get that a lot."

"I do want to join Red Mark. Making a difference, keeping kids safe." Ben leans back, gazing at Noah, who's still trying to balance the encyclopedia on his head. "My sister and I had a hard time when Dad died. Especially her. Cass... she was a mess. One night I found her in a river, drowning. I was thirteen, and she was fourteen. However I did it, I managed to pull her out. I tried to imitate people doing mouth-to-mouth. You know, from TV. I saved her then. And I kind of wanted to keep saving people, you know. But not as a doctor or anything medical."

I've known Ben fleetingly, only because he's Cass' brother. This is the first time I'm hearing his story. Now I know why Mark had been keen on taking him on board. "It's in you."

"I guess I've got to convince Mark."

"Hey, he wouldn't have had you guarding Noah if he didn't believe in you."

"Sam said I was too organized. Actually, I used to drive my sister crazy, too, with how I stored things."

I notice. He folds his clothes neatly, and it appears that he's utilizing all the storage available in his room.

"They'll take you, Ben."

"I guess. But I have to think about my Taekwondo school. At the moment, my friend is holding the fort. I haven't discussed what it'll be like if I join Sam and Mark."

"You'll figure it out. Do you have anyone? Girlfriend?"

"Nah. I was once in love with my best friend's sister, but it just didn't work out. That was a long time ago, though. I date and stuff, but nothing serious."

As I make myself another cup of tea, I receive a call from Mark.

"Mark, anything?"

"I'm close, Ivy. I think that boy's name is Wayne Tindall. And I've found an address."

24

MARK

It's already dark when I arrive in Livingston. The address I'm about to step into is the epitome of 'the worst house on the best street.' Its overgrown yard obscures the façade. Relying only on my flashlight, I find myself ducking under branches and jumping over shrubs to get to the front door.

According to neighbors, the man of the house has abandoned this place to live with another woman, but no one knows where. His only son Wayne and 'another boy' who fits the description of Ethan have apparently been coming and going at random. They were last spotted by a downtown shop owner three days ago.

There's no one tailing me. There's not even a car on the street at the moment. Without having to do further inspection, by looking at the faint light coming from the side of the house, I know someone's in there—an advantage of searching a house under the cover of darkness. The sweet odor lingering around the door tells me someone is having a party, albeit a quiet one.

The front door is unlocked.

"Wayne!" I call as the door closes behind me with a soft

creak. My Glock is in my hand, ready for any kind of eventuality.

The living room is empty, but when I turn a corner into what looks to be a reading room, I find a boy lying on a couch, puffing what I'm sure is meth. And if it's supplied by Mosaic, I bet it's the notorious EM2, which has been generously laced with fentanyl.

"Wayne? Wayne Tindall?"

"Hey, bro!" the boy says as if he knows me. But his eyes are clearly not focused.

I pull the smoke away from him, toss it to the floor, and snuff it with my foot.

"Where's Ethan?" I push his shoulder up so he sits straight, then kick the rest of his supply and paraphernalia off the table.

His arms flutter but too feebly to mount any meaningful resistance. "Chill out, man!" he slurs.

"Where is he?" I lift his chin up so he looks at me.

"Probably outside. Someone's gotta water the plants." He laughs hysterically. "Thank God for his fucking ammonia-rich piss."

I let him go and head deeper inside the house, navigating the narrow hallway. Everything smells in here. It's impossible to find Ethan just by following the scent.

"Ethan, you here?"

Both bedrooms are empty. The same with the kitchen and dining room.

Worry rises in me. What if he's not here? Where will I find him?

I keep exploring, walking out through the kitchen door onto the deck. I shine my flashlight beyond the deck's balustrade. It's a backyard, but unlike the front, there are only tree stumps, twigs, and dry grass here. Perhaps the watering system has killed all that used to live in this yard.

It looks like nothing. But the smell picks up again, prompting me to inspect under the deck.

There's a door. It must lead to some kind of basement.

"Ethan," I call. I duck under the deck to enter, but it's locked. "Open up. It's Mark Connor. I only want to talk."

It's awfully quiet, or perhaps because it's a steel door, I can't pick up any sound from the inside. I kick and charge at it.

Still not budging.

I bang on it. "Ethan! I know you're in there. Open up!"

The door is too sturdy. If I continue, I'll only be nursing a broken shoulder. I've got to find another way, and luckily, the frame is made of wood. I aim at a spot where the lock may be on the inside and release a few shots. It takes me three attempts to get to the precise position, but I finally manage to wreck the bolt and release the door.

I shine my flashlight into what looks to be a tunnel, slanting downward into a space about five feet underground.

My heart sinks. At the bottom, Ethan is lying on the ground, facing up.

"Ethan! Jesus Christ!"

His eyes are wide open. Froth starts to flow from his mouth.

I turn his body into a recovery position to stop him from choking on his own vomit. He feels stiff in my hands. I keep praying that I'm not too late.

I lay my phone on the floor, calling Zander on speaker.

"I need an ambulance. 433 North B Street, Livingston. Now!" I yell as I check Ethan's pulse.

Nothing.

"Fuck," I murmur.

I clear the boy's mouth.

"Paramedics are coming," Zander rushes out. "What's going on, Connor?"

"I've found Ethan, and he's not breathing."

Froth keeps coming out of his mouth despite me wiping it profusely.

"Ambulance should be there soon. Connor, do whatever you have to do. He's got to stay alive!"

"Come on, Ethan," I beg.

Once his mouth and throat are empty, I return him to his original position, lying on his back. I descend on him, giving the boy rescue breaths. Acidic and bitter tastes assault my mouth. The remnants of opioids and stomach content mix with his saliva—and mine. But I have to keep going.

"Don't you die on me, boy!" I keep up the compressions and mouth-to-mouth. "Don't you fucking die on me!"

I hear the ambulance coming.

"In here!" I shout.

I persist with giving him mouth-to-mouth, and I finally catch a faint breath from his throat. I feel his pulse. It's barely there, but the boy is alive.

"Ethan, hey." I wipe sweat off his face and clean his lips. "You're gonna be okay."

I cover him with my jacket as he starts to shake, then I pull him close, lying his head on my lap.

The noise made by the paramedics seems to alarm him. He tries to roll away from me, but I keep him in place.

"Hey, it's okay. They're here to help you."

He stares at me. I'm not sure if he's able to make sense of what he's seeing, but I feel his hand grabbing my thigh, clutching it as if asking me to stay.

I caress his face. God, there's so much of Ivy in him, especially those hazel eyes.

"I've got you, son. I've got you."

25

IVY

Noah is fast asleep. Not very often he runs out of energy, but after that session with Ben, he did.

I almost doze off by his bedside when my phone buzzes.

"Ivy, I found him."

I release a long sigh of relief. "He's with you?"

"Yeah. But..."

"But what, Mark?"

"He's in the hospital."

"Where?"

"Livingston."

"I'm on my way."

"Ivy—"

But I hang up. It's midnight, and it'll be two in the morning by the time I arrive there. But I don't care. I've got to get to my son.

"Zander," I call the captain.

"Ivy, I heard about Ethan."

"Give me an escort. I'm going to Livingston now. Your men will just have to catch me." I grab my car key and jacket, passing Ben on my way out. "Ben, you watch Noah. Stay in his room. I'm going to Livingston."

"I don't think it's a good idea."

"Zander will give me an escort. I'll be fine," I spout and leave.

God, Ethan.

What the hell happened to him?

Was there a confrontation? Did he try to attack Mark, and in return, Mark hurt him in self-defense? Or did Deuce try to kill the boy? Is Mark even okay?

I speed up. Zander's men finally catch up with me when I'm halfway there. As soon as I park my car at the hospital complex, I sprint into the building.

Barely a couple of yards past the entrance, I bump into Mark—literally—as I fail to stop when he steps in my way.

"Jesus, Ivy!" He hugs me. "You shouldn't have come here!" He peeks out, spotting a car lingering next to mine.

"They're Zander's men."

He sighs in relief. "Good girl!"

"Where is he, Mark? Take me to him!"

"Come."

"Was he shot? Was he... what happened?"

"He OD'd."

I feel my body shrinking as if something inside me is draining every cell and muscle. "But he's gonna be okay, right?"

"He'll be okay."

We take the stairs to the second floor, and right away, I see a police officer guarding a door. It must be Ethan's room.

A nurse stops us. "Sorry, we can't let visitors in at the moment."

"I'm his mother."

She cocks her head. "Okay. Fifteen minutes. That's all I can give you."

"Thank you."

The officer opens the door for me.

I stand mesmerized next to Ethan's bed. He looks just like any other boy, but he *is* my boy. The force that tugs me to him is bigger than anything I've ever felt.

"Ethan..." I whisper, holding his hand while trying to spot any sign of injuries. But he looks all right—apart from being unconscious.

"I'll make it up to you, Ethan. We've met... not even for a day. But I love you. I can tell you that much." I squeeze his hand.

No response.

I want to kiss his forehead, but I don't feel I have the right to—not yet. I have to know that he's okay with it first.

The door slowly opens. It's the same nurse who let me in. Fifteen minutes have passed like it was one.

"You can come back tomorrow morning. Maybe around eight," she says. "He may be awake by then."

I nod and walk out to Mark's open arms.

"He's still asleep," I murmur, my cheek on his shoulder.

"Let him sleep, then."

I nod. "Thank you. Thank you for finding him."

He kisses me. "So, what do you want to do now?"

"Wait."

"Here?"

"Yeah. I really want to be there when he wakes up."

"Okay. Let's go to the waiting room, then."

We sit with instant coffees in our hands.

"So he was with Wayne?" I ask. I still remember that boy's face under his ski mask—so young, so cold. Especially when he said his mother was dead.

"Yes."

"Did he OD too?"

"No. He was just high."

"So what's gonna happen to him?"

"He's with Social Services. He'll be put into witness protection."

"His father?"

"They haven't found him."

I put my head on his shoulder, my eyes getting heavier. Exhausted, we end up falling onto each other, sleeping in the plastic chairs that barely support our asses.

Until Mark's phone beeps.

"Yeah?" Mark answers.

Unlike his instant alertness, my eyelids take an age to open.

"Yeah... yeah. I know." He paces and pivots across the waiting room. I know he's talking to Zander.

As soon as he hangs up, he sits back down.

"JJ Marcusso is dead," he tells me.

"What?"

"His head was bashed with a fire extinguisher. In the laundry room, just before he was due to be transferred to PC."

"Suspect?"

"Not yet. But I guess he has a lot of enemies in there."

"Perhaps one who suspected Marcusso of colluding with prison staff or the police." It's not uncommon for inmates to target others they suspect are informants or simply threats. "Or me. What time is it?"

"Five." Mark taps at his hitching shoulder.

The gesture draws a smile out of me. "No, I won't sleep on your shoulder again."

"It's okay. Go on. I know you want to."

He can shoulder any weight—literally or not—for

however long. But sleep is the last thing on my mind right now. "No. Ethan may wake up soon. Actually, let's go upstairs and check with the nurse."

When we arrive on the second floor, things aren't what a hospital is supposed to be at this hour. It's chaos, almost a ruckus in here.

"What's going on?" Mark stares at the guard.

"The boy's gone..."

"How the hell!" Mark yells, grabbing his collar. Looking at his puffy eyes, I'm sure that guard has been asleep.

"He attacked an orderly who came in to check the bathroom, and then he stole his clothes."

"He walked out under your nose?" Mark tightens his hold on him.

"I'm sorry," the officer says.

I swear Mark is about to punch him in the face, and so am I!

"He left this." The officer hands Mark a piece of paper.

Don't look for me.

Exactly the same message as he left the Fultons.

So this is how it feels to have lost a son for the second time. It's like being stabbed with a blunt knife, then being freed of it, only for the knife to be pushed deeper into the same spot.

The two officers who escorted me to the hospital last night join us. "Attorney General, we have to go," one of them says.

Mark catches my hand. "Come on. We've got to get out of here."

"No. We've got to find Ethan. He won't be far."

"Ivy, you can't control him. He left, but not because Deuce took him. He wanted to disappear."

"He's just a child, Mark."

"You can't change him in one day. The more you chase him, the further he'll run. Trust me. In time, I'll find him again. And if anything happens to him, it'll all be on me. On me, Ivy."

And that just adds salt to my stab wound. "No, Mark. He's my son. It won't be on you."

"He's my son, too."

I don't know if it's his astounding words or just my body running out of rigor. But I hold him, begging him to support me. I need him to simply keep standing—I need him that much.

He almost cocoons my whole body as we head to his car. The two officers split up, one driving in front of us in their original car, the other behind us, driving mine.

I don't know what's on Ethan's mind. One thing is sure, that boy is capable of creating a lot of damage, especially if a figure like Deuce is behind him. What if I was faced with a situation where I had to choose between Mark and Ethan?

I can only hope that time will never come.

26

MARK

Almost a week after JJ Marcusso was murdered, the police have identified three suspects, but none of them has confessed. The more we think about it, Ivy and I believe that Marcusso's death is more than just a result of inmates' conflict. Ivy is pushing Zander to investigate if there's any outside party involved.

Following the incident, the Mosaic has gone quiet. No doubt, Deuce knows his identity has been compromised. The son of a bitch took Ivy from her home that night, hoping he'd scare her into surrendering to his demand. Instead, he choked on his own medicine. Now that Ethan and Wayne have been uncovered, too. He must be wary about what those boys might've revealed to the police. Although, in fact, they haven't said anything—and one has run away without a trace.

Meanwhile, Ivy has insisted on going back to business as usual. Both for herself and Noah.

"I'll be in meetings all day. I'll be inside the Capitol until late," she says as I drive her to her office. "Have a break. You need it."

Her ass swivels on the seat as she opens the door. Truly, I don't need a break. I never need a break from her.

I tug at her arm before she jumps out of my Jeep. "It's you who needs a break. Can you take leave or something? You're exhausted, Ivy."

Tiny wrinkles form between her eyes. "Well, I haven't taken leave in... I don't know how long."

"Even more reason for you to take it."

"I'll think about it."

She's not going to.

"Well, if you're going to be in the Capitol all day, I'm thinking I should go back to Livingston."

She casts me a cautious look. "You think he's still there?"

"I don't know. It may be his comfort zone, and smart as he is, he might be trying reverse psychology. No one would guess he'd decide to stay put after what happened. Or perhaps I'll find something else, a clue of some sort."

"Are you sure you want to chase him?"

I shake my head slightly. "Part of me says to leave him alone. But, you know, my gut tells me I should at least try to find where he is. Even from a distance."

"Okay."

I hold her by the waist.

"I love you. I mean it," she murmurs in an unsettling tone.

"What are you thinking, Ivy?"

"No. Nothing. Just the usual, be careful."

"You know I will. Because I love you too."

As soon as I arrive in Livingston, I return to Wayne Tindall's house. I start at the back, checking under the deck. The basement door that I busted that night is wide open, and the lock is still damaged. But no one's in there. The inside of the house is empty too. Not many neighbors are around, but those who are willing to talk to me say that they haven't seen any activity around here.

Back in the town center, I visit the shop owner who spotted Ethan and Wayne before I found them in the house that night.

"Nah, haven't seen him, Mr. Connor," he replies when I ask about Ethan. "The troopers have been doing mobile drug testing in the past few days, but I think the boy has left town."

"Any idea where he might've gone to?"

"Maybe Bozeman. It'll be easier for him to blend in and stay invisible there."

"Okay. Thanks."

I head to Bozeman before I return to Helena, calling Red Mark's trusty head of tech Cora-Lee Rancic on the way.

"Cee, get our guys in Bozeman to watch out for Ethan Fulton."

"Got it, boss. Do you want them to take him in if they find him?"

"No. Just get them to watch him and keep me in the loop."

"Okay," she affirms. Then I hear her talking to someone else.

"Is that Sam?"

"Ah, yeah, it's him. His first day back after parental leave. He says he'll call you."

I hang up on Cora-Lee to take Sam's call.

"Sam."

"Hey, buddy. How are you holding up?"

"Still searching for Ethan."

"Have you seen the latest news on Ivy?"

His heavy tone makes my forehead tightens. "Tell me."

"The press has found out about her and Ethan. There's a particularly nasty one—speculation that she had tried to abort her baby back then."

"Shit..."

I know Ivy is tough, but she has her limits.

"She needs you, Mark. And I hope it helps that I've completed Project Llama."

"You have?"

"Yeah. It's done."

"Thanks, man. I owe you."

"Hey, that was a small thing. You did the same for me and more." He pauses. "Grace is still here because of you, pal. And nothing will ever be big enough to make up for it."

"Shut up." I try to curb my emotions. "We're brothers."

"Hell, yeah. Now go and pamper your princess."

"You know Ivy is anything but a princess."

"Well, brother, you still have a lot to learn about relationships."

I end the call with a smile as I pull into a service station. But my smile turns into a gape as a figure leaps in front of me. Out of nowhere. Feline-like, discreet, and unmistakable.

I slam on the brakes, and the figure leans over the hood of my Jeep, hands planted down like a hunter zeroing in on its prey.

Those hazel eyes....

I RUSH to pick up Ivy from the Capitol. Her last meeting has barely finished.

"Have you seen what they say in the press about Ethan? That I tried to abort him?" she laments, surprisingly not picking up on my edginess.

"Yes. That's nasty, Ivy. But right now, we have to let that go. Let it remain speculation. The more you comment, the more they'll unpack it. With that note, go pack up."

"Where are we going?" Ivy puts her laptop and files inside her bag. She then rushes to put on her coat.

We make our way out. Her high heels clink against the marble floor.

"Have you requested your leave yet?"

"No," she replies, straight-faced as if I should've known her answer.

"Never mind. You can do it in the car." I keep hauling her through the long hallway, occasionally glancing at her shoes —however she manages to keep up with me in those killer heels.

We're out through the back exit. "Wait, your car is over there!"

"I know. That's my favorite car, but we're not riding in it tonight. We're using this."

She raises her brows, seemingly puzzled and, at the same time, impressed by my Lexus LX SUV.

But I know she doesn't care much about what land yacht I drive. She continues digging, "Mark, tell me what's going on. Or we're not going anywhere! Is Deuce on our tail now instead of the Helena PD on his?"

"The latter, Ivy. The latter. That's why I'm taking you to where I'm taking you now. I've been wanting to, but security wasn't up to scratch. Well, it is now—thanks to Sam. It'll be good for you and Noah."

"Mark, I don't appreciate you being cryptic at the moment."

"I'm not. I'm just asking you to trust me. And promise me, you won't scratch your skirt on the way there."

"I'm wearing pants! Seriously, where are we going?"

"To my other place."

"Right... we're going to your other place in your other car."

"In summary, yes." I open the door for her, driving east.

"Is Noah there already?"

"We're going to meet him and Ben halfway."

That seems to settle her a bit.

No one knows about this 'other place,' and I have insisted on no police presence. The last thing I want is a POTUS-like motorcade leading Deuce to my safe home.

"Talk to me, Ivy." Her silence is killing me, yet I'm running out of subjects to talk about with her. Perhaps I want to avoid the latest scandal the press is trying to stir up.

"Ben told me last night about the job that Red Mark turned down."

Her choice of subject incites a chuckle from me. It looks like she doesn't want to go near the scandal, either—instead, she wants to talk about *that* job.

"Miss Montana, is that it?" I tease her.

She hitches a shoulder up.

"Well, apparently, she needed a security escort as she embarked on her journey to become Miss USA."

"Did she really specifically ask for you?"

"Yeah. That's the problem."

"Huh..."

I enjoy the jealous vibe seeping from her. But truthfully, no one—*no one*—compares to my Ivy Wren. Not even Miss Universe.

Then I catch a small smile despite her trying to hide it. A satisfied, possessive smile. Oh, yeah, she wants me for herself.

About an hour from our destination, I slow down, allowing Ben to follow us. Noah waves at his mother from the back seat of Ben's car, making funny faces as Ivy waves back.

The sun has set by the time we reach the gate of my estate.

"Mark? What is this place?"

"Welcome to Silver Hill."

Her head whips left and right, trying to catch whatever sights she can in the dark. "Is it a farm?"

"A recreational farm on twenty acres of land, surrounded by a clear water river that shines like silver under the sun. You'll see it tomorrow."

"And you've secured the whole area? Or Sam did?"

"For you and Noah, nothing is too secure, and yes. We can thank Sam for that."

"You're too busy guarding me." She cups my chin.

"Well, this place was secure before. I mean, as secure as a farm could be. But now, we've got everything—wireless cameras, alarm systems, motion detector lights."

"Ben will say this is Fortress Connor 2.0."

I chuckle. "It's the place where I went when I needed a break from being married to the job."

"Really? Did you even have time for a break?" She challenges my explanation. "I mean, you always worked."

"Well. I did come here, although rarely. But I've got a neighbor taking care of the property. He's a retired Marine, a part-time farmer. You see that house?" I point at the top of the hill. "That's where we're going to stay."

"The lights are on. Anyone in there?"

"We'll see." I smirk.

We roll up to the front porch, and Ben follows behind us. Ivy takes time to survey the surroundings as if she was in a dream. By now, Noah has gotten out of the car, waiting for her.

I offer her my hand once I've opened the door. Her pensive face snaps back to reality, giving me a radiant smile.

Noah yanks her other hand, trying to show her a couple of bear carvings standing on each side of the porch. "Mom! This is cool, isn't it?"

"It is."

"Go on, take Noah inside." I punch in the front door code. "Ben and I will take care of the bags."

As soon as the door swings ajar, a canine nose slips out of the gap, pushing its way. After a few wriggles, the furry creature leaps out.

"Jasper!" Noah shouts, squatting to welcome the overexcited puppy. "Oh, you're here. You're here, boy! And you've gotten bigger already!" He pats Jasper's rump.

Ivy casts a glance at me, questions written all over her face.

Noah soon follows Jasper inside—at speed, as if racing to the end of the hallway. Meanwhile, Ben and I enter the house leisurely.

I take off my jacket, and Ivy slides in front of me.

"I recognize that." She eyes a sticker pasted on my shirt pocket.

"Well, the one that you saw before said, 'I hugged a puppy.'"

"Huh.... Now it's—"

I smooth the rolled-up edges of the 'I adopted a puppy' sticker.

"Okay... Missoula Animal Shelter," she mumbles, reading the small print. "So this was one of the puppies you *hugged* while I was with my dying mother?"

I pass her an innocent look while at the end of the hallway, Noah is rolling over, giggling, being decimated by the pup's ferocious licking.

"Who's a good boy? Who's a good boy?"

"Look at them." I chuckle. "You know, Jasper's my first dog in years."

Her head cocks. "And you chose a Great Dane?"

"Why not? They're pretty low maintenance, apart from their size."

"And their appetite?"

"Maybe," I ponder, imagining how big the mutt will get. But I don't regret taking him home. "Jasper had been overlooked so many times at the shelter. Besides, Noah loves him."

Her lips part in a smile, apparently agreeing with me.

With all bags accounted for, we head into the second living room.

The atmosphere changes. It's not the fire or the fragrant wood it's burning. It's the boy tending to it. Ivy is lagging behind, and she seems to stop moving. Without looking, I can sense her disbelief, excitement, and relief rushing across the room.

It's Noah who breaks the silence.

"Bro!" He unleashes his thrill. He runs to his big brother with open arms while Ethan, although reserved, cannot hide his smile.

Ethan did tell me he missed his little brother. He has been waiting since I took him here this afternoon. After our close encounter at the service station near Bozeman.

"Hey, Noah-boy." Ethan puts his arms around Noah. Against the eight-year-old's frame, his long arms could encircle it twice.

"Bro! This is unreal! You're here!"

Still behind me, Ivy grabs my arm. I step back, lining myself with her as she watches her two sons' reunion. She steps away from me, approaching her two sons.

Ethan gives a small wave—somewhere between a 'hello' and 'don't come any closer.'

"Ethan, you're all right." She halts, taking the cue.

He nods. "Um... I'm going to show Noah his room."

"Yeah. Okay. Okay." Ivy looks on, her feet planted firmly on the floor.

The two boys make their way upstairs. "Ben said there're llamas here. Have you seen them?" Noah asks his brother.

"Yeah. I'll show you them tomorrow," Ethan replies as they disappear into the room I've prepared for Noah.

Ivy keeps looking up.

"Give him time," I murmur.

She nods, clearing her throat. "Mark? How did you…"

"I didn't. He came to me."

Her face slants, and her lips form a little gape. "He came to you?"

"I told you to trust me."

"Well, I did. Because I'm here, and he's here. But… how?"

I draw her closer so I can kiss away her confused smile. "What can I say? I have a way with boys."

Ivy engulfs me in her arms, inhaling a deep breath right next to my ear. "Thank you. Thank you."

She should know. I always keep my promises, although this time, Ethan himself has contributed to it. But that doesn't change the fact that I will do anything for her.

Anything.

27

IVY

The smell of freshly-burned hickory wood rouses me. The curtains are still closed, but the room is already bathed in sunlight thanks to the wide roofline windows sitting on top of the wall behind the bed.

Straightening myself out of a fetal position, I slowly let my back fall, hoping to hit a wall named Mark. But I find myself alone in this huge, white-linen-covered bed.

As if on cue, Mark turns up, a cup of coffee in his hand. "Good morning."

"There you are." Still lying down, I stretch my neck to kiss him. I take the cup off him as he sits at the edge of the bed. "Hey...did I send you into exile again last night?"

"The bed's way too big for you to do that."

I kiss him again, unable to resist the taste of mountain air on his lips. "What time is it?"

"Does it matter?"

I frown. "There's no clock in here, and where's my watch? My phone?"

"You don't need them here."

I narrow my gaze, twisting my lips. "I guess not." I give in and then sip the coffee. Smooth milk froth spreads over my palate while the bold taste makes its way into my throat. "Whoa... this is great coffee."

"It's the usual."

"No way!"

"Well, what do they say? Everything tastes better when you're on vacation."

I put the cup on the bedside table and fall onto him, hugging his oh-so-warm fleece-clad body. And he smells like summer wildflowers this morning.

My arm makes its way to the inseams of his jeans, up to his crotch, drawing a restrained hum out of him. A strap of my pajama camisole drops off my shoulder, exposing part of my breasts, just over my nipples.

"Jesus... Ivy..." He caresses the curve where my neck and shoulder meet, waking the goosebumps on my skin.

Footsteps approach our room. "Mom, Mark, can I go with Bro to feed the llamas?"

I pull up the covers, and Mark stands.

"Of course, kiddo," Mark says while striding to the door, then opening it just wide enough for his head to peek out. "But don't let Jasper out. He's not familiar with this place yet."

Light stomping noises follow. I'm sure it's Noah scooting back downstairs. I smile at Mark—his dick is clearly happy to be in my company. "Tonight, okay? Tonight."

He releases a long breath. "So this is what it's like to vacation with kids?"

"Not even close!" I utter and get out of bed.

I stand by the window, absorbing the magnificent views as far as my eyes can see. Mark hugs me from behind.

"That's the river?" I point at the edge of the hill.

"Yeah."

"It does shine like silver."

He pecks the side of my neck. Right then I see Noah and Ethan walking toward the paddock, accompanied by a man who's holding a couple of buckets.

"Is that the caretaker?"

"Yes. Retired Sergeant Ramirez."

I stretch my arms and that makes Mark tightens his hug.

I chuckle. "I'd better get dressed."

"You do that. I'll wait for you downstairs."

I pad across the room, studying the open closet. Mark has hung out a few of my clothes—the pieces that are actually useful for this place. A pair of Wranglers, a flannel shirt, and a leather jacket. I put them on and head downstairs.

"There you are." Mark offers his hand, palm up. "Let me show you the rest of the lodge."

It looks like he's taking his role as host seriously, and I'm only happy to follow along with his hand in mine like it was our first date. Last night, we crashed into bed not long after Ben's express, restaurant-quality burger dinner, so I haven't really explored around.

"It used to be a hunter's lodge." Mark starts his tour in the front living room, while Jasper keenly follows our every step. "The previous owner expanded it—left and right. That's why you have these huge wings."

"What type of wood is it?"

"Douglas fir."

My eyes roam around the space. "Thought so." I recognize the straight, wavy patterns on the paneling and the distinct hint of red over the light brown base. "It's impressive. Did you have to do it up?"

"I bought it pretty much like this. I just added the llama farm and the security systems." Mark guides me to the second living room in the middle of the lodge. He points upstairs. "We've got five bedrooms, all with ensuite."

Jasper slides between us, rolling on the floor, exposing his belly.

I coo and crouch to give him a rub. "Oh, Jasper!"

After being distracted by some canine therapy, we continue. "You've seen this part."

I remember the large galley kitchen.

"Which Ben is clearly happy to claim as his own."

"Hey, guys!" Ben greets us. He's fixing something.

"And of course, this is the dining space," Mark carries on.

I look around. "We were here last night for dinner, right?"

"Yes."

"It looks so much bigger in daylight," I marvel, lingering in front of the biggest fireplace in the house. This must be where the hickory smell is coming from.

He walks me to the door and snatches a beanie off the coat hanger, putting it on. With that, he looks impossibly cute, reinforcing his baby-faced look.

"What's in there?" I ask about the room he seems to have skipped.

"My gym," he gushes.

Ah, of course. His body became like that not because of God—well, God planted the genes, but I know Mark maintains his physique meticulously. When he's not with me round the clock, he trains like an active Green Beret.

He puts a lead on Jasper's collar. "Should we get to the kids?"

Kids just came out of him naturally, and that seriously drives my maternal instincts off the charts. If I could marry him right here, right now, I'd do that. But there is a more pressing situation I've got to face head-on.

"Let's go, then."

We trudge hand in hand as Jasper calmly pads next to Mark. I look up at the sky. Ten-o'clock sun, it seems. It lights up the yellowing aspens, adding gold to the rays of colors decorating Silver Hill.

Despite the serenity, the closer we get to the llama paddock, the harder my heart pounds.

"I really don't know what to say," I confess to Mark.

"Let him start," he advises.

"Okay. Okay."

"Hey, Ethan. Hey, Noah," Mark calls out.

"Hi, Mom! You wanna feed the llamas?" Noah says eagerly while Ethan avoids eye contact with me.

"Maybe later, Noah," I say.

"Jasper!" Seeing the pup, he abandons the feeding bucket and runs toward the mutt, who, after a calm walk, suddenly goes berserk. "Good boy!" Noah hugs him.

Mark approaches Noah. "Hey, buddy, how about I show you a place where we can let him loose, and we can play fetch?"

"Oh yeah!"

"Come on, then," Mark tugs Jasper.

"Bro, you coming?"

Mark gently rounds his arm over Noah's shoulders. "Ah, why don't we let Ethan talk to your mom? You wanna hold Jasper's lead?"

"Okay," Noah says. As they start walking, the puppy goes in circles, wrapping Noah's legs with his long lead.

That fishes out a laugh from Ethan. And I take the opportunity to approach him. Together we watch Mark freeing Noah and showing him how to walk Jasper properly.

"Hey," I greet Ethan as the other boys make their way into the next paddock.

He twists his torso, avoiding my gaze, surveying the tall, fluffy creatures behind him. "Llamas... Out of any other farm animals, Mark keeps llamas," he says, patting one of the animals. "But this place is dope, though. Have you seen his gym?"

"Yes, it is a great place, but don't say that in front of Noah, please. Not using that word, I mean."

"I already have." He jumps back, trying to get away from a brown llama who starts nibbling at his sleeve. "Leroy, come on! I've fed you enough today."

I smirk.

He gives the llama more feed anyway, asking me, "So... you and Mark are gonna get married and stuff?"

"It's early days, but I'm hoping so."

"He's a tough guy. Tough guy. But he's different, you know." Ethan puts forth his opinion like it came from his hidden library of wisdom. "He's like the type of parent who'll give anything to his children. You want that latest Apple shit? I'll get you one, son. You want that sick pair of Kobe Elite? Here ya go!"

I giggle, but I can't help feeling he's describing Noah and excluding himself from what he sees as Mark's fatherhood style.

I pat the llama Ethan calls Leroy, hoping he'll finally look at me. "I don't think he'll spoil his kids like that. Not in a materialistic sense anyway."

"You'll see. You'll be the one who says 'no, you shouldn't do that.' And says 'I told you so' when your kids end up growing up brats."

I dismiss him with a laugh, then ask, "So, why did you come to Mark?"

He looks down, rubbing the sole of his shoe to get rid of a

pile of mud. "Well, I thought he tried to find me because he wanted to impress you. But he kept at it. So I figured he really wanted to find me."

"He did."

This time Ethan looks at me. "You see, I don't even know if I exist, okay? What Mark did—that felt good, you know? A guy like him wanted to find me—because he just did. He just *needed* to find me," Ethan explains.

I wish Mark were here to hear it.

We make our way out of the llama paddock, walking aimlessly around the fence.

"I hated his guts when I first saw him. Remember that night?"

"How can I forget!"

"You know, Mo—" He stops, wrestling with himself to find the right words. In the end, he continues, "You know, at Wayne's house. I was out, maybe dying, when Mark found me. But I know—I know what happens to junkies who overdose. Ugly things ooze out their mouths and noses, sometimes ears."

I feel sick imagining it—yet, Ethan's description heightens my respect and admiration toward Mark. So he gave my boy a mouth-to-mouth in that condition? Not many men would do that. Not many.

"But... that man..." He points at Mark, who is jumping and running while Noah and Jasper try to keep up with him. "That man gave everything he had. I knew it. I just knew. Otherwise, I wouldn't have been here. That's why. That's why I came to him."

"He's one hell of a man, I can tell you that."

"I spoke to Sandra Marcusso. Only moments before she was arrested."

"Ethan, you shouldn't have."

"I found out the truth about you."

I gulp, anticipating that truth.

He sighs. "So you really didn't know I was alive?"

"No. I didn't."

"Do you know my adoptive parents?"

"Yes."

"I'd always felt distant with them, you know. Dad was good to me, but there's just something in me, something in me that wanted to be out of that house. Moved somewhere. A village, an island, whatever. Somewhere I felt I belonged."

"Did Deuce find you when you were in Minneapolis?"

"Yes. Sandra had told him where the Fultons had taken me —this secret child of the Attorney General of Montana. And Deuce was exactly what I was looking for, what I was praying for. A leader. Powerful. Daring. No-nonsense."

I nod, accepting it although it hurts. "Are you still in touch with him?"

"No. I don't know if he thinks I'm his enemy or if he's still trying to get me back."

"Whatever you do, please don't go back to him."

"I know how you see Deuce. He's not a saint. But when he said he saved my life, he did."

One thing that Deuce did right was to lead me to my child I didn't even know existed.

"Tell me," he continues.

"Yes?"

"That night Deuce joked about me being his. Was that really a joke?"

"It was a terrible joke. He's not your father, Ethan. He can't be your father. I have tracked his history as Val DeMaria. He was a thirteen-year-old in Bozeman when you were conceived."

He nods a few times. "Cross your heart and hope to die?"

Like that, he looks like a child trying to convince himself he hasn't been tricked. "Yes. It's the truth. I wouldn't lie to you about something like that."

"So, who's my real father?"

I close my eyes. "I don't know. I'm so sorry, Ethan. But I really don't know."

His face remains neutral—perhaps he's been expecting it. "Okay. Okay. I guess that makes it easier."

I feel wrinkles form above the bridge of my nose. "What do you mean?"

He shrugs. "Whatever I meant."

I look him in the eye. "Do you hate me?"

He meets my stare. "Yes. I hated you like an enemy. But now that I know you didn't abandon me—"

"Ethan..." I step closer to him. "Can I hold you?"

His face crumples. "Ah! I don't know. I don't know..."

I step closer, and he stands still.

"I'm sorry I didn't find you sooner."

"It's not your fault."

His words wash over me as if I was immersing myself in silver water. I reach out my arms, my fingertips closing in on his shoulders.

"I guess you can hold me, as long as you're not going to—you know, do that stupid motherly crying shit."

I chuckle. "I'm the Attorney General of Montana. I don't cry that much."

"Good." He slowly welcomes my hug. First his hands, then his whole arms, and then... *him.*

I feel him, I absorb him, I breathe into him.

My son.

He's in my arms. I don't even feel the need to shed tears. This happiness inside me calls me to smile, be grateful, and enjoy the moment.

"So what do I call you? Mother? Mom? Ma?"

"Up to you," I whisper. "Up to you. You can call me Ivy if you want."

He lets go of his embrace. "I'll think about it, okay?"

"Of course." I rub his arm lightly, feeling like a mother who doesn't want her kid to leave home.

"Hey, do you think I can hang here for a bit? Until I figure out what I'm gonna do?"

The thought of losing him again weighs on me. But Mark was right. I can't control him. I can't shackle him just because I need to have him close.

"It's fine by me. But you might want to check with Mark. This is his place, after all."

"Yeah, all right." He turns to Mark again, watching him.

"Go on. And perhaps you may want to tell him what you told me just now?"

Ethan slowly steps away from me, angling himself toward the paddock to pat Leroy. But after a few moments, he makes a beeline toward Mark, who is still immersing himself in a game of fetch with Noah and Jasper.

"Hey, Mark, can I ask you something?" he calls out.

Mark turns to him as he jumps to catch the frisbee. "What's up, pal?" He then gestures for Noah to keep playing while he talks with Ethan.

I can't hear them, but from the looks on those guys' faces, I know the boy is pouring his heart out. At the end of the conversation, he steps forward and hugs Mark. That boy said he didn't want me to cry and do the motherly shit, but I'm sure he's hiding a tear or two in that embrace.

Right there, something becomes clear. This so-called vacation. A few days of leave, which I submitted last minute. It's not an escape from reality. It's a pathway *to* reality—the reality I've always wanted.

What I have here, the people surrounding me, they're not just a one-off. I want this to be forever. I want my family to be forever.

From the porch, the voice of Ben Winter rends the morning air. "Guys, brunch is ready!"

28

———

MARK

After a day of sweat and soil, llamas and dog, we decided to have an early dinner.

"Couple more," Ben passes me two empty glasses.

Dirty dishes keep piling up in the kitchen sink and along the benches—and I grin like heaven has arrived at my house. We ate as a family tonight, five chairs at my table, three long hours, and we passed more than just wine or salt and pepper. Laughter and love spread across the whole room. No one left the table without a smile.

Most of all, I won't forget Noah's face when Ivy told him that Ethan is his half-brother. I'm sure, to Noah, that's just the same as a full brother.

"I can do the dishes," Ben offers. "You cooked dinner. It's only fair."

"No, no. You cooked last night's dinner and today's brunch. And I think you're due to do some baking. Maybe tomorrow morning?" I wink and push the big man aside. "Sit down. Have more wine, or do whatever you want. I can take care of this."

"Okay. I'm gonna do my meditation, then." The big man excuses himself.

Of course, Sensei Winter needs some Zen time.

Ivy joins me after she wipes the dining table clean. "I'll help you."

"No, darling. You're on vacation. You should relax too."

"Darling?" She frowns, then ignores me as she starts drying off the clean plates.

That came out of the blue.

Ethan walks behind me. "Hey, man, thanks for dinner. Roast chicken was d—"

Ivy glances at him. I'm sure he was about to say 'dope.'

"Delicious."

I pat his shoulder. "Anytime, buddy. Glad you liked it."

"Um... is it all right if I go upstairs?"

"Of course."

"Where's Noah?" Ivy asks.

"He's already in his room," Ethan indicates. "You want me to check on him?"

"Yeah, if you can." Ivy beams. "Could you make sure that he brushes his teeth?"

"On it!" The boy runs.

She smiles to herself, then shakes her head once as if canceling a thought. Then she comes back to the pile of dried plates next to me, stacking them on the shelf. I peer into her behind her back. Wearing a tight T-shirt and snug jeans, the contours of her body are there for me to indulge in. Damn, that booty looks dope—um, well... delicious.

She comes back to the bench to dry the glasses. "What?"

"Nothing. You tired?" I ask.

"No, actually."

"Happy?"

"Very happy." She nudges closer to me and gives me a peck on the cheek. "Like Christmas."

It does feel like Christmas.

"So... what does it feel like, being a mother of two boys?"

"One who suddenly turned seventeen, and the other who's catching up fast?" she says. "It's like traveling along a time warp tunnel filled with happy gas."

I smile at her description. In fact, I feel like that too, even though technically, those aren't my boys.

I caress her hair, a question popping inside my head. It may be cryptic, but I think she'll understand. "Do you see the end of the tunnel?"

"If anything, I'd extend the tunnel so it has no end."

My eyebrows cock, and she hums. I rub her sides. This woman is slender, but she's got serious curves. "Is it because you want to have more?"

She blushes. "Maybe. But only with you."

"It's the best thing you've said all day." I knead her ass. If not for the surprise that I've prepared for her—or us—I would've abandoned the messes. Refusing to give in to my hardening cock, I stay cool. "Why don't you let me finish the dishes, and you go upstairs and check the last drawer of the first closet on your left."

"What's in there?" She suspiciously looks at me.

"Something that might help us extend the tunnel."

"Handcuffs? Whips?"

"Just check, okay?"

I leave her be, but I sneak out to observe her once she's out of the kitchen. The open ceiling of the lodge allows me to see the upstairs hallway. She's standing by Noah's bedroom door. I think Ethan is in there, too. I can hear him talking to Noah. She then bids them goodnight—which they reply with "Night, Mom!" simultaneously.

Once she's away from the boys' views, perhaps thinking no one else is watching, she flings her head back excitedly, her hands fisting victoriously in front of her chest. That's what every mother wants to hear—to simply be called 'Mom' lovingly. She deserves it. And however many more voices she wants to call her that, I'll make it happen.

A few minutes later, I join her in the bedroom. She's in the ensuite bathroom, brushing her hair, wearing—

That.

The blue satin nighty I bought for her yesterday while she was taking care of business in the Capitol. An impulse buy— but look at her! My magnificent Ivy Wren. Just now, I called her 'darling,' which I don't think she liked very much. She is a darling in my eyes though. Not like the sweet, demure mademoiselle kind of darling, but beloved, precious, and one of a kind. And in that sexy lingerie, God bless my manhood. She's become a darling who puts me in desperate need. Impulse has never looked so arousing.

I approach her, ditching my top and then my pants.

"I almost don't recognize you." My pecs glue to her back as I kiss the side of her neck. She has even put on some perfume —unlike her at this time of night. Lavender and rose. Lovely.

"Navy blue? The color of power?" she quips, whipping her head to the other side so I can kiss that side of her neck.

She has power over me, and I won't fight her. But there is something more to her power. "I'd like to see it as midnight blue," I murmur as my hands move up to cup her breasts, kneading them. "Dark, sexual."

She writhes and moans as I start thumbing her nipples, my mouth nibbling the flesh right under her ear, biting it. I exert a slight force on her chest, restricting her bucking. Then I skim my palm down over her ribs to her taut belly, and this time I keep coasting south.

Her skirt lifts as I reach for her panties. The soft lace plays against my fingertips. Without looking, I know it's the matching G-strings. My palm presses wide against her pelvis, tracing how much—or little—of her sex is covered. Her hand meets mine as if nudging me to feel her more.

My lips keep kissing her while I slip two fingers under the lace. As they glide in and out, guided by the sound of her sighing, I picture her beautiful folds. My tongue thirsts, but it has to wait. Right now, my hand needs her more.

Ivy's hips curl as I start circling her clit. She growls her impatience, and I feel a hand grabbing my cock. She shakes the shaft, sparing a finger so she can rub the tip at the same time. The urge to fuck her this second is as furious as the blood pumping through my veins.

But I maintain control. My hands stay in place, and my finger keeps teasing her clit. I want her to come this way.

Unexpectedly, she spins around, abruptly cutting me off.

"Ivy?" I call her name with a little agitation riding on it.

She rubs her satin-covered breasts against my bare pecs. "I want you." It sounds like a form of apology, but I don't think she's sorry at all. Her body snakes down along mine until she's at eye level with my cock.

"Ivy... this isn't the plan."

"Plan?" she utters breathlessly. "We're on vacation, darling."

This woman is unbelievable. "I'm supposed to finger you until you come, then fuck you silly until you come again."

That gets her thinking. She shoots me an admiring gaze, but boy, those eyes are on fire. With that, she strips my crotch bare. It looks like she's determined to do what she wants to do. And I let her have her way.

Still locking eyes with me, she wraps her fingers around my cock, then slowly slides her palm up and down my erection. Every so often, she thumbs the beads of precum spreading from my foreskin onto her knuckles. Her fist tightens, mixing long, slow strokes with quick shakes. Her free hand settles on my chest as if saying, 'just friggin' enjoy it.'

As I let myself fall into her spell, she intrigues me with half a grin, nipping her lower lip. Before I can decipher her intention, I feel the warmth of her mouth surrounding my manhood.

Shit...

This is definitely *not* the plan, and shamefully, my cock doesn't even care. It hardens and lengthens as if it deserves the privilege. In fact, my whole body doesn't give a damn about my rules of engagement—that is, I please her first, not the other way around.

But it appears the woman is enjoying this as much as I am. Her fiery eyes are doused in lust. *Don't you dare stop me.* And all I can do is to give her a hand—figuratively speaking—because what I'm giving is my manhood, getting it to work so she doesn't have to do all the heavy lifting.

I thrust in and out of her mouth, and that prompts her to relax her jaw. I stay shallow at first, and then once my cock is adequately lubricated thanks to her saliva, I go in deeper.

Her lips hum, and I can feel them vibrate around my flesh.

Oh, yes. She likes it.

I keep the slow pace of my pumping, reveling in the sensation of her tongue sliding on the underside of my cock, and at the same time, making sure I last.

But her greed escalates. "Ivy, it's my turn now," I huff when she jams the head of my cock against the bottom of her throat.

She lets it go slowly. And before she changes her mind, I pull her up, kissing her, lapping her glimmering lips—her saliva and my own precum included. I push her against the bathroom wall, pinning her. With a bit of force, I part her legs.

Heat blooms inside my balls, urging me to release. But I keep my erection away from her. No, I'm not giving it to her—yet.

I kneel, trailing my nose between her thighs, taking in the sweet scent seeping through the lace of her panties. She's always well-shaven, and I like that. It's as if she's got nothing to hide, welcoming me with all of her—skin and folds.

Her crotch projects forward as I kiss it. With my teeth, I grip the elastic strap of her panties, tugging them down until she's fully exposed.

Now, she'll do it my way.

29

IVY

Mark kisses his way along my inner thighs, sometimes moving his tongue to play around the center of my groin. Despite my persistent gasps, playtime doesn't occupy him for long. He soon heads deep into my entrance, quickly finding my clit, stroking it with the tip of his tongue over and over.

I writhe, I gyrate, but he's relentless—keeping my legs parted as he persists on that one spot. The spot that makes me explode to smithereens.

"Mark..."

Usually, I'd urge, 'please don't stop,' but the pleasure overwhelms me like a flood that they say only happens once in a century. He's got to know I'm on the verge, but he doesn't even slow down. He licks me until tears burst out of my eyes. My knees buckle under the endless arousal, but he pushes me back up.

In and out of the bedroom, this man is a giver. But this? He's never sucked me this hard for this long.

My legs strain, and my hips make a ridiculous move when he finally lets me go. Haze surrounds me. Blood rushes through every corner of my body. I come spectacularly.

The haze lingers for a while, and when I collect myself, I've been carried to bed, lying next to my man. His face is smeared with satisfaction that I've never seen on him before.

"That was so off-script," he grumps, trailing a finger up and down my belly. It looks like he hasn't even broken a sweat. "Round two?"

I huff. "Um... well... gimme a minute, will you?"

He guffaws, stretching his dimples. His adorable face remains full of vigor, in contrast to my defeated face. I'm defeated all right—by his determination to please me. And I've been pleasured beyond the core of my existence.

After catching up with my breath, I glance down at him. The poor man is still hard.

I lazily crawl up, curling around his buff body as if it's a pillow. Spikes of pleasure are still popping inside me, drawing me closer, binding me to him. I know orgasms can do that, but with Mark, they invoke closeness I've never felt with anyone else. And more than that, being with him like this heightens my sense of loyalty to him. Not that my loyalty was mediocre before. Four years of waiting—I've proven it to him and myself —yet it's faint compared to what's building in me now. The saying 'till death do us part' rings in my ears. I walk my fingers to touch his heart, and he does the same for me. I don't think even death will separate us.

As the tide of my afterglow recedes, I mumble, "We haven't tried to extend the tunnel, have we?"

"You need time, and that's okay."

I spread my palm wide, rubbing his abs. Even his belly button is tantalizingly cute. Meanwhile, I slide an inch lower, blowing air onto his nipple, then I extend my tongue to give it a lick.

He jolts.

"Is that good?" I mutter.

"Yeah."

"Hmm…" I do it again.

He puffs out a couple of breaths. Dimples once again pop on his face as he releases a sated grin.

For a while, I watch his chest rising up and down, taking my head with it. I feel safe. I feel free. And because of that, I let life's thoughts take over me.

My two boys, the time warp. And this man.

"I'm going to resign, Mark."

He holds his breath, slanting his body so he can see my face. "Ivy, what brought that on?"

"It's time to pick my lane. And it's not politics. It's not Helena. It's this." I point around the room, ending in the direction where Ethan's and Noah's rooms are. Then I put my hand on his chest. "I want to fight for what I have here right now."

"I'm with you all the way, Ivy. Don't do this just because you think you have to choose. You love your job, and you do good."

"It's not that I'm giving up, Mark. I still love Montana and its people. I'll still fight for the causes I believe in. Including fighting against the likes of Deuce and stopping them from poisoning our youth. But not as attorney general."

"Deuce is just a storm, and every storm passes."

"I know. But let's face it. After the magazine photo scandal, and the revelation about Ethan, people don't see me the same way. My presence is a distraction more than an anchor for them, and that's bad for everyone."

"I'm behind you whatever you decide."

"I know you are." I lift my head, kissing him deeply. "I'm not letting Deuce win. I'm just going to beat him another way. And with me letting go of politics, I know I'll gain a whole lot more. So yeah, I am going to resign."

He nods, but his eyes are studying me. "Something's still bothering you?"

I smile. With him, I'm allowed to be bothered by something. Even after a mad climax on my part, while he's still waiting for his.

"Ethan," I answer. "Sooner or later, he's going to run away again."

"Likely. Yes."

"And I'm worried he'll go back to Deuce."

"That means we'll have to make sure Deuce and the Mosaic are not part of the society anymore. That's the only way to stop Ethan from going back to him."

I lie back down on his shoulder.

"In an ideal world. Say Noah, Ethan, and our future children are with us. What kind of dad would you be?" I quiz him.

"Well, I'd like to be seen as a dad who's loving, kind, but firm."

I'm sure he already is. But I remember what Ethan told me. "Ethan said you'd be the type who would spoil his children."

Mark reflects on that. "He did?"

"He may be right, you know." I observe my man, who doesn't seem to agree or deny. He's got to know he can sometimes be a softie with Noah.

By now, I think his mind is no longer on sex. But despite my energy level hovering just over zero, I haven't forgotten that he probably came into this bedroom thinking he'd climax. And I'd hate for my man not to cum when we make love.

I shift myself up, sending an erotic breath his way. "Where were we?"

"You were... um, slightly overwhelmed."

"I want that baby, Mark." I rub his balls, and it doesn't take long for them to distend and for his shaft to stiffen from its semi-hard state. "Maybe one tonight and another...as soon as?"

Grunting seductively, he rolls me up so I'm on top. Now, this man is unfazed by literally nothing. Not even by me.

We look at each other as I ride him. This time it's not me or him. We lead each other, rising and falling together, giving pleasure to each other.

But I'm a woman who knows how to thank a man. Equality is not enough when you intend to honor a hero who has given so much, to reward a heart that has opened itself up unconditionally, ready to absorb pain or pleasure that may come its way. This time I'll prolong *his* pleasure. On and on, until he can't receive any more.

30

———

IVY

"So, this time you thanked me in your speech," Mark teases me as we walk along the boardwalk of Spring Meadow Lake.

It's a bright spring day, and I have just announced my resignation and declared my support for the fellow candidate with whom I have been competing in the primary. Between now and the general election, the governor has appointed her to be my successor. She's beaten me as the youngest attorney general in U.S. history by two months, and I'm proud. We share the same views, passion, and goals for our state. She's known for her aggressiveness, which worries some people. But I think she'll learn to rein it in once she experiences the real Helena.

"Of course. You're not my lover anymore." I plant a quick kiss on his lips.

Seemingly not satisfied with the brief contact, he spins me around, pins me against the balustrade of the boardwalk, and sears my lips as if we were alone.

I hear camera clicks.

"Let them," he murmurs against my lips. He presses my

back, really low, and kisses me rigorously as if giving himself a license to show the world I'm his.

Heat coats my cheeks, and it's not the sun.

"Damn you, Mark Connor."

He pulls me forward so I can stand up. "Do you think that'll make tomorrow's papers?"

"Maybe. But soon I'll be old news, and no one will care about that kind of public kiss anymore."

"Huh. At least for now, Miss Montana will see that."

I chuckle. "I hope so."

"Where life reflects, and the meadow of Helena sprouts to life," he recites a part of The Painter's note that gave us a clue to where Noah had been taken that afternoon.

"Only a few days, and I miss Ethan already."

While Noah, Ben, Jasper the puppy, and I have gone back to staying in Mark's Helena home, Ethan has decided to stay in Silver Hill, helping out with the farm.

"I'm surprised he's still there," he comments.

"Me too. But I know it's only a matter of time."

Mark gazes at the lake. "It seems like a long time ago. Where we started here."

"We started here?" I know what he means, but I challenge his point. "We started way before here."

He smiles, knowing I'm referring to Townsend. "You love bringing up that moment, don't you? I never felt so embarrassed."

"Embarrassed?" He's the perfect specimen of the male body, the epitome of a handsome hero—and he was embarrassed?

"Women barging into my office while I'm changing isn't my thing, Ivy," he defends himself. "What crossed your mind at that moment?"

"I thought... *turn around, turn around*. I was dying to see your ass."

He buries his face behind my neck while holding his laugh. Then he draws me away from the lake view. "My eyes weren't enough?"

At the time, he was bending down, releasing the cuff of his pants off his ankle. When he straightened up, I received a blank, petrified stare. Honestly, I didn't care that much about his eyes then. I let lust rule me for a few minutes—I sure as hell deserved it.

"Fine. Blame me for being shallow," I fess up.

He kisses my forehead as we continue our walk, hand in hand this time. "Hey, tell me. The other day when I asked you to check on my surprise at the Silver Hill Lodge. You mentioned cuffs and whips. Are you... are you into that sort of thing?"

I tidy his fringe that gets blown by the wind. Innocence fills his face as he waits for my answer. "No. Are you?"

"No."

"I like how you do it, Mark. Although, a smack on the butt every now and then won't hurt." I wink.

"Damn... give it to me, woman!" he hisses.

MARK HAS DRIVEN me to Silver Hill, and despite our last conversation ending on the subject of butt-smacking, it appears that isn't why we're here.

I stretch when Mark stops by the river.

"How's my sleeping beauty?"

Surprisingly, I did sleep all the way from Helena to here. However I managed to do that.

He adds, "Your body is thanking you for resigning."

"Maybe," I deadpan. I then look up the hill. "You don't want to check the house?"

"Ethan is out with Ramirez to buy feed. And apparently, the boy needs new shoes."

"New shoes?"

"Jasper's pee smell just won't go away, apparently."

I chuckle.

"Care to spend the afternoon with me on a private walk?" He steps to my side and opens the door.

Like a child, I leap into his arms. "Can you carry me?"

"If you wish, of course." He supports my ass with his elbows, walking toward the riverbank.

I flick a finger under his chin. "You can let me down now."

We walk along the sage-covered bank and make a turn onto a bridge that I've never seen before.

"This is so nice," I murmur, standing in the middle of the wooden structure, feeling the vibration of the stream running underneath us.

"Oh, look! We've got some snow geese." Mark points at a small flock that has just landed on the water. "I haven't seen any wrens around lately, though." He hugs me from behind, placing his mouth close to my ear. "Only this Wren."

In silence, accompanied by the sound of the stream, leaves rattling in the wind, and the sight of the blue sky spreading above us—the best Montana has to offer—I feel fulfilled. I have fought to get here, and this man made sure I didn't fight in vain.

I observe his hand gripping the railing, his fingers covering something.

"What does that say?" I unfurl his grip to see what's written on the wood.

Will you

"Huh. What do you think the person wanted to say?"

"I have no idea!" Mark stares at the two words, guessing. "Will you still love me tomorrow?"

"Must've been the previous owner?"

"Maybe." He points at the river. "Hey, pick which twig will pass the bridge first."

Is it because he grew up in New York that he didn't have a chance to play this game? He looks like a child seeing a river for the first time. I entertain him anyway. "The short one."

Then he hauls me to the other side of the bridge. "Gee, you won!"

"Yeah, apparently," I deadpan, watching his hand grip the railing the same way he did on the other side. This time I really look under his fingers.

marry me?

"Mark?"

Gazing at me, he gets down on one knee, taking my left hand while his other hand presents a ring.

"Ivy Wren. I took the long road to get to you. But here I am, humbled by your courage, touched by your love. I see the light because of you. And I want to be the light that shines on your darkest night and makes your day even brighter when the sun is out. I love you."

I squeeze his hand, inviting him to stand up because I don't want to be taller than him. But he stays down.

"Will you marry me?"

His eyes glisten. He had gone through the hurt that no man should ever endure. For him to come back after such devastation, I know his proposal is stronger than rocks, truer than diamonds.

"I will, Mark Connor." I get down on my knees too.

He chuckles. "That's not how you do it."

"Believe me, this is how *I* do it. You're my partner, my lover, my everything. Now my husband-to-be."

He slips the ring into my finger, then kisses my hand. And as soon as he looks up, I plunder his lips. There won't be another man's lips. There won't be anyone other than him. I've fought for this moment alone—well, besides Sam, who tried his best to advocate me—but the fight never felt hard, never felt wasted.

We smile at each other like we've just found out why we were put on this earth. Slowly we rise. As we walk to the end of the bridge, I see him smile, gesturing toward a spot on the wooden plank we're standing on.

And she said...

"Oh, Mark!" I never pictured him as a romantic, but it's literally written here.

"You'll have to make it official." He hands me a small chisel.

I kneel, clearing off some leaves to give myself space. Then I carve a *yes* which is probably too big compared to the rest of the words.

Mark blows off the wood dust. "Nice."

We continue our walk, following the meandering waterway. The silvery reflection hasn't stopped me from looking around as if I'd find more clues.

"That's it." He apparently notices my vigilance. "No more hidden words."

I kiss him.

I study the ring on my finger. It's platinum with marquise-shaped diamonds. I observe the asymmetrical design and pick up a figure of a bird on the right side of the main stone. "This is quite special."

"I asked an old friend to design it for me. He's in New York. He used to work for Chopard."

"Wow... you know how to impress a girl."

"You're not just some girl."

Hell, I'm not. But wearing his ring, being proposed to like that, I'm feeling all the emotions any girl would feel when a man declares his love and commitment.

"Can you juggle love and protection?"

He shakes his head, telling me I'm being silly. Of course, just because he's my partner in love, it doesn't mean he will stop protecting me.

31

MARK

I drop by the Red Mark headquarters after hours of shopping. Finding shoes for teenagers turned out more difficult than I'd ever imagined.

"Hey! The man of the moment!" Sam greets me from his desk. He then gets up, and his brotherly hug soon engulfs me. "Congrats, brother. I know I've said it on the phone, but it's good to tell you in person—" He stands straight, looking right at me. "Was I right, or was I right?"

I scoff, shaking my head futilely. There had never been a bigger, more persistent (sometimes annoying) advocate for Ivy and me than Sam. He has been there from the very beginning, believing in us despite my vow to swear off women. He even noticed sparks between us after Townsend.

"I'm proud of you." He taps my cheek like a father to a son. "You're not as pathetic as I thought you were."

"Hey, I know a thing or two about relationships, okay?" I land a playful punch on his pec.

"I believe you." His smile becomes weird.

"What?"

"I didn't know you could kiss like that."

I roll my eyes. I should've known. Clearly, it wasn't only Miss Montana who saw *that* kiss in the news.

"How's baby Phil?"

"He's getting louder and louder. I can't wait for him to grow up."

"No, you don't. You'd want your baby to stay young forever."

"I'm outnumbered by the girls, Mark. I need him to grow up so we're even." He combs his hair with his fingers. I notice a few more grays around his fringe. "Anyway, how're Ethan and Noah?"

"Yeah, they're fine. Noah is back to being Noah—with school and all, and Ethan is still hanging out at Silver Hill."

"So you've stopped being married to the job?" He elbows me. "It was weird to come here and not see you behind your desk."

"Everything changes when you meet the one."

He shoots me an 'I told you so' gaze one more time, then nods at my shopping bag. "What have you got there?"

"For Ethan." I show him the content.

Sam whistles. "Are those Kobe 9s?"

"Since when did you pay attention to basketball sneakers?"

"They're the famous ones."

"Apparently. And it's the Elite range." Whatever the hell that means. "One of his shoes was peed on by my puppy. Apparently, dog pee is more lasting than llama shit."

Sam laughs. "He'll be so happy."

"Yeah. As long as he keeps them." I nod at my own plan. Surely, he'll choose these over the pair he bought for himself. "So, what are you doing here?" I ask Sam.

He shows me a file. "I just interviewed this man. He's got potential."

The work at Red Mark never stops. Sam is back to working

full time now, but I know during his parental leave, he was still working in the background, assigning cases to our Helena personnel, while I have been keeping an eye on our men in Bozeman.

I skim the resume—another Green Beret. Then I study his photo. "Were you thinking of me when you decided to short-list him?"

"Come on, man. He looks nothing like you. And he doesn't talk like you. I guess he's less philosophical. I doubt he's read the Sun Tzu book."

The man has a scar on his face, but beyond his strong expression, I see a soft gaze.

"Why him?" I ask.

"He's capable, he's determined, and he was a dad."

"Was?"

"His girl mixed in with the wrong crowd, and she was found murdered. She was only fifteen."

"Shit... it might get too personal for him."

"Personal?" he challenges me, pointing at himself.

Indeed, Sam's brother was kidnapped when Sam was twelve. That was what drove him to push a case for Red Mark to specialize in finding missing children instead of guarding adults. It was more than personal, but he has put it to good use. Red Mark is where it is now, thanks to him. In the end, he found his brother alive and well, but he's still as determined in his work as he was before he was reunited.

"Worth a try with him, I guess," I relent.

"By the way, what are *you* doing here?" my partner queries.

I pat my pocket. "I just needed to get something from the tracker room."

"You found him?"

"Deuce? No. No. It's for, um... something else." I tap his

shoulder. "I'll see you around, pal. Send my love to Cass and Grace, will you?"

"Sure."

I halt my step and turn to him. "By the way, do they want Ben back?"

"They're keeping in touch. Cass is happy that his brother seems to have found his grove. And the pay is good, of course."

"I'll ask him to sign a contract when he's back here."

"Excellent."

ETHAN GAPES as he unboxes my gift. With his underground job, he would've had enough money to buy the pair himself. But for someone to actually give it to him, I can see that it doesn't happen often. I don't think he sees me as his father yet, but I have no qualms being at the receiving end of his gratitude.

"This is sick!" He marvels at the pair of gray sneakers. "Genuine, right? Not some Uncle Chi's high-end knockoffs?"

"Real ones." I smirk. "Put them on."

"Shiiiit..." The boy jumps and spins in his new shoes. "Thanks, man."

"You bet."

He looks at himself in the mirror, posing as if he had a basketball in his hand. Then he comes back to me. "Hey, can I come to Helena with you today?"

"Sure."

"And stay at your house?"

"Even better."

"Cool. Ben's there, too?"

"Yeah. He is."

"I miss his cooking," he admits with a chuckle. "And yours too."

With the life he leads, 'home cooking' has probably been erased from his vocabulary.

I look at the time. "Should we go now?"

Ethan examines my Lexus SUV, using his finger to wipe a dusty spot on the passenger door. "I prefer this to your Jeep, actually. It's older, right? But it looks more badass."

"You wanna give it a spin?"

"Nah. Let's go."

Ethan admires the dashboard, switching on the radio and leaving it at 'The Blaze,' a popular rock station. His head bobs up and down following the rhythm of the song that seems to say 'karma' a lot—and it's not "Karma Chameleon." Every now and then, he looks down as if admiring his new shoes.

After the song ends, he gazes at the road, seemingly losing interest in the radio.

"Thanks for helping out at the farm," I break the silence between us.

"They're intelligent animals, you know. Those llamas. Especially Leroy. He knows how to play ball." That brown llama is clearly his favorite. "I think they're better than cows."

"Cows are high maintenance. Llamas are more independent."

"Ramirez said that too." Before long, his attention is back on his shoes. "Hey, did Mom know about these Kobes?"

"Not yet."

He laughs. I bet it's got something to do with his remark about my potential tendency to spoil kids. "But she told you about this particular one? The Nike Kobe Elite?"

"She might've mentioned it, yes."

He laughs again. "I'm gonna tell her."

I shrug. "Fine by me." That feels surprisingly good. Parenting is easier when we have no secrets.

"She said you were a Green Beret."

"Yes, I was."

"Where did you go? Afghanistan?"

"Most of my career, yes. But my first assignment was El Salvador."

"El Salvador? What war was that?"

"War against the cartels," I explain. "We did intelligence-gathering and also supported the local force."

"Cartels? You mean coke and stuff?"

"Yeah, pal. Coke and stuff."

"Geez, man. Drugs—they're like your calling."

"They're everywhere, Ethan."

"The world needs them, Mark," he states calmly as if there's no other way to describe it.

"Yes, of course. For the right reasons."

"The reason is always to numb the pain. What else?"

I admire his intelligence. You can talk about drugs all day, but in the end, this boy has lived and breathed them, and I'm not about to condemn him. "True. But sometimes you've got to feel pain in order to live."

"Who decides whether to numb it or feel it?"

"Yourself. So you've got to be smart about it."

He sighs loudly. "You've been cool, Mark. But don't start going on about quitting or rehab and shit."

"No. I'm just telling you to be smart about it."

He leans back, playing with the string of his jacket hood. "Hey, man, I know you haven't asked me, and Mom hasn't either."

I give him a moment to tell me what it is, but he stops. "Yeah?" I give him a nudge.

"About Deuce."

I glance at Ethan, but he keeps looking ahead. "What about him?"

"I—I can't tell you anything, okay? I'm not gonna be your friggin' informant."

I nod. "I understand your point. I won't make you do what you don't want to do. But let me ask you a question."

"You've just got to find him another way."

"Let me ask you a question. Would you choose him over your mother or Noah?"

He cringes. "I wouldn't choose."

"If you knew Deuce was going to attack your mother or Noah, you wouldn't tell me?"

"I probably wouldn't be there to tell you. I'd be far away."

"A man has got to choose, Ethan."

"I don't know where he is, all right?" he raises his voice.

"Okay. I believe you. But you haven't answered my question. Would you let me know if your mother or Noah is in danger?"

"You'll probably find out first before me."

I believe that he has no idea where Deuce is, but his sense of loyalty to him is still apparent. Will it impair his judgment? I hope not.

The rest of the journey is spent in silence.

We arrive in Helena midafternoon. There's another car parked behind my Jeep, raising uneasiness inside me. I know whose car it is, and I hope I don't regret taking Ethan here.

"There he is!" I hear Ivy's voice as soon as the door lock clicks.

"Hey!" I head into the living room while Ethan lingers by the door, out of view from everyone.

Ty gets up from his seat and comes to shake my hand. He's still walking with a limp from his leg injury. Thank God none of the bullets had gotten his bones, or he'd be spending months in therapy. Apart from that, nothing seems to have broken the former SEAL.

"This is a surprise. Good to see you again, Ty."

"Same here, Mr. Connor."

Ivy gives me a welcome-home kiss while Ty settles back on the sofa. She tells me, "Noah was so happy to see him."

"I bet." Noah was close to Ty even though they were only together for a week. "Ben okay?"

"He was a bit jittery. Probably wondering if Ty was going to replace him soon. But he's okay. He's another special man in Noah's life, I guess."

Ben and Ty are special in their own ways—but I'll keep an eye on them just in case.

"And I've got a surprise for you." I invite her to look in the hallway.

Finally, Ethan shows himself.

"Ethan!" Ivy rushes to hug him. "It's good to have you here."

Soon, Ethan's gaze zeroes in on Ty. He sure remembers who that man is.

Ivy and I look at each other. She follows Ethan as he strides toward Tyler.

I flank Ethan on the other side while Ty meets him halfway. No doubt Ty knows he's the man behind the mask—the one who shot him while snatching Ivy from her house.

The former SEAL extends his hand. "Hey."

Ethan tentatively takes Tyler's hand to shake it.

"I'm Tyler. You can call me Ty."

Ethan acknowledges him, although keeping silent.

"All good," Ty assures him.

Ethan seems to return the man's expression of truce. "Yeah. All good."

Sometimes you don't need many words to express yourself

and be understood. Just like that, the two men seem to have put the past behind them.

"I'm just gonna play with Noah, okay?" Ethan tells Ty and me.

"Go on," I agree.

"He's in his room," Ivy fills him in. "Two doors down."

Ethan walks away, and soon I hear Noah's voice, welcoming him with familiar zest, followed by Ben complimenting his shoes.

I sit with Ty and Ivy.

Ty says, "He's a good kid. I have no hard feelings against him."

That is exactly why I hired him. He's got resilience, clarity, and the ever-important empathy.

Suddenly Noah joins us. "Mom! Today is the fourteenth. Dad is coming!"

Ivy quickly answers, "Yes. He is."

She and her ex-husband Darren have an agreement that Noah comes every second week of the month. With what's been happening, Noah has missed those opportunities.

"He knows we're here, right?" Noah checks.

"Yes, he does," Ivy replies.

"So, who's coming with me? Ben or Ty?" Noah asks innocently.

"We'll talk about it." I pull Ivy aside while encouraging the boy to go back to his room.

"How about both?" Noah presses.

"Wait in your room. We'll let you know." Ivy nudges him to walk away.

Standing in the hallway, away from the kids and Tyler, I look Ivy in the eye. "He's not going to San Fran today. Just hold on for a couple more weeks until we get Deuce. Why can't Darren stay here?"

"Look, it's not just Darren. Noah's missing his nanna too. She's in hospital after a fall, he really wants to see her."

I rub my forehead.

"Maybe he'll be safer in California anyway," Ivy suggests.

"He's not safe anywhere but here." I don't trust her ex-husband to provide security like Ben and I do, or Ty, for that matter.

"Ben or Ty can go with them," she insists.

I shake my head.

"I'm not going, am I?" Noah suddenly sneaks in.

"Noah." Ivy kneels in front of him. "You can play with Dad here."

"I want to see Nanna Dorothy."

"You've been speaking to her."

"Yeah, on video. But I want to see her, and I don't want her to die. I don't want her to be like your mother."

Ivy closes her eyes, pursing her lips.

"Noah!" I call out, but he runs out to the porch.

Ethan seems to notice Noah's distress. "I've got it." He joins his little brother. Soon Ben heads out to the porch.

Before Ivy can recover, she receives an incoming call from Darren. Ty rises as if knowing to leave us alone.

"Darren is outside," Ivy announces.

I open the door for him.

"Is Noah ready?" He's about to steamroll his way in. But I stop him, so we remain in the reception room.

"Not yet," Ivy answers.

His face tightens. "Ivy! Don't be so difficult."

"Darren!" I stand between him and Ivy. "She's not. I'm the one making it difficult. So blame me."

"Look, Connor. Stay out of this. And don't give me that 'I'm her man' shit." He glances at the ring on Ivy's finger. "I'm not afraid of you."

I step closer to him. "What are you saying, Darren?"

"Darren, please..." Ivy calls.

He points his finger at my chest. "You may be marrying her, but Noah is still my son, and you don't have a say in this."

"Oh, I do." Hell, Noah is my son too!

"Can we talk, just the two of us?" Darren sidesteps me to get to Ivy.

"No. Mark stays." This time she stands between us men. "Noah is our responsibility, the three of us. He has a say too."

I give Ivy a thank-you glance. She respects me that much.

Ivy restarts, "Darren, I'm not going to stop you from being Noah's father."

"Then don't make it so difficult."

"Listen!" she raises her voice. "It is difficult because a dangerous man is after us."

"Yeah... you and your danger. You quit, Ivy!"

"It doesn't mean it ends there!"

"And only he can keep him safe?" Darren points at me again.

"Enough!" I bellow.

"You want to take my son, Connor?"

"If I have to."

"Over my dead body!"

I jam my shoulder against him.

Ivy gently tugs at my arm. She says slowly, "Mark is just doing whatever he can to keep Noah safe. He's not trying to replace you."

She's so gentle. I guess when two men clash, she is the voice of reason, and I know Darren is softening, and so am I. I love Noah as my own son, but the reality is Darren is still his father. Noah loves him, and I can't change that.

"I can keep him safe, too!" Darren insists. "You see those men?" He points at two men lingering in his car.

Shit! I know them! They were my fellow Special Forces colleagues back in the day.

"California Hawkeyes," Darren states. "You recommended those guys, did you not?"

I surely did.

Ivy smiles. "I'm gonna make a decision. Noah goes with Darren today."

Darren grins, thanking her.

"On one condition," I determine. "Ben comes with Noah."

"Who's Ben?"

"Come with me." I usher Darren to the window in the dining room, looking down over the porch below, where four men of all sizes are trying their best to do a kicking routine while a puppy is inspecting the assembly. Ben, Ty, Ethan, and Noah. The Taekwondo master has certainly succeeded in distracting everyone from the prickly subject of parenting.

"Which one is Ben?"

"The giant," I answer. "So don't try to mess with him."

"Mess with him?" Darren scoffs. "I like him already!"

The unexpected answer prompts Ivy and me to look at each other. I guess the man started out being defensive because he was afraid of losing his son. Every good father would. Now that he's not seeing me as a threat, the man is willing to work with us, it seems.

He then asks, "So, who are the others?"

"That's Ty, the other big guy. He's Noah's former bodyguard."

"Oh... the one who got shot when Ivy was taken?"

"Yes. And that's Ethan."

Darren frowns. "He's too young and small to be a bodyguard!"

He has no idea what the boy is capable of!

"He's my first son," Ivy reveals after a brief silence.

Darren's brows knot. "Your... first son? So the rumor about you and a secret child is true?"

"Yes. I gave birth to him when I was eighteen. My mother lied to me. So all this time, I believed that he was dead."

"Oh, Ivy..."

"That's for another day. For now, rest assured—whatever happens, regardless of Mark and I being together, nothing changes between you and Noah. You are still his father."

"You mean it?"

"Yes."

"He'll be safe, I swear," Darren promises to the both of us, then faces Ivy. "I'm trying, you know. Our marriage, well, it is what it is. But I'm trying to be the best father I can be."

As if by instinct, Noah looks up. "Dad!" he yells from down below, and as though he was in a race, he arrives in the living room in no time. "Dad!" Noah hugs him. "I'm sorry I can't come with you today, but—"

"You are going with your dad," Ivy announces.

Noah's jaw drops. "Really?"

"Yes," she repeats.

"Really?" He looks at me.

"Yes, pal. You go with your dad and see Nanna Dorothy."

Noah comes to me and hugs me as tight as he did his father. "Thank you!"

"But Ben comes with you, okay? You listen to him, just like you do here."

"I promise," Noah affirms, jumping into Darren's embrace. "Can I take Jasper?"

"I presume it's the puppy?" Darren points at Jasper, who's running around the room as if greeting everyone all over again.

"Yeah. He's cool. He's potty-trained and stuff."

"Okay then."

"Dad, can Ethan come with me?"

Darren looks at Ivy for guidance, unable to respond.

Ivy rubs Noah's shoulder. "Noah, Ethan has to stay."

"Will he be here when I'm back?"

"Yes, he'll be here." I give my assurance to him as much as I do Ivy.

"I'll go and pack his clothes." Ivy then disappears into Noah's bedroom.

I step aside, letting Darren and Noah catch up, making plans for the days ahead.

I love Noah like my own son, and even if I have to share it with his real father, as long as the man behaves, I'm fine with it. Because I know it's the best for the child.

Outside, I see Ethan conversing with Ty and Ben.

As a father, you love all your children equally. But perhaps, Ethan will need just that little bit more. The void in him is big and deep, it's going to be a long road, but I'm up to it. When you've been brought down by something profound and then fight to rebuild yourself, your heart grows, increasing its capacity to love.

"All packed." Ivy approaches Darren with two duffel bags.

And with that woman—who makes it all happen—I still have plenty of space in my heart to love more. Perhaps someday, it will be full, or even overflow, when she and I have children together.

That's a damn fine future.

32

MARK

Bodyguards have two rules about sleep. Sleep with one eye open, and never ever sleep with your client. I maintained a clean sheet, and I'd never had a near-miss—well, apart from that night with Ivy in her bed before we argued about Rena.

Tonight, although Ivy isn't my client anymore, rule one still applies. Admittedly, it eases my mental load that my protectee is sleeping in the same bed, purring beside me.

I trail a finger along her cheek, prompting her to move closer to me. Her hand twitches on my chest, which I cover with mine. She has been sleeping soundly since we hit the bed last night—no attempt from her to banish me off my bed. Now my 5 a.m. eyes are telling me I should do the same as her.

An alarm blares. The back gate.

"Mark!" Ivy sits up, tugging at me.

The noise I never wished to hear.

"Stay here!"

No time to get dressed. I grab my gun, and only wearing a pair of boxer shorts, I pad out of the room. The front door is locked, but there is someone escaping through the back. Right now, he's trying to climb over the gate.

"Stop right there!" I yell, pointing my Glock at the intruder while glancing around in case there are more.

"Chill out, man!"

I huff, withdrawing my gun. "Jesus Christ!"

Ethan holds his position—arms reaching over to the outside of the gate while half of his body is draping on the inside. He's wearing all black, including a beanie and a pair of gloves. But I should've noticed his shoes.

He releases his grip and jumps back in. "Really? You've got different codes?" He repositions his drooping backpack, then looks at his hands as if wondering how he messed up his climb. The material is slippery, and you wouldn't readily notice that the gate is erected at a slight angle—precisely designed to stop climbers like him.

Clearly, he has seen my code for the front door that the alarm didn't set off earlier. But I do change it regularly, and I have different codes for the front and back gates.

I disarm the alarm. "Where are you going?"

He appraises my rushing-out-of-bed state, including my bare feet. I don't think he expected such a swift response from me. "I'm leaving. Can't you see?"

"Come back inside. We can talk about this." The wind batters my face and chest like it was winter.

"Nah, man."

"Look, this isn't a prison."

"Well, it sure feels like it. You should've run Alcatraz."

"You chose to stay here, Ethan. I told you I won't force you to do what you don't want to do."

"What about her?"

Ivy is standing behind me. "Ethan?"

He grunts. "I'm leaving, okay? You can't stop me."

"No, we can't, and we won't," Ivy says in her steely voice. "But at least have the courtesy to say goodbye."

"Well, goodbye." A bitter voice. He waves at us like he's going to school for the day.

"Ethan!" I yell at him.

He kicks the gate in front of him. "Let me out!"

"You're better than that."

He pivots and strides back to us.

"I don't have a problem with you." He points at me. "You're not even my father." Then he quickly turns to Ivy. "And you... don't make me hate you, Mom."

Ivy softens her stance. I know behind that face of strength, she is breaking. "That's the last thing I want. That's the thing that terrifies me—you hating me."

"Just think of the saying. If you love someone, set them free."

"I don't believe that," Ivy denies.

Her seriousness seems to take him aback. "You don't own me."

"No. I don't. But setting someone free is often confused with giving up on them. I can't do that to you."

A sarcastic smile forms on his face. "You claimed to be the defender of Montanan youth. I know you've saved a child or two—whether they wanted to be saved or not. Well, you did your job. You kept to your oath. When I found out you were my mother, I thought you were the biggest fraud in the history of the state. Then I found out the truth about what your mother did when you had me. Then I thought... maybe. Maybe she would be the one who understood me. Out of all possible mothers that I could've had, perhaps she was the right one."

"I understand you're not my possession. I'm letting you go, Ethan. I am. But I don't want this to be the end between us."

The boy bows his head. "I'm feeling like shit, okay? But I

don't wanna sound ungrateful." His eyes briefly wander to me. "Those nights at Silver Hill. I won't forget them."

Ivy dips her head, trying to stay composed.

I take half a step closer to Ethan. "They're yours to remember, but they're yours to have, too. Tomorrow, next week, next year."

"I know. You'll make it happen, I know. But I'm not made for that kind of shit. Sit around the table with shiny knives and forks, fine China, and crystal glasses. I roam alone. My steak knife is my fight knife. My napkin is my wound dressing. That's what I was born to do. You can't domesticate me."

This time Ivy shakes her head in dismay. "So be it. But from time to time, even a loner needs a place to see a friendly face. That place is us, Ethan. We're here whenever you need that safety."

"Goodbye," he says and eyeballs me to open the gate.

"Goodbye, Ethan," Ivy replies.

The boy's defenses are crumbling, so he turns away. I follow him to the gate while Ivy is leaving us to go inside.

As the gate slides closed behind him, his head turns toward me. "I've got an answer to your question, Mark."

That choice—Deuce or his mother?

"I will choose family," he simply answers and takes off in a sprint.

A dozen thoughts fly across my head. Inside the house, I find Ivy back in bed, sleeping on her side, looking at Ethan's baby photo we got from Minneapolis.

I slink under the covers, placing myself right behind her.

"You're cold!" Ivy turns and rubs me all over.

I guess I just needed to numb myself. "He's gone."

Ivy sets the photo on the bedside table. "I know this is for the best. I'd rather let him go knowing he still has some love for me than fight a losing battle. But the truth is, I'm not ready to let him go."

"You never are." I release a long breath, looking into her eyes, telling her this isn't the end. "Neither am I."

"What do you mean?"

"Ivy." I hold her shoulder. "As long as he's wearing his Kobe 9 Elites, we'll know where he is."

She doesn't blink. "What?"

"After I bought those shoes, I stopped by the Red Mark HQ. I fitted the left one with a tracker."

"No, you didn't..."

"I did. Call it intrusion of privacy, call me a paranoid dad. If he's back with Deuce, we've got to know."

She hugs me. "You don't know how much this means to me."

"So, I didn't buy 'em just because I wanted to win his heart."

"You're... I don't know what to say."

"I'll monitor his movements and get Cora-Lee at HQ to help me so I can focus on you. We won't lose him. I promised Noah he'll be here when he's back, and I intend to keep that promise."

She lies on my chest, clinging to my shoulder. The news seems to act like a sedative to her. Almost immediately, she falls back asleep. I'm close to doing the same if not for my phone ringing.

I carefully shift Ivy aside—she's really out, whatever is going on with her—then I head into my study to answer the call.

"Zander, talk to me."

"Can you ask Ivy to come back? Her successor is a piece of work!"

"Well, Captain, you just have to know how to deal with

different personalities. Ivy said she's a damn good lawyer, passionate about her work and all that. And you know Ivy doesn't say that often."

"I can handle personalities and passionate politicians, Connor. But there's a hard line between passion and micro-management—or crossing the line, for that matter."

"Wait until she runs for governor."

"Oh, God!" he frets. "Anyway, the Tindall boy finally talked."

Wayne Tindall, Ethan's friend from the Mosaic. "What did he say?"

"He told me about Deuce's last stronghold in Madison County. It's near Twin Bridges."

It's about a couple of hours from here. I quickly check Ethan's tracker. He's still in Helena.

Zander explains, "We've put surveillance in the area, and it looks promising. Local sheriff says he's been recruiting. Not kids, but mercenary-grade troops."

"What's your plan?"

"Capture or kill."

"Who's in it?"

"State troopers are in charge. The Madison County sheriff and us are there for support."

"The sooner this is over, the better. When's D-day?"

"Seventeen hundred today."

"Right. You'll keep me in the loop, won't you?"

"I'll check with the attorney general."

"Zander!"

He laughs. "Of course. I know how important it is for you and Ivy."

As soon as the call ends, I contact Cora-Lee at Red Mark headquarters. "Cee, watch tracker RM12774511."

"Got it. The target is in downtown Helena."

"That's it. If you see him leaving the city, call me."

"Okay. May I know who we're tracking, sir?"

"Ethan Fulton."

"Understood."

I pace the room, the dozens of thoughts in my head having multiplied, and uneasiness stirs in me. Ethan knows about something, and I can't let the boy face it alone.

"Cee, get Ty to come over to my place."

"On it."

AFTER HAVING SLEPT AGAIN FOLLOWING our early dinner, Ivy finally wakes up—only to puke out what looks to be the soup I made for her.

I clean her mouth with a warm towel. "Should I make tea?"

"No, thanks," She sighs feebly as I help her up. "I just want to sleep."

"You've taken your meds?"

"Yeah. I don't think it's got anything to do with my low blood pressure." Barely stepping out of the bathroom, she spins around and kneels in front of the toilet bowl.

"Ivy Wren..." I rub her back. "We need to go to the doctor."

"I'll be fine. I think I'm just catching a cold or something. Could you warm up the heat pack, please?"

"Of course."

I put the heat pack in the microwave, still keeping an eye on her. I don't want to get ahead of myself, but—

"Mark?"

"I'm coming."

Ivy is sitting in an armchair, looking out the bedroom window.

"Sitting down seems to hold it," she says as I place the pack on her belly.

She approves with a small smile. Her face...could it be *that* glow?

"Have you checked where Ethan is?"

"He's still in Helena."

"Is Wayne Tindall still in witness protection?"

"Yes."

"He can't be seeing him, then? I wish I knew his other friends."

Then I see Zander's name flashing on my phone screen. "Sorry, I've got to take this."

I run to the study.

"Tell me you got him," I rush out my words.

"Jesus... Connor." The captain breathes out hard. "It was a mess. A fucking mess!"

I quickly check Ethan's tracker. He's still in Helena. Could he have left his shoes behind and traveled somewhere else? But the tracker is moving, a walking pace, showing that he's heading south within the city boundary.

"Fucking Deuce wasn't there," Zander continues after pausing, no doubt cursing and swearing to himself like he does when an operation is fucked up. "His men were there though, about thirty of them. We'd never seen that kind of numbers before. One of mine was injured, and two troopers are dead. But that fucking son of a bitch wasn't there."

"Goddamn it! Surely he's running out of place to hide."

"Someone must've tipped him off. And—" He pauses again.

Zander is never speechless twice in a row.

"What, Zander?"

"Never mind the mercenaries. Those kids who were still

loyal to him, and they defended him like he was fucking God. Troopers had to shoot two of them dead."

The muscles around my neck tighten. "Hell! Was one of them Ethan?"

Zander is shouting at someone in the background.

"Zander! Was one of them Ethan?"

My voice seems to attract Ivy's attention. She stands on the doorway of my study, her face as white as a ghost.

"No. Neither was Ethan."

I shake my head, letting Ivy know there's nothing to worry about. But she lingers.

Zander asks me in desolation, "How long have we worked together, Connor?"

The Helena PD captain has been there with Red Mark since the beginning. "Four years, thereabouts."

"How many kids were killed in our joint operations?"

"Zero."

"Yeah. Exactly. We save them, not butcher them."

"Lure them to Helena. Make it your jurisdiction, not the troopers'. And Red Mark will back you up."

An incoming call alert pops on my screen. Cora-Lee—and I know what she's going to tell me. The tracker map is showing Ethan leaving Helena southward. Wherever Deuce is, I think the boy's going to get him.

The easy way out is to give Zander the information, but with the state troopers and the local sheriff involved, and two of their own dead, their priority is Deuce. They'd shot two boys. I'm sure they won't hesitate to do it again. They'll do anything to get him. I can't risk the same thing happening to Ethan.

This is the uneasiness that has been stirring inside me.

I've got to do it without police support. Red Mark is my only ally.

And just in time, Ty arrives.

"Zander, I've got to go," I say and hang up.

"What was all that?" Ivy asks.

I let Ty in while explaining to Ivy, "Zander had a big raid, believing they'd got Deuce. But he wasn't there. I've got to get to Ethan."

Ivy nods heavily. "He still regards Deuce as his father, deep in his heart."

Ethan said he would choose family. But who did he mean?

Ivy adds, "He will defend him."

"And I will defend *him*." I put on my bulletproof vest and my tactical belt. I'm carrying two guns, suppressors, spare ammo, and my trusty army knife. "Ty, stay with Ivy. Get Cora-Lee to share Ethan's tracker. I'll be communicating with her too."

"Yes, Mr. Connor."

Ivy hugs me. "Be careful."

"Next time you see me, he'll be with me." I kiss her, then eye Ty.

The former SEAL nods.

"Aye, sir."

I take my Jeep along the I-15. Ethan could be going toward Twin Bridges. We're almost halfway there. Perhaps Deuce has another hiding place nearby. But the tracker slows down as it hits the city of Butte.

I'm closing in on him. There's only one car in front of me, and I overtake it, yelling, "Pull over!"

The woman driving the sedan looks at me, her car coming to a complete stop. I'm ready to shoot—I'm not going to be fooled by a scared woman.

"Please, I don't want any trouble. If you want money..." She eyes my Jeep and perhaps realizes money isn't what I'm after.

I point my gun at her, peering inside. No one else is in the car. "Open the trunk!"

It's empty.

Fuck.

"Sorry to bother you, ma'am. Have a good night."

He's got to be here!

I watch my boots tapping the ground. The dot is right here —I'm circling it.

Welcome to Butte, the Copper City! There are ten thousand miles of tunnels underneath the city, and I've got to get down there somehow.

"Cora-Lee! Ethan is underground. Find me an entrance."

"O-okay... I'm working on it, sir."

She has never had to track an underground city before, and I'm not sure how many of the tunnels are mapped out.

"I don't care if I have to barge into someone's house, a church crypt, or a sewer. Find me the nearest entrance."

"Still working on it, sir." I know she's typing furiously. "How about through someone's barn?"

"Let's hope it's not under a stack of hay."

"Or a sleeping cow."

I chuckle as she guides me to the farm in question. "Where is it, Cora-Lee? There are three barns here."

"Keep going, about fifty yards. It should be on your right."

The barn is half empty. I hope I don't have to dig, because Ethan's tracker is getting away from me fast.

"You should be around it, maybe three or four feet away."

I stomp the ground, looking for a sound of a hollow space. There is a trap door.

"I love you, Cee!" I exclaim and jump in.

I hurry down the ladder. The first tunnel I encounter is no deeper than ten feet, and it is leading me to Ethan's tracker. With its low ceiling, I have to hunch as I run deeper into it.

The tunnel merges with a bigger one, and I see movement. Three men—they're all of similar build. But the one charging ahead, I'm guessing, is Deuce. One of his guards is walking right behind him while the other is on his side, carrying someone.

It's Ethan on that man's shoulder.

I shoot the man guarding Deuce. For the first time, I see the Mosaic leader face to face. But before I can shoot the son of the bitch, the man carrying Ethan unleashes relentless shots at me, covering himself with the boy's body, forcing me to take cover.

Soon I hear a metal object rolling against the stony ground.

Fuck!

33

IVY

I open another box of tissues—the second one today. I blow hard into one, making my ears ring, but my nose is still clogged. I've got no time for a cold, yet... here it is. I'm curled in bed like a hopeless kitten. My body has zero energy while my mind is running rampant. Ty is waiting in the living room, checking on me every now and then. The sweet guy even makes tea for me, but honestly, at the moment any liquid tastes like jacuzzi water.

"Anything from Mark?"

"No, ma'am. But I'm sure he's getting close."

"Where's Ethan now?"

"He's in Butte."

I nod. "I'm going to go back and lie down." I pull up the covers.

"I'll be right outside if you need me."

Not long after I close my eyes, my phone beeps—not the usual tone. It's a video message which I don't often receive.

Ivy Cavanagh. Soon Ivy Connor. Congratulations are in order.

My hair stands at the back of my neck. The man is still wearing that white mask, but his sandy voice is unmistakable.

It looks like he's still holding onto his ego despite his identity having been found out.

Before you get up and tell whoever is minding you, just know that Ethan is with me. Like any good son would do. When his father is in danger, he rallies behind him.

He pans the camera to show a figure lying on the floor. The room is dim, surrounded by stone walls. I think they're in some kind of old basement. Deuce shoots the footage close-up, first on Ethan's face—fog forms around the lenses, showing he's breathing—then his arm, his sleeve rolled up. Unfortunately, I can't make out if Ethan is still wearing his Kobe 9 sneakers.

They went all out on me this afternoon. Fools! I do have an escape plan, but I'm not done with you. You will pay for what you've done.

He takes out a syringe, injecting something into Ethan's arm. The boy is motionless.

"No... no... no..." I tremble.

For every twenty minutes you're not here, I will inject twenty milligrams of my signature fentanyl cocktail into his system. Yes, the notorious EM2. You know how potent it is. So, you don't want to gamble with how many shots your son can take before his heart gives up. Then his brain.

He swings the camera back to himself.

Come alone. No funny tricks.

Oh, and don't bother with your fiancé. He tried, and he failed.

I muffle my scream when Deuce pans to his right, enough for me to see another body behind him. That's my man? Lying in his own pool of blood?

Take the I-15 south. Keep going, and you'll know when it's time to stop. I'm watching your every move. Alone, Ivy. Alone.

That man is full of tricks. Although my gut says he's not fucking with me this time.

I call Mark—it keeps ringing, but he's not answering.

This isn't happening. So that is really Mark? With that much blood, I don't think he'll survive. If Deuce hasn't already killed him.

I write a message for Ty. *I just need a head start. Deuce has been drugging Ethan. And he has Mark – he's bleeding badly. Track my phone, and I'll call you when it's safe to follow me.*

After putting the message on my bed, I plod out of my room.

"Ms. Cavanagh, are you feeling better?" Ty asks.

"Marginally." I hold my head. "Hey, I've got to get my meds from the car."

"Let me get them."

"No, no. My car is a mess. You won't find them. Um... another cup of tea would be nice, though."

"Of course."

I hurry to my car while unlocking the back gate. As soon as the gate opens, I speed through and lock the gate back.

"Ms. Cavanagh! Ms. Cavanagh, stop!" Ty yells.

Unlike Ethan, I know all the codes around the house, and I know how to change them.

Ty keeps calling me. Unable to get his car out, he climbs over the gate, running as fast as a man can, despite his still-recovering knee. I know he intends to guard me with his life, but at the moment, my life doesn't mean shit. I'm not his responsibility.

When I can't see him anymore, I receive a call.

"I'm sorry, Ty. I've got to do this alone."

"No, you don't! Give me the code, Ms. Cavanagh!"

"I will. When I've got enough head start." Right now, I know I'm being watched, and I can't risk being seen with someone. "They've got Mark. I saw him. There's a lot of blood, Ty."

After about half an hour on the I15, I see a car merging behind me, and another soon catches us up.

"Tyler, 45113890."

Before the faithful guard affirms, a car speeds up, driving alongside me, then pushing me to the side of the road. I lose control, followed by my car coming to a halt, hitting a tree.

My world spins, and I can't make sense of what's happening—only a hand covering my mouth and a heavy thud on the back of my head.

34

MARK

I never thought I'd see a grenade again beyond my Green Beret days. But there it is, exploding like I was inside an insurgent's safe house.

Still trying to combat the ringing in my ears, I crawl out of the abandoned dump loader I've been tucking myself under. If it wasn't for that heavy equipment, I would've been blown to pieces, like the supporting beams and the ceiling of the tunnel in front of me.

I take a couple of seconds to assess my surroundings and to steady myself after the blast.

I'm cut off. I've got to turn back.

The signal from Ethan's tracker is still on the move. There's got to be another way in. Sweat covers my face, and more is drenching my back as I trudge to the start of the tunnel.

I arrive at the ladder, but as I start climbing, I'm halted by a spike of pain. My left leg.

"Shit!" I thought I'd pulled a muscle, but looking at a rip in my pants and feeling the sensation of flesh splitting, I'm sure a piece of shrapnel has gotten my calf.

Pain can wait. Right now, I've got to move on.

And my wound turns out to be the least of my worry. As I reach the top, a man is waiting in the barn, a hunting rifle pointed at me.

"You're trespassing!" he exclaims. I'm pretty sure he's the farmer owning this place.

"I am, and I'm sorry. My name is Mark Connor from Helena. Call Red Mark Rescue & Protect tomorrow, and we can chat about this."

"No. We chat now!" He raises his aim straight at my chest.

I've got no time to waste. Luckily, the man is willing to get up close and personal with me, allowing me to grab the barrel and yank the weapon away. He loses his grip without even trying to fire. I point my Glock at him while emptying the rifle's magazine, confiscating his bullets. "Call me tomorrow."

I throw away the rifle, and with the old man watching me like a statue, I dash back to my Jeep. My phone has become the next casualty of the night. I must've smashed it as I rolled over to avoid the blast. It won't even turn on.

I use the radio to reach the Red Mark command center. "Cee, find me another entrance!"

"Mr. Connor! You're alive!"

"Who said I wasn't?" I rip the first aid kit open and patch up the gash on my calf.

"I lost contact with you and... and Ty told me Deuce had taken you."

My blood pressure shoots up. "What the hell?"

"He said Ivy saw you bleeding. Deuce must've tricked her about your death."

"Tell me she's safe!"

"She's trying to get to Ethan. Deuce has been drugging him."

"Shit!" I punch the steering wheel. This is fucked up! "Where's Ty?"

How the hell did he lose Ivy? She was sick as. Perhaps she used her sickness to trick him—but how?

A bodyguard can only do so much. If their protectee decides to slip out of their protection, sometimes there's nothing you can do.

Especially when your protectee is a mother who's hell-bent on saving her son.

Still, it's no comfort for me.

Cora-Lee explains, "Ty's off to get Ivy. He was tracking her phone. I had been too. She was heading to Butte, but we lost her about twenty minutes ago. Hang on. I've got Ty on the line. Ty, come in."

"Have you got a signal back from Ethan?" I hear Ty saying.

"Yes, although it comes and goes, they must be deep," Cora-Lee replies. "Where are you?"

"I'm about ten miles north of Butte. I've found her car."

"Fuck!" I yell.

"Mr. Connor? Thank God!" Ty exclaims.

"Is she in her car, Ty?" I desperately seek an answer.

"No, sir. From the tire marks, I think two cars have gotten her. I'm sure they're heading to Butte."

Deuce—I swear I'm going to nail the son of a bitch's ass!

"Gents, I've found another entrance." Cora-Lee sends me a coordinate. "It's under a bridge. I really hope it's not underwater."

I don't care if it's covered in hot lava.

"I'll meet you there, boss!"

"Join me in hell, Ty!"

35

IVY

My head feels heavy, and I know it's not because of my cold. Whatever they used to hit me with! I'm now sitting on the ground, leaning on something.

I slowly open my eyes—I've seen these stone walls. It must be the same place as the one featured in Deuce's video. It's not a basement. It's a fucking mine! How the hell is Mark or Ty going to find me?

I grope behind my back. I'm leaning against some kind of low wall, perhaps a well or a shaft. Beyond the wall, I can see a pair of legs and those Nike Kobe sneakers...

"Ethan! Ethan, can you hear me?" I shift myself sideways to see more of him.

But a man stops me. He's got blood all over his shirt—if it's not fake, it's certainly not his.

"Prick!" I spit.

Soon I hear laughter, and the face of Val DeMaria comes into view. No mask. The phantom has revealed himself in front of me. I've seen that face in photos and sketches—straight, narrow, no smiles. In the flesh, behind that cynical laugh, I somehow feel closure. Our unfinished business is no more. There he is, as plain as the night. Every line on his face tells me he's ready to admit defeat. His eyes are black like a crow's, but there's no rigor behind them.

"I didn't think I'd pull it off, but wow." He laughs again.

Yes, he has fooled me. But his voice—he's forcing himself to be loud. Its sandiness no longer exudes power. Instead, it sounds like uncertainty.

"I wonder, Ms. Cavanagh. What if this man climbed into your bed one night?" He passes a new shirt to the man smeared in fake blood. I'm sure it's his guard. "Would you let him fuck you? You wouldn't even know the difference, would you? Perhaps you'd moan like you'd never been fucked before. This man, well, he's pretty well-endowed."

The guard smiles dirtily while exposing his torso, putting on the clean shirt slowly, acting like the star of a show.

I ignore the guard to gaze at my sworn enemy. "Then your asshole must've been as loose as a used rubber band."

He restrains his grunt. "Oh, you're pissed. I know you're pissed. Aren't you supposed to stay level-headed under pressure? Isn't that your best quality as a lawyer?"

Maybe. But level-headedness won't get me anywhere right now.

He crouches in front of me. "I guess your heart is bigger than your head, after all. That's what love does to you. It debilitates you, turns you into an irrational mess."

I spit at him.

He pants, wiping his eye. "Don't blame yourself. I know you would've come anyway, whether your lover was in the picture or not. That's what mothers do, huh?" He nods at Ethan.

I refuse to listen to his pathetic speech, digressing my attention to my son. His legs are moving. "Ethan! Say something. Tell me you're okay!"

"Oh, he's all right," Deuce dismisses me, pulling my head by the chin so I face him.

"Let my son go. This is between you and me." I shift myself closer to him. "It took you two years to groom that boy, just to get to me so you can avenge your dead mother. After all, you are the bastard. Val DeMaria."

"My father begged for mercy!" he barks. "He knew that without him, she would be dead. I saw the slaughter. The blood is on your hands, Ivy Cavanagh."

"Your father killed a family! Including their four-year-old daughter. He roasted them alive! Where was the mercy in that?" I groan. I still remember the remains of that child, wrapped in her mother's charred arms. "Your mother had a choice. But she decided to be a double agent for those warring gangs."

"She did what she had to do!"

"No one forced her to."

"You know nothing! My mother had survived many ordeals. Only to be brought down by a woman sitting behind her desk. Someone who supposedly had honor!"

"I didn't kill your mother. Those gangsters did, and your father let them! Now your father is dead. That means your revenge is over and done with, isn't it? Why are you keeping me?"

"You made me do it!"

"You tried to impress him by getting him released. But you were never enough for him, were you? No matter what you'd done, he never even gave you a second look." I titter, taking whatever small win I can. "Who did you pay to kill your own father? A con man? A wife beater? And you tried to teach me a lesson about family?"

"Because of you! He told you too much, that ungrateful old man."

"He didn't!" I say it to his face. "He didn't tell me anything! You killed him for nothing!"

He strikes me.

"You can hit me until your knuckles are covered in blisters, but you won't be able to wash your hands of your father's blood."

Behind me, Ethan is squirming in pain.

I whip my head away from Deuce, calling, "Ethan!"

Deuce gets up, watching him for a while, then pierces a syringe into his vein yet again.

"Stop it! Kill me! Take your revenge! But just stop what you're doing." My voice gets erratic. "Walk away from here. Be a father to him. I know he looks up to you. He wanted to be with you. He tipped you off about the raid this afternoon, didn't he?"

Deuce growls. "You think?"

I narrow my gaze.

"One of the sheriff's men did. Proved that money still talks."

I release a breath. So my son didn't try to save him?

Deuce continues, "But you're right. He wanted to be with me, and you know what? I wasn't about to let him go. So we met."

"Why didn't you just leave Montana? Execute your exit plan."

"I told you I wasn't finished with you. And you know... that boy got fishy along the way. I thought... maybe you and your Red Mark hillbilly had gotten into his head, and he'd started to side with the police, just like his friend."

"He wanted to be with you. Take him, take him while he still worships you."

"Worships me? I don't know about that, Ms. Cavanagh. He's a son of a bitch. I can't really trust him."

"I know he's special to you. You two have forged a bond. I know that."

"Let's ask the man himself, shall we?" Deuce gestures to his guard to drag Ethan to us.

I look around. There's no sign of the two men who hijacked me. Perhaps they're stationed outside, along with Deuce's remaining men. I can only speculate that they are expecting company—and I hope it's Mark and Tyler.

Ethan is waking up, crawling toward us.

"Stand up, son," Deuce commands.

My son looks around. "What the fuck is this place?" His gaze lowers and finds me on the ground.

I meet his stare. "I understand, Ethan. You want to be with that man. You go. Don't look back."

He turns to Deuce. "What the hell is she doing here?"

"I've got business with her."

Ethan tries to get to me, but still under the influence, he offers no resistance when Deuce hauls him back.

I give Ethan a defiant gaze. "I know you've got to go. I don't own you. You've made your decision, and I respect it. Just know that—" I pause. "That I'll be with you wherever you are."

"So touching," Deuce says, hand on his heart.

Ethan raises his hands, surrendering. "Let her go, and we can escape together, Deuce. She won't do anything. She just wants me alive."

"Look me in the eye, Ethan," Deuce says. "And tell me you're still mine. *Blood or nothing.*"

"Just let her go," Ethan repeats.

"We'll rebuild the Mosaic. I will take you. We'll be bigger and more powerful than we've ever been. Blood or nothing."

"Yeah. Blood or nothing. Come on, let's go."

"Good. Let's go." He wraps his arm around Ethan's neck and then throws a sharp look at his guard.

Before I can do anything, the man hauls me up, throwing me over the low wall I've been leaning on.

I don't even have a chance to utter anything. After diving into the mouth of the well, my head hits the water. So cold it feels like my body is piercing an iceberg.

In between my chattering teeth, I can hear scuffles coming from above.

"Get her out of there!" Ethan yells. He sounds further now.

"She'll survive a few more hours. Let's see how fast that Red Mark prick gets to her. My guess is it'll be too late. If he's not dead already."

"Get her out of there!"

"Or what? Do you want to kill me? There." Deuce's voice is challenging Ethan. And there's a noise. I think he has tossed his gun to the ground for Ethan to pick up. "Shoot me."

"Just go, Ethan!" I don't know if my trembling voice carries. Perhaps it does because soon, Deuce's guard throws a cover over the well.

Silence.

Darkness.

I shake hard, vomiting air as there's nothing left in my stomach. This is no basement cage, but my mind knows no difference. I'm not afraid to die, but I am terrified of how long I have to endure this.

My arms flutter to stay afloat as numbness crawls over my legs. I can't feel anything from the waist down. I don't even know if I'll survive the next ten minutes, let alone hours.

36

MARK

Despite its proximity to a creek nearby, the second entrance Cora-Lee has found is, thank God, dry as a bone. Judging by the size—and the newer doors and locks—it looks to be one of the entrances still in use.

I relay my finding to Ty over the radio. "There's a door under the second arch of the bridge." I attach a suppressor to my Glock, then shoot at the locks. "I'm going in. I'm not sure how deep this tunnel goes. If you lose signal, do what you do best, brother."

The former SEAL had toured Afghanistan multiple times. In one of his last operations, he led four of his men and two innocent civilians out of the rubbles of a mosque that an insurgent group had blown up. Under constant fire, too. I know I've got a trusted partner.

"Copy that, sir. I'm about ten minutes away."

The tunnel is dark, full of debris. Some piles are almost as high as the ceiling. After about half a mile of what feels like an obstacle course, I arrive at another set of doors. Faint light seeps through the gap, disturbed by moving shadows.

Changing into stealth mode, I slink along the door, pulling it ajar—just enough for me to see in.

And then aim, and release two rapid shots.

The two men manning the doorway are down. I wait, anticipating more resistance. But I find myself alone until the tunnel bends, leading me to an opening. And I've never expected to see such a scene.

"Go on. Shoot me!" Deuce taunts Ethan, who's pointing a gun at him. Beside Deuce is another man, armed and ready to shoot the boy.

I halt my steps, gluing myself against a stone wall. There's a beam just wide enough to cover me, but I wish the tunnel had led me to the other side of the chamber because from where I am, Ethan is blocking my view of Deuce.

Scanning the space around me, I'm sure they're the last three men standing. Worryingly, though, there's no sign of Ivy.

I'm only a few yards away, but standing on the same level, I won't be able to take Deuce and his guard quick enough before one of them gets me or Ethan.

"You won't do it, Ethan. If you wanted to kill me, you would've done that a long time ago. You would've done that two hours ago. Deep down, you know what real love is, and who has it."

"Get my mom out of there!" Ethan commands, still pointing the gun at Deuce.

There? Where? There's nothing but walls around here.

Ethan steps forward. Deuce stands tall. I can't see his face, but I imagine he's smiling condescendingly. It's a different case with his arms, though. I see them—and one of them twitches. The other man moves from his stand-down position, getting ready. Behind me I hear faint footsteps.

Deuce slides his arm behind his back. His hand is out of view, but I bet he's reaching for a concealed gun.

I have no time to line up my sight.

"Ethan, down!" I yell while leaping, knocking the boy down with my shoulder while my body twists in the air, facing Deuce.

Things happen in slow motion. Two shots are fired—Deuce's hisses past my ear, and mine is firmly lodged in his chest. But there is another shot—if that has come from Deuce's man, I'm sure it's heading my way, and he would've had time to get it right.

I fall, rolling to cover Ethan, who's insisting on shooting at Deuce.

"Ethan, down!" I stop him from getting up, blockading his body while examining my enemies.

The Mosaic leader is dead. And to my surprise, so is his last man.

"Mr. Connor!"

Of course, Tyler Hunt was the one firing the last shot.

"Mr. Connor, are you okay?" Ty checks on me while my attention is still on Ethan.

"You okay, Ethan?" I pat him all over.

"He was going to fucking shoot me," Ethan rages.

I did what I did to protect the boy physically. But more than that, I wouldn't let Ethan live with guilt for killing someone he used to adore. The kid is not a killer.

"Where's your mother?" I ask.

"In there." He points deep into the tunnel. It's dark, but what I see gives me chills and boils my blood at the same time.

She's in a well?

"Ivy!" I shift the wooden cover and shine my flashlight down. I see her, barely floating. Her mouth gapes, and her arms bent rigidly in front of her chest. "Ivy!"

She doesn't respond—doesn't even try to look up to

acknowledge me. If not the cold, her fear will threaten her safety.

"I'm coming down!" I yell, taking off my bulletproof vest, and get completely topless. It's about fifteen feet to where Ivy is. I have to be as light as possible, and as soon as I get to her, I have to warm her—and the only way to do it is by using my body heat.

"You're gonna crush her!" Ethan says when I climb over.

The well is only about four feet in diameter. He's right. There won't be enough room for me to land in the water without hitting her, but—

"I'm not gonna jump, son. I'm going down the green-beret way." I enter the well—my hands and feet spread wide, clinging to each side of the walls.

"Fuck me..." Ethan murmurs as he watches me chimneying down the well.

Only now, I'm reminded of injured calf. Shit it stings like there's a dagger lodged in it.

"Find a rope or anything that can help get us out," I instruct Ty, then I look down. "Ivy, hang on. I'm coming."

Finally, I hear the water underneath me move, then I hear her voice. "Mark..."

"I'm here, Ivy Wren."

The only movement she makes is trembling. I've got to get her out fast.

My feet almost touch the surface of the water. But I can't afford to get wet, at least not my torso. I make a small swing, so I'm hanging across the diameter of the well like a hammock—my heels planted on one side while my back is glued to the other side of the wall, supporting the weight of my body.

Mother fucker! I bite off the pain that wracks my leg while tugging her arm toward me.

"Come to me, Ivy."

"Mark…"

As soon as she's close, I use my army knife to cut her drenched jacket and blouse.

"Climb on to me."

She forces herself up, but her legs seem to be weighed down. I pray that she's not wearing jeans. I dip lower, letting my legs get submerged. The cold water is numbing my gash, but I know I'll pay for it when I'm out.

Relying on my back and feet to support my weight, I reach out to her, snaking my arm under her buttocks. Thank God she's wearing light pants.

"Come on. You can do it. Lift yourself, and I'll do the rest."

I haul her up, and that seems to get her legs to move.

"Come on, Mom!" Ethan encourages from the top.

After a couple of failed attempts, she finally manages to climb over, throwing herself onto my belly. I hold on to the stony wall so hard that I'm starting to shake. After drawing quick breaths, I steady myself, sustaining her weight.

Ivy is still shivering profusely, but she drops her chest onto mine.

She exhales deeply. Her wet bra is still on her, but it's thin. We're almost completely skin on skin. As her chest rises and falls, I feel her soaking up warmth from my body.

"Take it in, take it in, Ivy." I shake my wet hand and blow warm air into it, settling her shivering jaw. Her breathing steadies somewhat, but she's still so weak she can't even hang onto me.

My feet slide, and we both droop. I utilize all my muscles to give me a push. We can't afford to go back into the water.

I look up. Ty has just come back.

"I can only find this, Mr. Connor. It's not long enough." Ty shows me a piece of wire rope, about five-yard long.

Dammit.

But you'll have to work with what you've got.

"Throw it down!" And The rope lands on my shoulder. It's a typical lightweight, general-purpose mining rope. Its strands are galvanized, but it's pretty thin at three millimeters, flexible enough for what I have in mind.

"Okay, Ivy. Here's what we're gonna do." I can't tie the two ends together, so I weave the wire around her and my belts. "We're gonna climb together, okay?"

She nods—no sliver of doubt.

"This rope will secure you to me. All I need you to do is put your arms around my neck and hold on."

Her head bobs again, assuring me she's in, although her lips are still shivering.

"Ready?"

Despite her weakened state, she manages to cling to my neck as I haul myself up. Gravity tugs me back, testing my endurance and will.

"You've got this, Mark!" Ethan shouts nervously. Meanwhile, Ty bends down, arms reaching, ready to catch us, although he's still far away.

I release a bellow for every push I make—like a weightlifter who's about to break his own record. My calf is in splitting pain as if the flesh had been stripped off the bone, but I keep going.

"Mark..." She notices my struggle.

I puff, gathering energy. "I'm fine. I'm fine, Ivy." I grunt loudly, telling my legs not to give up on me. By now, I'm relying mostly on my glutes. With frigid air wrapping around our bodies, weighed down by our wet pants, I'm almost at my limits.

But I feel Ivy move. Her feet that have been dangling all this time are now supporting us from underneath my ass.

Thank God for her long legs! Then she slowly places her hands on the wall, climbing with me.

"Come on, let's finish this!" My determination grows, fueled by her will. I know she won't let me fight alone.

"You're close, Mom! You can do it!"

Ivy slips, but with me as her safety net, it doesn't stop her from getting back to battle.

"Imagine what we'll do once we go out," I pant. We're only three feet away from the top.

"A mug of hibiscus tea sounds friggin' good."

I chortle. "Hibiscus tea it is, then."

"Ms. Cavanagh, give me your hands!" Tyler yells, and soon he catches Ivy's wrists. I release her belt, unraveling the wire rope that has kept her attached to me. Ty then hauls her up, helped by Ethan.

"Mom!"

"Ethan!"

I push myself for the last time as Ty hooks his elbows under my armpits, dragging me over the wall.

"Welcome back to hell, Mr. Connor."

I pant furiously. "It's frozen over, Ty!" Then I swing my head toward where Ivy is. Ethan has given her his sweater, and he's holding her tight.

Ty drapes his jacket over my shoulders. "I called Zander before I went in. He's coordinating things with Butte PD. They're on their way."

His attention then lands on my leg. He knows I'm hurt. His medical kit is already out of the bag. Now he's rolling up the cuff of my pants all the way up to my knee. Then he removes the soaked bandage. "Jesus, Mr. Connor."

"Better than dead, I suppose."

"I guess." He takes one more look at the gash.

"It's just a frag."

His eyes raise to me then carries on with the task at hand, dressing the wound expertly, better than I did myself. I watch him, recalling the first day he turned up at the Red Mark HQ. The guy had confidence. He walked like a soldier, yet he wore his heart on his sleeve. "I owe you one, Ty."

"Anytime, sir," he smirks. "Pay rise on the cards?"

I keep my expression neutral, although I've already got plans for him—and it's more than just a pay raise. I pat his shoulder and shift my position to observe Ivy and Ethan.

"Are you warming up, Mom?"

"Yeah."

"I wasn't going back to him, Mom. I agreed to meet him because I wanted to kill him."

"It's okay, Ethan. It's over."

"I couldn't kill him. I'm sorry."

"There's nothing to be sorry about. It's over. We can move on now." She rounds her arms over her son's back.

Much as I want those two to continue their bonding, I can't wait any longer. I have to be with her—I've got to have her in my arms.

Seeing me coming over, Ethan gets up, staring at the dead body of the man who used to be his leader. It's face-down, the man's shooting arm bent next to his shoulder. I think Ty had kicked the weapon away from the corpse.

"He was going to shoot me! He was going to fucking shoot me!" Ethan kicks the body and spits at it.

"Hey, easy, son. Easy." Ty draws him away.

I join them, reluctantly leaving Ivy.

"I'm cool! I'm cool!" Ethan frees himself from Ty, walking away to the other end of the chamber, sitting on a pile of rocks.

Ty gestures for me to go back to Ivy, telling me he'll keep an eye on Ethan.

"Mark! You're hurt!" Concerns mar her face as she notices the bandage on my leg.

"I'm okay. Ty has fixed me up." I sit next to her, and intense scrutiny flies from her gaze. "It's nothing. A piece of shrapnel got me."

"Deuce tried to blow you up?"

"He used a grenade to blast an entrance," I clarify. "You okay? You were amazing down there—I mean, helping us climb."

She scoffs lightly. There's a lot she wants to say, I can see it, but her attention is back on Ethan. We hear Ty's calm voice as he approaches the boy, "Hey, can I sit?"

Ethan moves aside with a nod. The scene warms me. That's Ty. He'll never hold on to the past, and he's an advocate for healing. Just by being next to him, I know Ethan is opening up.

"He'll be fine," I murmur.

She smiles then leans on me. Our skin meets again in places where our jackets expose it. Her rosy cheeks slowly return. "You called me amazing? You didn't look human in there, Mark. How the hell did you do that?"

"Which part? The heat or the scaling?"

She chuckles. "You were as warm as a radiator down there." She caresses my pecs. Her fingers are warm now, and they feel like cotton wool had been dabbed against my skin. "But the climbing... seriously."

"I had you. That was how." Really. In the military, training is an enabling mechanism. It's purpose that takes us over the line. It's no different with us tonight. She was the fuel that got us home. I did it for her, and with her.

We start hearing people storming into the tunnel. "Butte PD!"

"In here!" Ty answers. "I'm Tyler Hunt. I made the call to Captain Zander from Helena PD."

"Is that Ethan Fulton?"

"Yes," Ty says, standing protectively next to Ethan as the officer looks a bit too eager to approach the boy.

In the end, the officer keeps his distance. "You're okay, boy?"

Ethan nods.

"Let's get you two out of here," the officer says.

Ty agrees. He knows Ethan shouldn't be here when those officers examine Deuce's body.

"Mom!"

"It's okay, Ethan," she assures. "You go with Ty. Mark is here. He'll stay with me."

As Ty and Ethan leave, the officer in charge instructs his men to check on the bodies. Then he strides to Ivy and me. "I'm Sergeant Peters."

"I'm Mark Connor."

"You okay, sir?" He gives me a blanket while spreading another over Ivy.

"Yeah. And this—"

"Ms. Ivy Cavanagh." The officer greets her, securing the edges of the blanket so she's wrapped tightly. "You're okay, ma'am?"

"Yes. I'm fine."

He then surveys his men, who are flipping Deuce's body so it lies on its back, no doubt checking his identity.

"That's Val DeMaria, a.k.a. Deuce. The leader of the Mosaic," I confirm.

One of the officers checking the corpse affirms to the sergeant.

"Paramedics are coming. We'll get you out of here soon. Captain Zander is on his way. For now, stay here."

We're left alone while the police assess the crime scene.

"I can't wait to go home, Mark," Ivy murmurs.

"Sure. But first, we've got to get you to the doctor." I caress her belly.

She smiles, kissing me. "Maybe."

"You know, Ivy, you asked me a question which I haven't answered."

She cocks her head. "I can't believe I let you get away with it. What question was it?"

"You asked if you were my duty."

"Ah... that night, when you said that Ty would take over, and then you stormed off my bedroom."

"I wasn't thinking straight."

"You were being true to yourself, and that's a good place."

"Truth is, you're not just my duty, Ivy." I caress her cheek, clearing wet strands off her face. "Duty has a scope. Duty is what I do for others. But what I have for you... is devotion. All of me that I faithfully give to you."

She pushes herself up, reaching my lips. Her hand slowly slips under my jacket, holding onto my pec. She tastes different. It's not the water from the well... I swear, she's different.

37

IVY

Mosaic is no more. Although the war against fentanyl, and other drugs for that matter, is still far from won, the peace of knowing Deuce won't haunt us again is a victory.

Following the final showdown, Mark and I manage to get Ethan to seek help—for his drug use and Deuce's death. Surprisingly, he asked Ty to accompany him in some sessions. I guess Mark and I were too close to Deuce—he wanted to kill me, and Mark killed the man—so perhaps Ethan seeks a neutral person.

But I think he feels safer with Ty. Safer—not only because of the former SEAL's incredibly big heart, but also because of what he went through when he was a teenager. Mark told me Ty's best friend died of overdose. It became one of the reasons he decided to join the Navy, as a dedication to a friend taken too soon.

Ty knows loss. Ty knows drugs. And Ethan seems to relate to him.

Today though, my son decides it's time for him to leave Helena.

"You'll come to my birthday, right?" Noah passes him a hopeful look.

"Of course. Just send me the invitation," Ethan answers, patting Noah's shoulder.

Noah gives his big brother a hug when noticing a car coming. His best friend Dylan and his mother are here to pick him up from school. "I've got to go, Bro."

"Go on. I might see you at school sometime." Ethan winks, no doubt reminding him of the days he was only known as 'The Painter.'

Now it's just the two of us.

"I guess this is goodbye," Ethan sighs. "But not the end."

Those were my words—ones I told him when he ran away the last time. I know he'll be all right, but there's a sting behind my heart, a motherly kind. "Take care, okay?"

"I did say goodbye to Mark last night."

"I know."

"I spoke to my dad too. I mean, Terry. I might see him in a couple of weeks."

"Good. I'm sure he misses you." A bitter-sweet feeling scrapes at my chest cage. Regardless of what has happened, Terry Fulton is still Ethan's father. But the last thing I want is for Mark to be left out. "Look, Mark has an urgent meeting, but he asked me to give you this." I draw his hand and put a key in it.

His hand freezes in front of him as he gapes. "You serious?"

"He said it's yours."

"Unreal!" he exclaims, hugging me, almost jumping. "Well, I'll um... I'll call him." He rounds the four-wheel-drive, all smiles.

"You'll be careful, won't you?"

"I will." He can't stop beaming. "Told ya he spoils his kids! But this is sick!" He inspects the car one more time, wiping away some dust from the driver's side door. Then he turns to me. "By the way, no one has answered this."

"Answered what?"

"Tell me, how the hell did Mark find us?"

I hum, trying to keep a secret I can't keep anymore. I flick my gaze down at his shoes.

"What?" he eyeballs me. "What? No! No fucking way!"

"Language, Ethan."

"He... wired my Kobes?"

"The left one." I smirk.

"Shoot!" He takes off the left pair, removing the inner sole. There's indeed a chip-like object wedged in there. "Fuck..." He sighs softly, but his eyes flare wide. "Bastard!"

"Hey, that's my fiancé you're talking about. And he's a good man. Don't call him that."

"Sorry. Sorry. That... dude!"

"If it wasn't for that tracker, we both would've been dead."

He raises his brows, accepting my argument. "So, what'll happen to me when you get together with Mark? I bet you're planning to have more children?"

"Yes. But nothing will change between you, me, and Mark. We're family, Ethan. You'd better get used to it."

"I'm learning," he admits. "I always wanted to have siblings, though. I wondered what it'd be like, especially when I was alone. When I found out about Noah, I was... I don't know. Proud. I planned all sorts of stuff—good and bad, I suppose. Not *bad* bad, but naughty."

I had almost forgotten about what those two were up to when Ethan took Noah to the lake. "I'm sure you're wiser now."

"If I have more brothers or sisters, I'll be better. Yeah. Better."

"Good to know." Tickles attack my gut, imagining the house overrun with kids.

"Do you remember? When we were with Mark's llamas that day. I asked about my real father?"

"You said it was easier that I didn't know who he was," I repeat his statement.

"Yeah. Well, that was because—that meant I could have Mark as my father. Clean slate. No chance of some weirdo turning up at my door claiming to be my real dad."

That pierces my heart in a wonderful way.

"Why don't you tell it to him when you speak to him?"

He chuckles. "Nah. Nah." He ponders. "Well.... Maybe. One day. Just don't ask me to call him 'dad,' okay?"

He waits for my reaction, but I keep it to myself, looking for him to say more.

"Look, Mom. I'll keep calling Terry 'dad' even though it's hard for me to see him as my father now, after all that has happened. I'm not trying to forget him or ignore what he's done. He's a wonderful man. But there had always been a lump inside—something that kept nagging, telling me something wasn't right.

"On the other hand, I see Mark as my father because that's how I wanted, or dreamed, my father to be. Not because of this, okay?" He fiddles with the car key. "I'm thrilled, but he can't bribe me!"

"So what is it about Mark?"

"He's tough—yeah, tough. What he did in that well was... incredible. Yet, he's a cool dude. He tells things as they are and sees me as I am—genuinely. But I can't call him 'dad.' It's hard to explain, but—"

"I understand. I'm sure Mark does too."

"Maybe I'm just too old to start calling another man 'dad.'"

"And you're not too old to keep calling me mom?"

"You're different. Moms are always... moms," he chuckles. "And you're badass." Then his lips clamp shut. "Can I say that?"

I shoot him a teasing smile. "Yeah. Badass is good."

"Look, I don't know when I'm gonna be back. But if it's okay, I'd like to drop by sometime to see Noah. I mean, not just on his birthday or with pre-arrangements or something. Impromptu, you know. Maybe surprise him at his school. Because I certainly won't know the code of the day." He gestures at the gate.

"All you need to do is call, even when you're at the door, and one of us will let you in. But a surprise is doubly welcome, I guess. That's what family is."

He gives me a peck on the cheek. "I'll see you around."

"Yeah, see you around. God, Noah will miss you."

"Mom, *you* will miss me. I know."

His hand reaches for the Lexus SUV door, but he whips around, hugging me, even kissing me. With that, I know he's no longer my lost son.

"Drive carefully!" I take the opportunity to act like a typical worried mother.

He pulls the handle. But once again, he stops. "Wait! Is this car wired too?"

I shrug.

"Mom... is it?"

"I don't know, Ethan. Find out or leave it."

He growls, clutching at the key. He stares at me for a long time, then decides to dive in. Hell yeah, that machine is too irresistible for a freedom-seeking teenager.

38

MARK

What I love most about Silver Hill is the sun. Although in the height of summer, its rays are gentle, as if respecting the earth, not wanting to overpower the water, trees, flowers, and grass from being the main characters in this landscape.

Today it's no exception. With the soft afternoon sun breaking out of the clouds, the hill serves as the perfect backdrop for our wedding. The sage-filled riverbank frames the table arrangement—dressed in white and fern green. The bridge that witnessed our engagement has been decorated, complete with a wedding arch made of local tree branches and the hill's best summer blooms.

My best man Sam is standing by me next to the arch. I look at my watch. Fifteen more minutes.

"Surely, you can't be nervous for Ivy. You know she won't stand you up."

"Jesus, Sam! Of course not. I just don't want to mess up my vows."

"You, my man, will never mess up anything." He flicks away a pollen off my tux, then going back to perfect my bowtie

—must've been the third or fourth time he's done that. I think he's the nervous one.

I look up the hill—it looks quiet up there. I've honored the tradition of not seeing the bride on our wedding night, so I let Ivy have the house for herself. She spent last night with Cass and some of their friends, along with the kids, while I stayed put in my Helena home. It wasn't so much of a stag party. We boys, including Sam and Ben, opted for a quiet one—playing board games and having a few beers. We were even in bed before midnight!

"Do I look okay?" Sam asks.

"Yeah."

"I think I've gained a few daddy pounds," he quips, buttoning his suit.

He's still as ripped as I remember. "What daddy pounds?" I tap his abs.

Around us, guests are laughing and chattering under the marquees. Everyone who means to us is here—except one person.

"Where the hell is he?" I mumble.

"Give him time. He may be late. Teenagers!" Sam tries to play it down. "Hey, I miss our time together."

"Don't get melancholic now, Sam," I warn him.

"I mean, those days when there were just the two of us. Boots on the ground."

"Those were good days." I gaze at Ben, who is mingling with the guests, carrying baby Philip while Cass is still with Ivy in the lodge, no doubt doing her matron-of-honor duties. Chatting with another group of guests is Ty. That charmer seems to be a hit with the ladies, although I'm not sure if love is on his mind at the moment—considering his recent breakup.

"You know, Sam, we've gotta admit, it's time for the next generation of Red Mark to make a difference."

Sam observes the two young Red Marks. "Ben and Ty will be a formidable duo."

I cock my head, agreeing.

Ty excuses himself to answer a call, and as if tugged by some kind of telepathic power, he runs to us. "Hey, gents!"

"Just the man!" Sam responds. "We were just talking about you."

"Me? What?" His eyes switch between looking at me and Sam. "Nah, no, man. I'm not the next one getting married."

"How do you fancy being the alpha of Red Mark?" I hint at him.

"Mr. Connor?"

"What he means is, what do you think about becoming Red Mark's head of ops?"

Her eyes flare in anticipation. "Seriously?"

"It's yours if you want it," I say.

"Sure! Um... but..." His head tilts up toward the hill. "For now, we should focus on the wedding. Your bride's coming, Mr. Connor."

Sam and I shift our gaze to follow his. A decorated Rolls-Royce Silver Cloud is making its way down. It's her, all right. And I can't wait.

I ready myself, and just as I see her car approaching the river, Sam asks, "How was the ultrasound the other day?"

"You're asking me now?"

"Just trying to get your mind off your vow."

"Dammit, Sam." Ivy has given me permission, so I whisper the news to Sam.

My best friend can only gape, then smile and give me a tight embrace as if we were the only ones here. When he lets go, he quickly fixes my bow. "Sorry. I messed it up. But geez, brother, that's... that's wonderful."

Almost every head turns toward the car that has just arrived. I can't see much of Ivy as Cass is obscuring her, perhaps on purpose. As soon as the passenger door opens, I see Noah stepping out, along with Jasper the Great Dane puppy who, at nine months, is already taller than a full-grown retriever. The mutt is carrying a *Here comes the bride* sign on his collar, swinging his legs too fast. Noah has no hope of catching him. Ivy and Cass haven't even gotten out of the car.

Jasper sits next to me, and finally, Noah catches up. He slides some treats into the pup's mouth, then smiles at me. The boy is so cute in his mini tux, but my attention is still ahead when flower girl Grace, Cass' daughter, steps out.

And she finally emerges.

There's my partner, my best friend, and the woman I'm spending the rest of my life with. She's the only thing I see. Wearing an angelic lace and chiffon dress, her long, flawless leg flashes out through the high slit on her skirt as she strides toward me. In her hands is a bouquet of fresh roses and ferns. But it's her who truly shines.

She shines.

The former attorney general is no blushing bride, but elation is apparent on her face. Uninhibited, unpretentious. There's even a hint of impatience in her stride. Her hair has now grown to just above her shoulders. In the sun, it shimmers, along with the beads of pearl adorning her head. Her incredible hazel eyes are looking straight at me. I am, too, the only one she sees.

I take her hand as soon as she's close.

"Right on time," the celebrant murmurs playfully.

Of course, 'fashionably late' is never part of her. I'm never worried about her standing me up. Our bond is too strong to let anything get in the way of our union.

How I want to kiss her already. But I simply smile, running my thumb over her finger, feeling the engagement ring.

As the celebrant is concluding the brief introduction and formalities, Ivy starts looking around.

Nervously she mutters, "Mark... where is he?"

My heart shrinks. It would've been perfect, but sometimes things just ought to go wrong. "I'm sorry, Ivy."

Her long lashes splay across her face as she blinks, her head nodding slightly. I wish I could soothe her. I just hope that Noah and I are enough to make up for Ethan's absence.

Sam moves forward, handing over the ring to her.

The celebrant prompts Ivy to say her vow. Sudden movement in the crowd catches my eye. A boy wearing a sleek blue suit is shuffling his way through, finding a seat next to Ty. My goodness, that boy has pulled one out of a hat!

Ivy beams as Ethan gives her a discreet wave. Her eyes twinkle just that much brighter. It's going to be perfect, after all.

"Mark, I'm not one who runs out of words to express how I feel. But today, I am." Her smile stretches. "Because how I feel in this very moment is too deep to dig, too profound to utter, and too heavenly to describe. But today is not about words. It's about my heart, and the whole of me that I vow to give to you. I'm yours till my last day. Please take this ring as a symbol of my promise."

She gently takes my hand, sliding the ring into my finger.

I hook my fingers over hers, holding on, begging her to stretch the moment. This isn't redemption. This is love in its simple form—a man and a woman who love each other, supported by those who are dear to us.

"Mark?" The celebrant gestures to me.

I take Ivy's left hand. "Ivy Wren, I had built a fortress to keep love at bay. But what we've gone through together has proven that we are both meant to fall in each other's arms and get up together to start this new life. I love you..." I stop to sniffle. "And I always will, for the rest of my life. Please take this ring as a symbol of my promise."

"You may kiss the bride," the celebrant says.

I can't wait to kiss her, but as I promised Ivy a couple of days ago, there's something I've got to do first.

"Actually, I have something else to say," I tell the celebrant and then turn to the guests. Ivy smiles at me, knowing what I'm going to say. I clear my throat.

"To our sons," I smile at Ethan and Noah. "Our *three* sons and *our girl*." I touch Ivy's belly. Everyone gasps. I nod at them as Ivy squeezes my hand tight.

I continue, "And however many future children we may be blessed with, I love you all, and I promise I will be the father who will protect you, come what may. And I will be there for you no matter what—troubles or triumphs, hurt or joy. You can count on me."

Sam is the first one to cry, and he soon makes me teary. He has been close to crying in front of me when dealing with his own turmoil, and he always managed to compose himself. But apparently, today, he's really lost his shit.

"Now, you may finally kiss the bride," the celebrant repeats.

I kiss my beautiful, beaming bride. I keep it soft but long, relishing her warmth.

"Best day of my life, Ivy Wren," I whisper against her parted lips.

"Wait until the twins are born," she replies. "Or the moment when they smile back at you."

She has really pictured it for me. In the small corner of my heart, I'm hoping that the babies have her eyes.

I put my hand on her belly and continue kissing her. Confetti falls from the sky, and cheers fill the valley.

Ivy Wren Cavanagh. I made her wait. I might've left a little crack in her heart. But she's always been the only one. Near or far, she's in my heart—even when we were apart. Her tenacity, compassion, and love will always humble me. She's not my duty. She's the woman I will be devoted to until I take my last breath.

THANK you for reading *Her Devoted Protector*.

Grab the next book, **Her Steadfast Protector**, and follow the journey of former SEAL marksman Tyler Hunt. When a mysterious young woman begs him to find her little sister, how far will he go to save the girl—and confront the truth about the woman he's falling in love with?

If you haven't already, grab the first book in the series, **Her Unbreakable Protector**, and read the story of Sam and Cass —and how Mark risks his life to save Sam's adopted daughter, Grace.

Join my newsletter for release updates, free books, and more ➜ alessakelly.com.

ALSO BY ALESSA KELLY

Fighting for You: From Strangers to Fearless Lovers

She's ready for a soulmate. He's sealed away his heart. When attempted murder brings them together, can they survive long enough to find love?

Longing for You: From Secret to Fearless Lovers

He's a notorious mercenary boss, she's a no-nonsense oil tycoon. When legal entanglements take them on a collision course, will they rise to beat unsurmountable odds?

The Hartley Brothers Series

Hold Me Forever

She's a traumatized survivor. He's a closed-off veteran. Can two lost souls find safe harbor together?

Cherish Me Forever

Two wounded hearts. When unexpected love comes within their grasp, can they learn to trust before it's ripped away?

Standalone

Protecting Her

He's a disgraced ex-cop. She's on a mad quest for justice. When they're trapped in a deadly game, can they escape into each other's arms?

Join my newsletter for release updates, free books, and more ➜ alessakelly.com.

THE MEANING BEHIND THE RED MARK LOGO

Red Mark is named after its two founders, Samuel Redley Kelleher (nicknamed Red) and Mark Connor. The fox is their mascot; it's a resilient and resourceful animal with sharp tracking instinct, and one of the most protective in the canine family.

For every heart that has been broken

www.ingramcontent.com/pod-product-compliance
Lightning Source LLC
Chambersburg PA
CBHW032148050726
47591CB00001B/129